Just Like
Other
Daughters

Just Like Other Daughters

COLLEEN
FAULKNER

KENSINGTON BOOKS
www.kensingtonbooks.com

KENSINGTON BOOKS are published by

Kensington Publishing Corp.
119 West 40th Street
New York, NY 10018

All Kensington titles, imprints, and distributed lines are available at special quantity discounts for bulk purchases for sales promotion, premiums, fund-raising, educational, or institutional use.

Special book excerpts or customized printings can also be created to fit specific needs. For details, write or phone the office of the Kensington Special Sales Manager: Kensington Publishing Corp., 119 West 40th Street, New York, NY 10018. Attn. Special Sales Department. Phone: 1-800-221-2647.

Kensington and the K logo Reg. U.S. Pat. & TM Off.

ISBN-13: 978-0-7582-6684-2
ISBN-10: 0-7582-6684-7
First Kensington Trade Paperback Printing: November 2013

eISBN-13: 978-0-7582-9149-3
eISBN-10: 0-7582-9149-3
First Kensington Electronic Edition: November 2013

10 9 8 7 6 5 4 3 2 1

Printed in the United States of America

For Maura, for all the lives you've touched and the hope you give to special people and their families. Thank you.

Just Like Other Daughters

1

I lost Chloe twice. The first time, she was six. We were in Wal-mart. I still, to this day, don't know how it happened. My daughter was there one minute, hanging on to the cart, singing "Itsy-Bitsy Spider" in that husky little voice of hers. Then she was gone. I have never been so terrified in my life.

Until today, maybe. Now.

Losing your six-year-old in a public place is every parent's nightmare. You imagine all the possibilities. You're certain she's dead. You *know* a pervert has kidnapped her. You see the headlines in tomorrow's paper. You hear your tearful interview on the local news, begging the perv to bring her home, unharmed.

I've never been the woman who needed to one-up others. We all know one of those. If you have a headache, she has a migraine. If you stub your toe, she's sure hers is broken. But losing Chloe in that Walmart was worse than the usual lost-child-announced-over-the-public-address-system situation. My six-year-old couldn't speak her own name clearly. Not even her first name. She could sing "Itsy-Bitsy Spider," but she didn't know her phone number, or her street address. All she knew was that we lived in a red house . . . except that it wasn't red, it was yellow.

The house has always been yellow. My ex and I bought the

house on Ivy Drive, in the little college town of Port Chapel, on the Eastern Shore of Maryland, the fall before Chloe was born. I didn't like the yellow, but Randall said we would repaint it. Financially, the house was too good a deal to pass up; we used the inheritance from my grandmother to make a hefty down payment.

The location was ideal, just on the edge of the college campus where my husband, the literature professor, taught. He could walk to work in his tweed blazer and wool cap. Later, I learned the location was also convenient for him to meet his grad students alone in his office to have sex with them on the leather couch I bought him his first Father's Day.

I digress. Back to the yellow house.

I wanted to paint it white. I'd always dreamed of a white house with green shutters on a quiet street. Like my grandparents'. Randall and I agreed the day we went to settlement to paint the rambling Victorian white with green shutters. I was at an OB appointment when Randall met with the painters. It was mild for late January and he was in a hurry to have the peeling paint tidied up before there was snow.

And when I arrived home, the painters were painting it yellow. I called Randall at his office. He called me back two hours later. It was too late, he said. The paint had been bought. It was nonrefundable. The house would look better yellow than white anyway, he told me. He told me a lot of things that I didn't question. Until I was older. Wiser. At least, wiser to him.

So I always wished it was white. But it was yellow. And Chloe could never remember the difference between yellow and red, so she called it our red house.

I walk to the window and gaze out. It's winter, but there's no snow on the ground. Just dead leaves, dead branches. The same deadness I feel inside.

I think about that day in Walmart when Chloe was six. I'd been so terrified that it took me a moment to move, to find my voice. Then I ran from aisle to aisle, calling her name, trying not to panic, knowing logically that panic wouldn't help.

I've always been able to think logically, even in the most emotional of times. But that day, my emotions were lodged in my throat, threatening to spill out between the aisles in hardware.

Cleanup on aisle twenty-two. Mother's puke.

I found her within two minutes, three tops. By the time I spotted her, my heart was pounding so hard that I couldn't catch my breath. "Chloe!"

She turned to me. She'd been studying doorknobs. Or maybe the boxes of screws beside them.

"Chloe?"

"Mama Bear." She pointed at a pack of shiny brass screws. She was all smiles. She hadn't missed me or realized *she* was missing.

That perfectly round, flat face, almond-shaped eyes, putty nose, and tiny rosebud lips. All telltale signs. When I close my eyes, I still see her as she was that day. Small and round. Red-blond hair pulled back in a messy ponytail, blue corduroy pants, a light blue shirt, blue sneakers with sparkles on them. She loved blue. Blue like her eyes. Her father's eyes.

Chloe, my precious daughter, was officially diagnosed with Down syndrome, or Trisomy 21, at eleven days of age. I knew within seconds of her birth. During my pregnancy, I'd read about all the things that could go wrong. I don't know if I had *known* she wouldn't be what Randall was expecting, or if it had just been my usual slight paranoia. When I was pregnant, my OB had said it was common for mothers to worry about the possibility of birth defects, and that I should relax and anticipate a healthy baby.

Chloe wasn't a defect. I refuse to ever look at my child that way . . . or allow anyone else in my presence to do so. And she *was* healthy. But she would never be what Randall had wanted. A "normal" child, whatever the hell that is. What he wanted most, what he dreamed of, was a scholar, a son or daughter to attend his alma mater, Princeton. What he wanted was all the things Chloe would never be.

I lean so close to the window that my breath fogs the cold glass. In literary analogies of a broken heart, images of *fragmentation* are often used. My heart isn't a thing in broken pieces. It's like something that's seized up. Frozen. I touch the foggy, cold glass, but they're not my fingerprints that appear. They're Chloe's.

I hear her husky giggle. She's no longer a child and her fingerprints are no longer tiny. She's twenty-five, almost twenty-six, standing here at this same window.

"Come on, Chloe. We're going to be late." It was only three years ago, but it seems like . . . another lifetime. When I close my eyes, I can smell her still, *here* in this room. Her room. Does a mother ever forget the scent of her child? I fight the tears that sting the backs of my eyelids.

I see myself in the reflection in the window. I watch myself walk around her bedroom, the walls painted a pale blue, picking up dirty clothes: panties, socks, her pj top. "Get dressed."

She's here, standing at the window, breathing on the glass, then pressing her fingertips against it. She's wearing flannel pajama bottoms, slippers, and a pale blue bra with little hearts on it. She doesn't have very large breasts. Really, a cami would do, but she likes wearing a bra. It makes her feel like a woman, I think, instead of the child she will always be.

"Get dressed," I repeat, tossing her dirty clothes into her hamper. She's so fastidious about some things, like where her comb and hairbrush go in her bathroom. Lined up side-by-side, parallel to each other, perpendicular to the edge of the sink. If I move her hairbrush over an inch, I'm in big trouble. So, why is it okay for her to leave dirty underwear on the floor? "You're going to be late to Miss Minnie's and I'm going to be late to class."

"Teacher's late. Late, late." She pronounces the words as if they're a tongue twister. She's worked hard with her speech therapist, with me, with the mirror, to speak clearly. I'm proud of her, but I don't have time to be the proud mama this afternoon. It's my first day teaching Sue Chou's British Literature 101.

I can't for the life of me figure out why I'm nervous. It's a one hundred level class. I could do it with my eyes closed: Charles Dickens, Jane Austen, Lewis Carroll. I have a doctorate in Comparative Literature. I've been with the department (Randall's department) for nineteen years. I don't teach freshman classes. I don't have to. I'm only doing it as a favor to Sue, who's gone to California to bring her mom back to put her in a retirement home. Alzheimer's.

I'm jealous. Not of the retirement home or the Alzheimer's, of course. The having a mom part. I wish I had a mom to put in a retirement center. Mine's been dead since I was twenty-two. Ovarian cancer. A long, sad tale that I don't have time to think about right now. Dad lives in Boca Raton with his second wife, Gloria. I don't care for Gloria, but it's not really an issue because I don't care for Dad, either. The feeling's mutual. It took him exactly four months after my mother's death to marry Gloria. She'd been my mother's home care hospice nurse.

"Chloe, put your sweater on. Put your jeans on." I point to the blue knit pants we've agreed to call jeans. She can't wear jeans; at least I can't find any to fit her. She's built like a fireplug; five three and a size sixteen with a weird waistline not made for blue jeans.

Chloe has moved from fingerprints to handprints on the glass pane. She seems utterly enchanted by the phenomenon.

"Please?" I beg, holding out her sweater.

"All right, already," she grumbles.

It comes out more like "Awight, aweady." She talks as if she's Elmer Fudd with a mouth full of marbles. I understand her perfectly . . . most of the time. Other people . . . not so much. But we're working on it.

"Sweater, underwear, jeans, socks, *and* shoes," I remind her. Everything is laid out on her bed.

"What's today?" she asks, finally tearing herself away from the window.

"Tuesday." I pull a sock out from under her bed. Shoot for the laundry hamper.

"I don't go to Miss Minnie's on Tuesday. Not on Tuesday," she repeats firmly. "Not on Tuesday."

I miss the hamper. "You go on Tuesdays now. Because I'm teaching a class." I remain patient, even though we've had this conversation at least half a dozen times in the last week. Chloe doesn't adjust well to change. That doesn't mean she *can't* adjust, according to our family therapist; it just means we need to give her the tools.

She thrusts out her lower lip. "Not on Tuesdays."

Just once in a while I'd like to forego *the tools* and have her do what I ask her. Not put up a fight.

I pick up the sock next to the laundry hamper and drop it in. "You're going to Miss Minnie's for a couple of hours, then your dad will pick you up."

She struggles to get the sweater over her head. I fight the urge to help her.

"Then you're going to Chick-fil-A, for dinner," I say brightly. "Just like every Tuesday night."

I keep the bitterness out of my voice. This is the sum total of Randall's commitment to his relationship with his daughter. His weekly date with Chloe at Chick-fil-A. He picks her up here in his silly little fluorescent yellow smart car; he takes her to the fast food place; they have chicken sandwiches, fries, and diet lemonade; and he returns her by six thirty. Less than two hours a week. That's how much time he spends with her.

And now it will be three hours, because of the change in my schedule.

"Do you think it's wise, modifying Chloe's *sked?*" he asked.

I'd stopped by his office. It's difficult to get him to return my phone calls. "*Sked?*" I'm impatient. With him. With Chloe. With my students. With everyone, these days. I feel like I need a change. Maybe that's why I agreed to take Sue Chou's class in her absence. Because I was bored with my life. And I thought teaching an extra class would help? Maybe. Or maybe it was the idea that I might have time to meet David after class for coffee . . . before going home. Was that what was driving me? Did I think I was going to go all wild and crazy and have a coffee date once a week?

"Chloe's schedule," Randall said.

Only he pronounced it *sheh*-dule, as if he were British. Which he isn't. He's just an ass, an ass with a Ph.D. in Comparative Literature, a wool blazer, and a tweed driving cap.

"Skeds were used early in the century, mostly for sports—"

"I know what a *sked* is," I interrupted. I stood in front of his desk, my hands in my coat pockets. I'd walked over from my cubby office down the hall, which, unlike his corner office, had no window.

He'd kissed me for the first time in front of that window twenty-seven years earlier. I was a grad student and his teaching assistant. He'd been helping me with a paper on the Changing Meaning of the Victorian Family in the Work of Elizabeth Gaskell. I'd only had a couple of boyfriends before that, and mostly boring sex (except with bad boy Tommy LaGeedo, who had dumped me a few months before). I was still smarting from the breakup when Professor Monroe came on to me.

Randall is fifteen years my senior. At the time, he seemed so . . . mature. So . . . unlike Tommy LaGeedo. So brilliant and . . . exciting.

I try not to think about what would have happened if I hadn't let Randall kiss me that night. If I hadn't gone back to his apartment with him. Shared a bottle of pinot with him and dropped my panties. Maybe Tommy and I would have gotten back together? Tommy had worn men's knit bikini briefs. They'd fascinated me as much as the jumbo-sized package inside.

"Alicia—"

"Randall." I lifted my gaze to meet his. At the last undergrad reunion, I'd chatted with Tommy. He was still married to his first wife, his only wife; they had three great kids. Two were at Stanford. Maybe Randall should have married him.

"Chloe's schedule." Randall, always Randall, never Randy, always spoke as if he were standing in front of a lecture hall. He had become a perfect caricature of a literature professor. "I fear it's unwise to make any serious alterations—"

"She likes Miss Minnie's. And you guys will have a little more time together. Maybe you can take her back to your place." *And let her hang out with you and Kelly*, I thought. "Play a game or something. I'm teaching her to play Go Fish."

Kelly was his fourth wife. Thirty-five years his junior. Oddly enough, like me, and Ann (wife number three), Kelly had been a grad student here at Thomas Stone University when Randall met her. Randall had been separated from his first wife when we began dating, although they were still living together. Something he failed to tell me when he plied me with wine and Emily Brontë quotes that first night. She'd been out of town, leaving him free to *entertain*.

"I think we should talk this through," Randall puffed. "A change in Chloe's schedule could potentially—"

"Inconvenience you?"

"Must you always interrupt me, Alicia?"

I walked to the door. "Pick her up at four thirty at Minnie's. There's a charge for every five minutes you're late. Don't be late or you're paying, not me," I warned. I rested my hand on the doorknob, feeling like a total bitch. Knowing I can be at times, but who isn't, with their ex-husband who cheated on them with a younger woman? Several younger women. With bigger breasts and smaller waists. Young women unencumbered by a mentally challenged child. "I'll be home by seven thirty."

"I thought your class ran until six thirty."

Three hours. He didn't want to spend three damned hours *a week* with his daughter. With *our* dear, sweet-natured, stubborn daughter.

I remember vividly, at that moment, wanting to strangle him. I wanted to kill him and wait until late at night to drag his body out of Ballard Hall. His head would *thump, thump, thump* as I dragged him down the marble steps. I had it all worked out. I'd put him in the trunk of my Honda. He'd fit; it was a big trunk. I'd dig a hole in the backyard near the rosebushes where the soil was soft. I'd plant him there. Throw in his driving cap. Maybe, in the spring, I'd even add a couple more rosebushes. Yellow teacup roses. And I would never, *ever* tell. That's how people usually get caught; they brag. I wouldn't need to brag, not even to my best friend, Jin. The satisfaction of the deed would be enough.

But I didn't kill him. Instead, I just looked at him, my face carefully constructed to hide my emotions. How could I still be hurt all these years after the divorce? It wasn't the divorce that still caused the pain. It was the fact that he didn't love our daughter. Not like he should. Not like she deserved. "We agreed that I would make these kinds of decisions, Randall," I deadpanned. "Chloe can handle the change."

Chloe can handle the change. She handled the change, all right.

Tuesday. I don't go to Miss Minnie's on Tuesday. I go Wednesday. And more days. Mom is a dummy head. I'm not a dummy head. I get the days mixed up sometimes, but I know I don't go to Miss Minnie's on Tuesday.

I go to Chick Filly on Tuesday. With my dad. Not Miss Minnie's.

Mom tells me to get dressed. She has to go work at college. But I don't want to get dressed. I want to make handprints on the window in my bedroom. The glass is cold.

I don't want to go to Miss Minnie's. I don't want to go to Chick Filly with Dad. He reads his paper when we eat. He doesn't talk to me. He thinks I'm a dummy head. He doesn't know I'm smart. He doesn't know that I can order my sandwich by myself. I can tell the lady I want diet lemonade. I practice saying the word sometimes because it's hard words: *diet lemonade*. Every time we go, I think Dad will let me tell the lady what I want. I say, "I can tell her."

But he never lets me.

I think that's because my dad doesn't like me. I want to tell my mom. Then I wouldn't have to go to Chick Filly with him on Tuesday. But that would make my mom sad. She loves me. She wants me to go to Chick Filly.

She loves me and I love her. That's why I put my sweater on when she tells me. Because I love her mostest in the world.

2

"Alicia." He half-stands, then, maybe thinking better of it, sits again. Before I reach the table he's picked by the window, he pops up again.

"David." I feel awkward. *He* obviously does. I wonder if it was a mistake to ask him to meet me for coffee. Too forward? Too early in the relationship? Maybe I misinterpreted and there *isn't* a relationship. When you're fifty, time isn't on your side.

I switch my coat to my left arm, which is already holding my briefcase, so I can hug him with my right arm. We touch cheeks, but we don't kiss. Again, awkward. We kissed last week at the end of our date. On my doorstep, like I was sixteen again. It was a real kiss that, while it hadn't set me on fire, had warmed my toes.

Has David decided he isn't attracted to me? Am I a bad kisser? Has he agreed to meet me for coffee only because he couldn't figure out how to politely turn me down? It's all I can do not to groan out loud the way Chloe does when she becomes frustrated.

"How was your new class?"

"Fine." I drop my coat over the back of the chair, set my briefcase on the floor, and sit across from him, not next to him. The shop smells delicious, like coffee and caramel. And maleness. David smells as good as the coffee. It's been a while since I've dated. I've forgotten what it feels like. The nervousness. The excitement. I've forgotten how good a man can smell whom you haven't been pissed off at for twenty-five years. "Good," I add, nodding. Like an idiot.

"I ordered you a cappuccino." He looks around. It's a nice café on Main Street. The kind you expect to see in a college town. Quaint. The owners, Steve and Michele, use real china. Floor-to-ceiling bookshelves line two walls; patrons are urged to bring in books they've read. Borrow books they haven't. "Decaf," he says. "I got you decaf because . . . you know. It's late in the day. I drink decaf this late in the day."

David Collins is an attractive man somewhere in his fifties; tall, slender, with a clean-shaven face and a full head of barely graying hair. His skin is pockmarked, probably from teenage acne, but it doesn't bother me. I like his smile. And the fact that the day we met a month ago, at a cocktail party, he had acted as if I fascinated him. We talked about the Brontë sisters and the Orioles and sourdough bread.

"Great." I smile, settling myself in the chair, feeling flustered and insecure. Wishing I didn't. We've been on two dates: first coffee, then dinner and a movie. He hasn't met Chloe yet. Chloe doesn't like anything new: food, clothes, or people. It's not that I'm trying to hide Chloe from David. It's more the other way around. What would be the point of getting around to him meeting Chloe if nothing came of this? Which is probably how this will play out.

It always does.

"I've taught the class before," I say, fiddling with the paper menu on the table between us.

"I just ordered coffee, but are you hungry?" David rests his fingertips on the menu. Close to mine, but not touching. He has nice hands: clean fingernails, no wedding ring indentation. Of course, men don't always tell the truth about their marital status. I learned that the hard way.

"We could order something," he says.

I'm too nervous to eat. I'll stuff some leftover spaghetti into my mouth later, when I get home. "Just the cappuccino," I say.

It's his turn to bob his head. We're bobbleheads having coffee.

I don't know why this is so hard. I like this guy. He's interesting. . . . No, actually, he's a little boring.

A CPA. Good with numbers, I assume, but a little dull in the conversation department. But what am I expecting? What do I want? What's wrong with a little boring? Randall was exciting and look where that got me. David probably thinks I'm boring, too. If there were a contest, which one of us would win, me or David? I mean, honestly, what's duller, a CPA or a literature professor at a small, private, liberal arts college?

I scoot forward in my chair. If I'm going to do this, I tell myself, I'm going to do it right. *I* invited him for coffee. *I* wanted to see him. *I* should act like it. "So, how was your day?" I smile. Make eye contact. I *engage*.

He smiles back. "Um . . ."

I push my thoughts and worries of the day aside and I listen, I really listen, and I enjoy the hour we spend together. He promises to call me later in the week and I head home, happy. Feeling appreciated. Actually feeling as if something might come of this, of David and me. Like my life might really be changing.

Turns out I'm right on one count. Wrong on the other.

"Mom!"

I hear Chloe's voice the minute the front door opens. I'm in the kitchen, eating the leftover spaghetti.

"Mom!" comes my daughter's voice again, this time with a little panic in her tone.

I swallow a lump of cold noodles. "In the kitchen. Coming." I grab a hand towel off the kitchen island as I go by. I wipe my mouth and toss the towel back on the counter.

"Mom!"

I walk down the hall in my sheepskin slippers. It's barely eight o'clock, and I've already changed into my sweatpants and taken my contacts out. I push my rimless glasses up the bridge of my nose. "I'm coming, Chloe. Hold your horses."

When she sees me, she runs across the foyer and hurls herself into my arms. When she lets go, she grabs both of my hands. Her chubby hands are much smaller than mine; her bitten-down fingernails are painted blue with sparkles. She and the other girls at Miss Minnie's have been playing beauty salon again.

She sounds breathless. She's excited about something, which makes me smile. She doesn't often come home excited from visits with her father. "Did you have fun?" I ask. "With your dad? Let me guess, you had a chicken sandwich, waffle fries, and a diet lemonade?"

"Minnie's. I had fun at Miss Minnie's."

"Slow down," I advise. She's difficult to understand when she gets excited or emotional.

"Miss Min-nie's," she repeats carefully, enunciating each syllable.

I drop a kiss on her forehead. She needs a shower; her hair has that musky smell of three or four days without shampooing. She still wears her hair in a ponytail the way she did when she was a little girl. I've been told I should cut her hair short to make it *more manageable* for Chloe, but I can't bring myself to do it. Her red-blond hair is just too pretty; besides, when dirty (more often than not) it looks better long than short.

I shut the door behind her, catching a glimpse through the outer door in the vestibule of Randall pulling away from the curb in *Stupid Car*. I don't know why I hate the car so much. Maybe because it represents him in my mind. It's all fake: the caring professor persona he presents at work, his concern for the environment, his love for his daughter. He drives that yellow car because he likes to draw attention to himself, all the while pretending he doesn't. I lock the door. "What happened at Miss Minnie's?"

"A boy," Chloe gushes.

There's something in the tone of her voice that makes me turn around and look at her. I realize then that her cheeks are rosy. From the cold? Or is it something else?

"A boy?" I echo.

Chloe starts to fight her way out of her coat. "His name is Thomas!" She puts too much emphasis on the first syllable of his name. "He's new."

"Thomas is new at Miss Minnie's?" I pronounce the name correctly. I have to tuck my hands behind my back to keep from helping Chloe with her coat. Our therapist has given me the task of allowing her to be more independent, of helping her realize what a capable young woman she is. It's hard. So hard. "Did he just move to town?"

"He goes to Miss Minnie's different days. Different days," Chloe tells me, sounding more like Dustin Hoffman in *Rain Man* than I care to admit. But Raymond was autistic. Chloe is not. Unlike the character in the movie, Chloe has no problem with emotion. In fact, one of her problems is that she often feels too deeply.

She's got both arms behind her back now, as if she's wearing a North Face straitjacket. "Different days," she repeats as if the information is critical.

"Ah. So he's been going to Miss Minnie's, but you just haven't met him? Because you haven't been going Tuesday afternoons." I stand by the coatrack, knowing that eventually she'll get her coat off. There's nothing wrong with hanging it up for her, I reason. I'd do the same for Jin if she were standing here. "Is Thomas nice?" I ask.

"Apple juice," she cries excitedly. Her right arm pops out of her sleeve and she looks triumphant as she finally manages to get out of her coat. "He likes apple juice. I like apple juice. I love apple juice." She draws out the word *apple*, making it sound like *aaa-pull*.

I smile as I take her coat. "You do love apple juice, don't you? Did Miss Minnie have juice in cups today or in juice boxes?"

Again, the grin that melts my heart. I would do anything for my child who isn't a child anymore. I'd throw myself in front of a bus to save her. I'd lie on the backs of crocodiles to build her a bridge. There's nothing I wouldn't do to help her climb a mountain.

"Juice boxes," she says.

"Come help me load the dishwasher." I hang her coat up next to mine on the rack and head for the kitchen.

"Mom! Listen to me! I have to tell you!" She balls her hands into fists. She's annoyed with me. She's easily annoyed and prone to temper tantrums. We're working on that, too.

"Tell me? Tell me what? I heard you. A boy named Thomas came to Minnie's and you had apple juice."

"*No*, Mom."

I stop in the hallway and turn back to look at her. She's standing in the same place, her fists at her sides. Her chin is jutted out and her eyes, with her Mongolian eye folds, are narrow. Whatever's going on, Chloe means business. "What, Chloe?"

"I'm trying to tell you," she insists.

I cross my arms over my chest and wait.

"He loves apple juice and me and Thomas . . . we're gonna get married."

I smile. "You can't marry Thomas. You don't even know him. Come on." I wave to her. "Help me load the dishwasher."

"I'm gonna marry Thomas," Chloe repeats. This time with a foot stomp. She has tiny feet. She wears a size five, compared to my boat-sized nine-and-a-halfs.

"Marry Thomas, and leave me?" I chuckle. "No way, Chloe." I turn for the kitchen.

"I love him," Chloe insists.

"You don't love him. You love me," I call over my shoulder. "And your dad," I add as an afterthought. Divorced mothers are supposed to say things like that. "Come on. Dishes, then a shower and then a movie. You can pick the DVD."

"But, Mom, I love him!" Chloe cries passionately. She still hasn't budged.

Maybe I should have been concerned at that point, but I wasn't. Chloe is passionate about everything: the order of her DVDs, her fear of crickets, her love of Mrs. Paul's fish sticks . . . and apple juice.

"*Beauty and the Beast? Aladdin?* Or maybe *The Princess and the Frog?*" I tempt. Chloe loves Disney movies. She can't remember that her father's wife's name is Kelly, but she remembers that the monkey in *Aladdin* is called Abu.

"*Moooom*, you're not listening to me." Chloe shuffles down the hall.

It's funny how things are said, things happen, and you have no idea at the moment just how significant they are. What's the saying? Ignorance is bliss? That evening I was in pure bliss.

After I watch *Aladdin*, when I brush my teeth, I look at my face in the mirror. I feel different, but I don't look different. I look the same. Thomas says he loves me and we can get married, but I still look the same.

Mom doesn't understand about me and Thomas. She doesn't understand about apple juice. I love apple juice and I love Thomas. Thomas loves Thomas the Tank Engine. He has a shirt and backpack and Thomas the Tank Engine stuff at his house.

He says I'm pretty.

I look different than other girls. Not pretty like my mom. My mom is pretty.

My eyes are squinty and I don't always speak good. People look at me when we go to the grocery store. Because I look different. Because I have Down's.

Thomas doesn't have Down's. He's not a dummy head. He's smart. Really smart.

Thomas says I'm his girl.

I spit toothpaste into my sink and put water in my cup to swish.

I was Mom's girl, but now I'm Thomas's girl.

I like to be Thomas's girl. I want to be his girl on Wednesday. That's why we have to get married.

"She said she *loves* him?" Jin is smiling. "You think it's serious?"

I eye Jin across the breakfast table, closing my fingers around my warm coffee mug. "She met him once. Chloe's never been interested in boys. Or girls," I add for Jin's benefit.

Jin's all the things I'm not: gorgeous, confident, athletic. She's also a lesbian, which on certain days, when I'm finding my relationship with Randall particularly difficult, sounds awfully appealing.

"She's twenty-five years old, Ally." Jin is the only one who calls me Ally, the only one who has *ever* called me Ally. I'm not an Ally. I'm too uptight, too controlled to be an Ally. But I like that she calls me it anyway.

"She doesn't like boys. Not in that way."

Jin sips from her coffee mug. She's Chinese, first-generation American. She has amazing dark hair, perfect skin, and dark eyes that turn both men's and women's heads. She's been my best friend for twelve years, ever since she and her partner, Abby, moved in next door with their eight-year-old son. She and Abby split up almost five years ago. Abby took a position with a law firm in Baltimore, but Jin stayed on at Stone. Jin is an art professor and a very talented sculptor and painter. I don't understand her modern paintings or the creations she forms out of clay and metal in her studio/garage behind the house. But I see their beauty.

Chloe, on the other hand, sees things in Jin's work that astound me. Chloe knows nothing of art or artists. She can't draw a stick person or a box. But she *gets* Jin's work. Jin thinks Chloe *picks up on the emotion* of the piece. I think they're both full of shit. I don't get how a piece of artwork made of canvas and oil paint or clay and iron washers can have emotion.

"So what are you going to do?"

"Do?" I eye the Pop-Tart Jin is munching. She nabbed it from the cabinet when she came in the house. They're one of Chloe's favorites, so I buy them for her. It has white sugary frosting with sprinkles, and when Jin bites into it I see the number-something red-dyed strawberry filling. I tell myself it looks disgusting, but it looks delicious. I've had a hard-boiled egg this morning. Started a new diet. I lick the tip of my finger and touch the crumbs Jin has dropped on the round oak kitchen table. We have a dining room, but I use the table in there as a desk. We haven't used the dining room as a dining room since Randall and I divorced. I press the crumbs to my tongue. "About what?"

Jin lifts a perfect, dark eyebrow. She has them waxed. She has her lady-parts waxed, too. I try not to think about that.

"About the *boyfriend*."

"She doesn't have a boyfriend," I whisper.

"A fiancé, then?" Jin takes another big bite of the Pop-Tart.

Now she's just baiting me. I want to snatch the Pop-Tart out of her hand and cram it in my mouth. I take a big gulp of black coffee. "Chloe does *not* have a boyfriend," I repeat. "They drank apple juice together."

"I've had some damned good relationships based on less."

I sit back in my chair, thinking. I look up. "You don't think . . . she would let a boy take advantage of her, do you?"

"He's not a boy if he's her age. He's a man."

I frown. I've always made certain Chloe was protected. She's never left alone, not even in our own house. Besides not being able to make good choices about stoves and candles, she's too sweet, too trusting. She's also an affectionate girl. Physically affectionate. It's taken years for me to get her to not hug strangers.

I've always had a fear that if a predator were to tell her she was pretty, or offer her Gummy Lifesavers, she'd get in a car with him.

I look at Jin. Her new haircut is cute. It's chin-length and asymmetrical in the front. Very hip for a fifty-year-old woman. Self-consciously, I tug at my ponytail. My hair is the same color as Chloe's. Or hers as mine, I suppose. Pale red. Thick, a little wiry. I've always envied Jin, with her shiny black China-doll hair.

"Maybe I should talk to Minnie," I say.

"And say what?" Jin crumples the silvery Pop-Tart wrapper. She's still chewing. "But you could check him out, I guess. Do a little recon."

I hear Chloe clomping down the steps.

"Mom! Mom!"

"In the kitchen," I call. I look at Jin. "You think I should check him out?"

She shrugs as she gets up. She has a nine-thirty watercolor class. "Why not? I still check out Huan's female friends on Facebook. When he was in high school, I checked his cell phone messages and listened in on his phone calls," she says, seeming unashamed of her lack of respect for her son's privacy.

"He's not her boyfriend," I say, louder than I mean to. *He's not her boyfriend*, I repeat to myself as Jin goes out the back door and Chloe walks into the kitchen with pink bunny slippers on her feet.

❧ 3 ❧

I have no intention of *checking Thomas out*. Really, I don't. I think
Jin ought to be ashamed of herself. What would Huan think if
he knew his mother was Facebook stalking his friends?

I manage to get myself on a high horse for a few minutes, but
I don't stay there long. The truth is, Huan probably wouldn't be
all that surprised by his mother's behavior. Or upset. Jin was a
Tiger Mom long before Amy Chua coined the phrase. I don't
completely understand the phenomenon, but I understand it's
more common than not with Asian Americans, this drive to see
their children succeed at almost any cost to the child's psyche.
Her child rearing techniques had been a constant bone of con-
tention between her and Abby.

Jin insisted Huan (conceived by in vitro fertilization from a
Chinese American sperm donor) begin violin lessons at the age
of four. Abby wanted him to play T-ball. He still takes violin
lessons and practices regularly, even though he's living away from
home. Jin limited his extracurricular activities so he could concentrate on his music and academics. And she has always expected her only child to excel in every class he takes, beginning
in nursery school. He graduated from the local public high school

as valedictorian, and I have no doubt he'll graduate from Brown summa cum laude. Of course, the fact that Jin ever allowed her son to even have friends in high school is proof that if she is a Tiger Mom, she isn't a good one. And never once, as long as I've known her, has she belittled or tried to intimidate or shame her son into doing what she wants him to do. That's not to say she wasn't or still isn't above manipulation.

"Miss Minnie's!" Chloe declares excitedly.

I eye Miss Minnie's red front door from where I've parked on the street in front of her contemporary single-story house. Miss Minnie, with the help of two part-time employees, runs a private daycare for mentally and physically handicapped young adults. The men and women who attend Miss Minnie's are between the ages of twenty-one and thirty-five, or so. There are three who attend every day from nine to five, then another five who, like Chloe, attend a certain number of hours each week. Minnie Wellston is a registered nurse who, when she recognized the need for such a care facility for her Down syndrome son and couldn't find one, opened one herself. Her Adam died of leukemia eight years ago. I hadn't known her then, but Minnie had apparently decided that even though her son was gone, this was still her calling.

Minnie had been a lifesaver when Chloe aged out of the public school system at twenty-one. Randall and I had decided not to apply for Social Security for Chloe and kept her out of the state system. By not accepting Social Security's financial support, we felt we had better control of our daughter's life. Fortunately, we could afford it. But that had meant finding something to do with Chloe while I taught and held office hours. There had never been any discussion of Randall caring for Chloe. He was busy with his career and his wife, and he did, after all, see Chloe every Tuesday night for dinner.

I tried leaving Chloe home alone one day, just after she "graduated" from high school. Looking back, I wonder what I was thinking. I was going to be away just long enough to get a haircut and a touch-up on the color. I was born a redhead; I'm determined to die one, even if possibly toxic chemicals are necessary.

I think I left Chloe partly because of the pressure I felt from the outside world. Randall, our family therapist, even the girl who checks us out at the grocery store, all thought I was being overprotective. Chloe seems so independent to other people. So capable. And she *is* capable. She can do so much more than I thought she would ever be able to. More than I could have imagined when those original blood tests came back all those years ago and her genetic disorder was confirmed. Chloe was twenty-one years old, for heaven's sake. She could certainly be left home alone for two hours.

That morning I gave her tons of instructions: do not go outside, do not answer the phone, do not take a bath, do not use the stove. Instruction piled on instruction, more than she'd ever been able to handle. My fault again, but I was so nervous and excited. I *so* wanted it to work out. I kept thinking that if she could just stay at home alone for three or four hours a day, I could figure out how to continue to teach my three classes a semester. Honestly, I think I was also looking for a break. Just a little time for myself. And I wanted to feel normal. I wanted my daughter to be normal.

It was a Tuesday morning. It was June. I was gone two hours and three minutes. I didn't even let my stylist blow-dry my hair. After an hour, I just wanted to get home. I just wanted to know that she was safe.

I saw the fire trucks when I turned down our street. There was no mistake. They were in front of *my* house. And in *my* driveway. But my house wasn't engulfed in flames. I couldn't see any smoke.

But I could smell it.

I parked my car in the middle of the road. A fireman tried to stop me as I ran across my lawn, but I shoved him aside. I just kept calling Chloe's name. I'll admit it. I was frantic. Chloe's all I have. *She's all I have*, I kept thinking.

I found her on the neighbors' lawn. The Watsons, next door. Both Al and Beth were at work, their two children at a summer play program. Chloe seemed unhurt, but I could tell she'd been crying. Hard. Her eyes were red, her nose was running, and she was taking in great gulps of air. I pulled her into my arms. When I held her, I could smell her familiar scent, tinged with smoke. I've heard that a woman can pick out her own baby, blindfolded, going only by smell. I believe it.

Huan was with Chloe. "What happened?" I asked, not giving either of them time to answer. "Tell me what happened. You're not hurt, are you, Chloe?" I looked to Huan. "No one's hurt?"

Huan was fifteen or sixteen at the time. He looked scared. He had been home that morning because school was out and he hadn't started his enrichment class yet. I'd checked with Jin the night before. *Just in case she has a question*, I'd said. Huan has always been good to Chloe. Very understanding. And kind.

"Huan, what happened?" I said, finally calming down. A little.

"I'm really sorry," he said. "I didn't know what to do. I heard Chloe screaming so I went next door. She was under the kitchen table. The microwave was on fire. There were flames shooting up the cabinets."

"The microwave caught fire? That doesn't make sense." I was talking fast, not sure exactly what I was saying. "We had the whole place rewired. There was faulty wiring?"

"No. No, I don't think so." It was obvious he was upset, but he was playing it cool. He was a teenager; cool was important. "It wasn't the wiring. At least I don't think so." He looked at Chloe.

She was hanging on to me for dear life, her face buried in my breasts. She was making a wet spot on my T-shirt with her mouth.

I waited for Huan to go on. That was the day I noticed the tattoo behind his ear. His hair was longish at the time, but when he pushed his hair back out of his face, I saw it. It was some kind of

Asian symbol. There would be a huge blowup when Jin saw it, but at that moment, Huan's tattoo seemed insignificant.

"She was trying to cook something in the microwave. I think she cooked it too long."

I put my hands on Chloe's shoulders and pushed her back a little so I could look her in the eyes. "You tried to cook?" I asked.

"I didn't cook. Didn't use the stove," she blubbered. "You said no stove. No stove."

"You weren't supposed to cook anything. Not in the stove or the microwave. I left you apples and peanut butter for a snack. You weren't supposed to cook," I said again. *And if you started a fire*, I thought, *you were supposed to call 911. You weren't supposed to crawl under the table and hide.*

We'd practiced dialing 911. I'd disconnected the phone and we'd practiced over and over again. How to push the buttons, what the 911 operator would say, what Chloe was supposed to say.

"Chloe, what were you trying to cook?"

Her lower lip trembled. She didn't answer.

"Chloe?"

About that time a firefighter, in full regalia, walked over to us.

"This your house, ma'am?" He had a handlebar mustache and one of his front teeth was chipped badly. I remember wondering if it had happened while fighting a fire. The firefighters in Port Chapel are all volunteers. This guy, and all of his buddies, risk their lives to save our houses, and possibly our daughters, for free.

"I'm Alicia Richards." I don't release Chloe to shake his hand. "Chloe's my daughter. Huan lives next door in our duplex."

"That was a smart thing you did there, son," the fireman says. "Hardly any damage to the house because you were so quick to call." He hesitated, glancing at Chloe, who was still hanging on to me, her fingers bunching my T-shirt. "This young lady's very lucky she wasn't hurt."

Then he looked at me and I could see it plainly on his face. I shouldn't have left my mentally handicapped daughter at home alone. *I* was responsible for this fire. *I* knew Chloe couldn't handle being left alone. If she hadn't screamed, if Huan hadn't heard her—

Tears welled up in my eyes. "Can we go inside?" I asked.

"We had to shut the main circuit breaker off. You need to get an electrician out here to rewire behind the microwave. I wouldn't recommend popping the electric back on 'til you've had it inspected." He pulled his fireman's hat off and wiped his damp forehead with a clean white handkerchief he produced from his pocket. It was probably in the mid-seventies that day, but with all that gear, he had to be roasting.

"Would it be okay if I just go in to get a few things?" I asked, thinking that Chloe would need her stuffed bear, Boo Bear, and we would both need a change of clothing in case we ended up having to spend the night at a hotel. Something I didn't even want to consider. Chloe was already so upset; having to spend even a single night in an unfamiliar hotel room might unhinge her.

Ultimately, I ended up paying an electrician time and a half to come out that evening and check the wiring. He had to replace something, but then he gave us the okay to stay in the house. In the following days, I called the claim in to my insurance company and made arrangements for repairs to the walls and cabinets, and splurged on new granite countertops. I argued with Randall over having left Chloe alone. He didn't remember our conversation two days before discussing the possibility. Selective memory on his part.

And I began looking for someone to stay with Chloe during the day when I had to work. It wasn't so much the fact that she'd started a fire in the microwave trying to make popcorn (probably by setting it for an hour instead of a minute), but that when the fire started, her response was to hide under the kitchen table. In the same room as the fire.

I told myself that maybe the day would come when Chloe could stay home alone. But that day wasn't it.

I had the summer off, but when fall came, I found a sitter willing to come to the house. Mrs. Jameson advertised that she sat for the elderly, but when I interviewed her, she said she had no problem with handicapped adults. Chloe disliked Mrs. Jameson from day one. She said Mrs. Jameson smelled funny, which she did. Chloe missed her schoolmates and was bored with Mrs. Jameson and the soaps she watched all afternoon. Chloe threw one fit after another until I did my homework and found Minnie.

Minnie was a godsend. She provided the kind of structured environment Chloe liked and needed. They did crafts, watched movies, played music, and went on field trips. But all activities were on a strict schedule, with plenty of warning, which was perfect for Chloe.

"Mom?"

I glance at Chloe in the passenger seat. She's pulling on the door handle. "It's locked," she says.

I hit the UNLOCK button on my door and start to get out.

"Mom. What are you *doing?*" Chloe asks me, enunciating her last word very clearly.

I get out of the car. "I thought I'd walk you in. Say hi to Miss Minnie."

Chloe's IQ is somewhere around 48. She's not a smart girl. But that doesn't mean she's not intuitive. Particularly when it pertains to me.

"I don't want you to come," she says. Her brow creases. "Don't come."

It's cold out. The wind is blowing off the Chesapeake Bay and cuts through my dark green fleece jacket. My office hours start in half an hour. I have a student coming in. I have to scoot. But I can't help myself. If this Thomas whom Chloe has been babbling about is here, I want to meet him. "I just want to say 'hi.'" I walk around the front of the Honda, keys in my hand.

Chloe looks at me and slams the door, making no bones about her annoyance with me. There are days when she begs me to walk her to the door. Now, suddenly, she's Miss Independent. I'm not sure if I like it. I mean, we've been working for years on her being comfortable doing things, going places, talking to people, all without me, but the idea that she doesn't want me to be here hurts my feelings a little. Dr. Tamara, our therapist, says I'm as dependent on Chloe as she is on me. Damn if maybe Dr. Tamara isn't right.

I hit the remote on my key ring, the car beeps, and I walk up the sidewalk toward Minnie's front door. After a minute, I hear Chloe tromping behind me. She has a particular gait, sort of a side-to-side lope that is probably a by-product of the way she carries her weight on her small frame. I'd recognize her footsteps anywhere.

I take the steps. Chloe bangs up the metal wheelchair ramp that runs beside the steps.

"I don't want you to come," she repeats. "I don't," she whispers under her breath angrily.

The door opens and a young man stands in the doorway. He's very tall, compared to Chloe. Maybe five-foot-nine or five-foot-ten. He has shaggy blond hair and bright blue eyes that are framed with glasses. Which sit crooked on his face. Very Scandinavian looking. He doesn't have the physical characteristics of Trisomy 21, but I can see by his features that he's mentally challenged.

He spots Chloe and starts to jump up and down and clap. All one hundred and ninety pounds of him. "Ko-ey!" he cries.

Chloe runs up the ramp, pushing past me, her canvas bag from the public library swinging on her chubby arm.

It's not hard to guess who this is.

Chloe throws herself into his arms and he hugs her, lifting her tiny sneakered feet off the ground.

It's on my tongue to remind her that we don't hug strangers, but *obviously* this isn't a stranger.

"N . . . Knock, n . . . knock," the young man says.

Chloe looks at me. "You're supposed to say 'who's there?' " She looks at him. "Who's there?" she hollers.

"B . . . banana."

Again she turns to me. "You say 'banana, who?' " She looks up at him. "Banana, who?"

Thomas bursts out laughing and then Chloe laughs.

No punch line? I smile. "Are you Thomas?" I ask. "I'm Chloe's mom."

"K . . . koey's mom," he repeats. He speaks fairly clearly, despite his stutter, in a hoarse voice. He's a nice-looking young man, but his eyes are too close together and his mouth hangs open. There's a little drool in one corner of his mouth.

When Chloe was growing up, I was very diligent about teaching her how to keep her mouth closed. I knew my daughter would always look different from the other girls her age, but I felt there were certain ways she could fit in better socially. I taught her no burping or farting in public . . . and no drooling.

Thomas still has his big hands around my Chloe, though he's at least put her down. She's resting her cheek on his plaid flannel shirt. The look on her face startles me. She looks so . . . so . . . enamored.

"Alicia." Minnie appears in the doorway and smiles. "Good to see you." She looks at my daughter in this man's arms. "Chloe, we've been waiting for you. We're starting art class in the sunroom." Minnie looks back at me.

She's as tall as I am, a slender woman whose age I couldn't guess, but she has to be every bit of seventy. She wears her gray hair long, pulled back in a ponytail. Most days, she's in a chambray shirt and jeans. She reminds me of Jane Goodall, who came to speak at the college the previous year about her Roots & Shoots Foundation.

"Would you like to come in?" Minnie asks me. "See what we're up to today?"

I hold up my hand. "Thanks, but I can't. I have office hours shortly." I give a little laugh. I'd been so eager to see Thomas and now that he's standing in front of me, I just want to get in my car and go.

Minnie must see the discomfort on my face because she gives Thomas a tap on the arm. "Enough with the hugs, you two. Chloe, hang up your coat and put your bag in your cubby. Then show Thomas where to find the smocks we use when we paint."

I like the way Minnie talks to my daughter. She keeps her requests short and to the point, but she speaks to her as if she's an adult and not a child. It's obvious she respects Chloe. And cares for her. Chloe isn't always treated with respect. Or even common courtesy. Especially not in public. She looks so . . . *damaged* that many people make certain assumptions. Either they talk loudly to her, as if she's deaf, or they totally ignore her. Minnie never ignores Chloe.

Thomas and Chloe go into the house. Chloe doesn't even say good-bye to me.

Minnie smiles at me again. Her hand is on the door. She's telling me, without saying, "In or Out."

I take a step back. "Thomas is new?"

"He's been coming a few weeks. His mother wanted him to ease into our program. First just Tuesday and Thursday afternoons, but this week, we're increasing his hours. He and Chloe hit it off right away yesterday. As you can see," she adds, glancing over her shoulder then back at me.

"I can see." I look up at her from where I stand on the sidewalk. I feel like I need to say something else, but I don't know what. I suddenly have this overwhelming feeling that I need to protect my daughter. From what? Watercolor painting? This man/boy? This urge to run inside, grab Chloe's hand, and take her home is irrational. It's silly. I force a smile. "Well, have a good day. See you this afternoon."

"You have a good day, too," Minnie calls cheerfully.

She closes the door, and I walk slowly back to the car. I unlock it and get in. I'm upset and I don't know why. Chloe wants so badly to have friends. To have a life. Why am I not happier for her?

I mean, I *am* happy for her, but . . . somehow my feelings are hurt. And something else, a feeling I can't quite define. Again, as if life is changing and I don't see it, I don't hear it, I don't smell it. But I feel it in my bones. In my gut. In my heart.

I think about Thomas's arms around Chloe. There wasn't really anything inappropriate about his embrace, other than that he hasn't known her twenty-four hours yet, but . . .

She said she was going to marry him . . .

I push the thought aside. It's beyond the realm of possibility.

I start the engine, but I don't pull away from the curb. I rest my hands on the steering wheel. What kind of mother am I that I'm not thrilled my daughter has a new friend?

My cell rings and I pick it up from the console. The caller ID says DAVID. "Hello?"

"Alicia . . . hi, it's um, David."

I smile. "David, hi."

"Did I catch you at a bad time?"

"No," I say, checking the time on the dash. "I just dropped my daughter off and I'm on my way to work. I have office hours, then two classes, back to back. Women Writers and a Byron Seminar." I'm tickled he called. Is it because I really like him or is it just that it feels good to have someone interested in me?

"I was wondering . . . the 1939 *Wuthering Heights* is playing Friday night at the old cinema downtown. Would you . . . like to go? I mean . . . if you can find someone to stay with your daughter. Unless . . . you think she'd like to come?"

I laugh and turn up the heat in the car. There's snow in the forecast. "Chloe's strictly a Disney girl. But I'd love to, if my girlfriend can keep Chloe. Jin's always bugging me to go out and do something, so as long as she doesn't have plans, I'm sure it'll be fine." I feel like I'm rambling. "So that's a yes. Probably."

"Great," David says, sounding a little less awkward.

Did he think I was going to say no? I smile at the thought that I could make anyone nervous like this. "So how about if I call you tomorrow?" I turn down the blower on the heater. "And let you know."

"Seven o'clock. That's what time the show is," David says. "We could go out for something to eat before . . . or after. Whatever you'd like."

I'm still smiling when I disconnect.

I'm glad when Mom leaves. I'm glad she doesn't come in Miss Minnie's. Miss Minnie's is my college. I went to high school. Then you go to college. But Minnie's isn't Mom's college. She goes to her own college.

I always liked my college, but now I like it better. I like it better because Thomas is here.

I look at Thomas and he smiles at me. His smile is so big that I can see his teeth.

I sit next to Thomas at the big table and wait for Miss Minnie to give me a paintbrush. Usually Ann sits next to me, but today I tell her no. Today I tell her not to sit in Thomas's chair. This is Thomas's chair next to me now. Not hers.

Ann was nice and didn't cry when I told her to sit in a different chair. I'm glad she didn't cry. Sometimes I want to cry when I can't sit in my blue chair.

Ann was my best friend but now she isn't. Now Thomas is my best friend.

Miss Minnie gives me a paintbrush. She gives Thomas one, too. And Ann and JJ and Melody. She doesn't give Abraham a brush because he sits in a wheelchair and his hands don't work good. Sometimes I let him use my hands, but not today. Today I want to paint a picture for Thomas. Usually I give my pictures to Mom, but this one will be for Thomas.

I always paint clouds. Blue. Mom says clouds are white but I like them blue. I stick my brush in the blue paint.

"You like blue clouds, Thomas?" I ask.

He looks at me and his mouth smiles and his eyes smile at me.

I want to paint blue clouds every day so Thomas will smile at me every day.

I walk into the house that evening, Chloe in tow, and see water dripping down through the ceiling onto the hardwood floor of the foyer. "Jeez," I groan.

I'm already in a bad mood. I had a student stay after class to argue over a grade. It happens all the time, but this little chit practically threatened me with responsibility for her impending suicide if I didn't give her a B+ on her C paper about nature and society in Byron's "Childe Harold's Pilgrimage."

Then I picked up Chloe and she talked nonstop about Thomas all the way home. He wants her to go bowling with his church group. It was all she could talk about. Bowling on *Wednesday*. With Chloe, anything that's going to take place in the future is on Wednesday. She can recite the days of the week, in order, and she can pick out a numbered day on a calendar, but she doesn't really understand the calendar.

Then, at the grocery store, Chloe tried to carry a glass container of orange juice and dropped and broke it. Then she cried and made a scene. It's amazing how far a quart of orange juice can go.

As I pull off my scarf and hang it on the coatrack, I look up at the spreading stain. I just painted the ceiling in the fall. After another leak in the pipes.

"Mom, it's dripping. Mom," Chloe says, standing in the puddle of water in the center of the foyer. She looks up and a big drop of water hits her in the forehead. She bats at her face but doesn't move. "Mom."

I grab her arm and pull her back. "Get out of the water, Chloe."

"It's wet," she says heavily. "Wet." She smiles. "Rain in the house."

"It's a leak. It doesn't rain in the house." I sigh and add my coat to the coatrack. "Can you put the groceries away?" I point to the cloth bags we set down inside the door. "I'll call the plumber." I start for the staircase to double-check that the leak is coming from a broken pipe rather than a bathtub overflow, which Chloe has done before. But I don't hear any water running, so I'm not hopeful.

"Tacos," Chloe says.

"Yup. We're making tacos. I'll show you how to brown the meat. You can make the tacos." I head up the stairs. "Take off your coat. Take the groceries into the kitchen and start putting them away."

A minute later I'm headed back down the steps. No bathtub overflow. I can't see any water, which means it's probably the bathroom pipes in the wall or floor again. Chloe is standing in the foyer, coat still on, groceries still on the floor. And she's *still* looking up at the water dripping from the ceiling.

"For heaven's sake, Chloe." I drop two towels in the puddle of water. "I thought you wanted tacos." I rest my hands on my hips, knowing impatience gets me nowhere with my daughter. "If you want tacos for dinner, you have to get out of your coat. Take the groceries in the kitchen. Put them away." I point at her, at the groceries on the floor of the foyer, and then in the direction of the kitchen.

She shuffles backward and begins to struggle out of her coat. "I want to go."

"Go where?" I ask. I grab one of the bags of groceries but make myself leave the other for Chloe. "I'm going to call the plumber."

"Bowling. I want to go bowling."

"You don't even like bowling." I head for the kitchen.

"I like bowling with Thomas," she says firmly.

"We'll see, Chloe. I'd have to get the details from Thomas's mother." Chloe's not good on details or following up. I don't see this whole bowling adventure with Thomas ever happening because Chloe won't be able to get the necessary information and I'm just not that interested.

I flip the light on in the kitchen and set the grocery bag on the counter. A can of black beans rolls out, off the counter, hits the hardwood floor, and rolls under the table. I leave it, going to the phone. If Chloe really wants to go bowling, I wonder if I should look into it. I wonder if I'm letting my feelings against organized religion keep Chloe from doing things she'd like to do. The bowling trips are, apparently, sponsored by Thomas's church. There are several churches in town that sponsor activities for mentally handicapped adults. Is my anger with organized religion getting in the way of my daughter's happiness?

Truth be told, I'm not so much angry with *religion* as I am with *God*. I just never got over Him making Chloe the way she is. I never quite bought the whole "she's a special gift from God" thing that people tried to tell me when she was born. Would any mother, given the choice, choose a handicapped child over a healthy, normal-brain-functioning child? I know. Totally politically incorrect. But it's not about me. It's not that I care how hard this is for me. It's about Chloe and the way she has to struggle to understand the simplest task. How frustrated she becomes with her own limits.

Jin says it's a karmic thing. That Chloe's soul has been sent to earth in her body, with her limited mind, to teach her lessons she'll be able to use in her next life. That idea actually appeals to me. Am I a closet Buddhist and I just don't know it? I wonder if there's a sangha that would take Chloe bowling.

I was born a Quaker. As a child, I grew up in a Quaker congregation. I drifted away from my Quaker roots in college and never found my way back. Never wanted to, though lately, I've found myself thinking about those days. About the peaceful silence of Meeting and how it made me feel.

I pick up the cordless phone and scroll through the saved numbers. My plumber's on speed dial. I hear Chloe knock over the coatrack. It happens sometimes. "You okay?" I call. I can't find the number.

I hear Chloe upright the coatrack. "Okay," she calls. She's grumpy. Probably hungry. Tired. I know how she feels. I finally find the plumber's number and hit the CALL button.

I assume I'll have to leave a message. I'm surprised when the phone clicks and I hear an actual, live human voice.

"Hello?"

"Mark. It's Alicia Richards." He lives on the street behind us. I can see his back door from mine. Handy, considering how often I need a plumber in this house.

"Hey, how are you?" he asks pleasantly. He has a nice phone voice.

"Um. Okay. Good." I see Chloe tromping into the kitchen, carrying the grocery bag. She sets it on the table rather than the counter and begins to unload it. She carries one item at a time from the table to the refrigerator or a cabinet. At this rate, it will take her half an hour to unload one grocery bag. I turn my back to her so I don't have to watch. "I'm well," I say, "but there's a pipe in my foyer ceiling that apparently isn't."

He chuckles at my bad joke. "Gushing or dripping?" he asks.

I don't know why, but I laugh. Maybe because the first time I called him in the fall for a leak (our previous plumber retired), he had to tell me to go shut off the valve under the kitchen sink so the water wouldn't continue to pour into the cabinet and onto the floor. "Just dripping," I say.

"I'm on a call right now, but I can be there in about an hour. Will that be okay?"

Somehow, his cheerfulness makes me feel better. "Sure. An hour it is."

"See you soon, Alicia."

"See you soon." I hang up and look at the phone. That was easy. I always expect there to be problems, no matter what I'm trying to do. When there isn't, I guess I'm pleasantly surprised. When I return the phone to its charger, I'm still smiling.

"So, Chloe." I clap my hands together. "How about tacos?"

She's struggling to get a half-gallon milk carton on the shelf in the refrigerator door. "How 'bout bowling?" she answers, surprising me with her cleverness.

"How about we see?"

✺ 4 ✻

An hour and a half passes. Chloe and I make ground beef tacos. She goes upstairs to put on her pajamas and then we begin to clean up from dinner. Mark-the-Plumber still hasn't shown up. I pick up a wet towel from the foyer floor and add a dry one. The steady *drip, drip, drip* is giving me a headache. My own personal Chinese water torture.

When the phone rings, we're doing dishes. I'm rinsing; Chloe's loading the dishwasher. Chloe is an excellent dishwasher loader. Better than most. It took her a while to learn how to arrange the dishes, but once she knew how to do it, she did it exactly the same way every time. And exactly right. Her father never learned to load the dishwasher in our six years of marriage. I suspect he's still doing an equally poor job on marriage/dishwasher number four.

The phone continues to ring as I dry off my hands on a Cinderella dish towel. Chloe's purchase, not mine. I hope Mark isn't calling to tell me he won't be able to make it tonight. If he can't make it until tomorrow, I'll have to shut off the water pump. Chloe hates it when I shut the pump off. (It's an old house; they leak. It's part of the charm, I tell myself all the time.) No matter how many times I tell her there's no water, she tries to get water. She tries to flush the toilet.

The phone is still ringing.

"It's for me," Chloe says, placing a white plate just so in the lower wire rack.

"It's not for you." I frown as I pick the phone up off the counter. She always says the phone is for her, but it never is. Her father doesn't call her. *My* father doesn't call her. She has no friends, except for those at Minnie's, but they're not the kind of friends who call. "Unless you want to talk to the plumber," I tell her.

"It's for me," she repeats. "Not a plumber. Not."

"Hello?" I say into the phone.

"C . . . can . . ."

It's a heavy, male voice. Loud. I recognize who it is, even though I've only heard him speak a couple of words.

I hear a woman in the background.

He starts again. "C . . . can I p . . . please talk to K . . . Ko-ey?" He's speaking at a deafening volume.

"It's Thomas," Chloe says. She jumps up and down and claps her hands. "I told you. It's for me."

"Thomas?" I say, holding the phone a little bit away from my head so he doesn't damage my eardrum. I can't hide my surprise. "Is this Thomas?"

"This is T . . . Thomas," he says. Then his voice is muffled as he speaks again, obviously to someone else in the room with him.

There's a pause and then I hear a female voice. "Hello, this is Margaret Elden, Thomas's mother."

"Oh, hi. This is Alicia, Chloe's mother."

"Thomas is trying to get ahold of Chloe. Is she there?" the woman asks. She sounds older than me. Quite a bit older. "He's nervous." She chuckles. She sounds nervous, too. "Calling a girl. It's his first time."

"Um . . . Yeah. Sure. Just a moment, please." I cover the receiver with my hand. "It's for you, Chloe. It's Thomas."

She shakes her head. "I told you," she says loudly, with excitement. "Thomas. I told him to call me."

"You know our phone number?" I ask, suddenly seeing my daughter in a new light. She's never been good with numbers. She can count, but the actual digits and their meaning evade her.

"On my bag. Inside." She puts her hand out for the phone. "In case I get lost. In case I can't find my mother. Call this number. My number."

I'm still staring at my daughter. Some of her hair has fallen out of the elastic at the nape of her neck and brushes her cheek. Something about the kitchen lights, maybe, but she looks different to me. "You wrote down our phone number for Thomas?" I ask incredulously.

"Hello?" I hear Thomas say. He's back on the phone again. Still loud. "K . . . Ko-ey?"

Chloe giggles and claps a hand over her mouth. "Thomas called," she says in a stage whisper.

"Just a minute," I tell him. I hold the phone out to my daughter. "Chloe? You wrote down your phone number for Thomas? You copied the number off your bag?"

She wipes her hand on the same pink and white towel I used, only she's more meticulous. She's drying each finger. "I showed Thomas." She nods emphatically. "Thomas, he wrote it. With his blue pen. He likes blue pens."

"Here." I offer the phone.

She tentatively holds it to her ear. "This is Chloe. May I ask who's calling?" she says, as I've taught her to answer the phone.

"It's okay, hon. It's Thomas. He's calling for you. You can just talk to him." I close the dishwasher door that's between us.

"Thomas?" she says into the phone.

"K . . . Koey!" He's so loud that I can hear him four feet away.

Her face lights up. "Thomas!" she says. "You called me. On the phone. You called me."

I can't help smiling because she's smiling. She's been saying she wants a friend. Maybe this will be nice, having Thomas for a new friend.

I cross my arms over my chest, watching my daughter as she grins from ear to ear.

"You called me," she repeats. She's apparently as surprised as I am. "Thomas."

"I ate . . . ate d . . . dinner," I hear him say after a long pause.

"I ate dinner," she says. "Tacos." She hesitates, trying to think what to say next. "I made tacos. Did you eat tacos?"

His mother must have told him to speak more quietly because I can still hear the rumble of his voice, but not what he says.

Chloe turns her back to me. I fold the dish towel.

Then Chloe walks out of the kitchen, scuffing her bunny slippers as she goes. I watch her go, resisting the urge to follow her and listen in on her conversation. She certainly has the right to a little privacy on the phone.

Five minutes pass as I finish cleaning up the kitchen and start the dishwasher. I hear Chloe giggling. She sounds the way I imagine a teenage girl must sound on the phone with a boy. It's the kind of experience I've missed out on, my daughter being different from other people's daughters. She's never had a boyfriend, never gone to a homecoming dance. Certainly never had the thrill of a first kiss.

Chloe's in the living room. Another five minutes pass. I flip through the day's mail: electric bill, Visa bill, and a bunch of junk.

I can't imagine what Chloe and Thomas are talking about. She can certainly ask and answer questions, but she's not much of a conversationalist. It's just not the way her mind works.

"Chloe!" I call. "The plumber might be trying to call. If the phone beeps, it means another call is coming in."

She doesn't answer me.

"Could you tell me if the phone beeps, Chloe?"

She comes back into the kitchen and lowers the phone stiffly to her side. "I want to go bowling." She blinks, her lips pursed. She's looking very serious. "Wednesday."

"Next Wednesday?" I ask. "Today's Wednesday. Do you mean next Wednesday?"

She raises the phone. "Wednesday?" she asks Thomas. She lowers the phone after a second. "Saturday," she says. "Ten o'clock."

I can tell Thomas is talking in her ear. "In the morning," he shouts.

"In the morning," Chloe repeats.

I hesitate. "You want to go bowling? I thought you hated bowling."

"I want to go bowling. With Thomas. Wednesday."

Chloe talks about doing all sorts of things that aren't really feasible. Last week, she watched *The Rescuers Down Under* on DVD and insisted she was going to Australia. On Wednesday.

"Who else is going bowling?" I ask, amazed that I'm doing this for the first time in my life.

Chloe goes places with me, Jin, her father, and Miss Minnie, but with no one else. She doesn't have that kind of relationship with anyone else and she's not capable of going without one of us to a place like a bowling alley. She's just not high-functioning enough for that kind of independence.

"It's not going to be just Thomas, right?" I ask.

"Are you going, Thomas?" Chloe asks into the phone. She listens, then looks at me. "Thomas is going."

"But who's going *with* Thomas? Thomas isn't going alone with you, right?" I toss the junk mail into the recycling bin near the back door. I met Thomas. He obviously isn't able to drive. He has to be going with *someone*. "Is he going with his mother?"

Chloe speaks to Thomas again, then tells me, "Thomas's mother doesn't like bowling."

"Can I speak to Thomas's mother?" I ask. I don't mind if Chloe goes bowling, if she wants to, but she has to have supervision. Even finding a public restroom can be hard for Chloe.

Chloe hands me the phone.

"Hello, again," the mother says.

"Margaret, hi," I say. This feels so weird. "Chloe tells me Thomas has invited her to go bowling."

"I'm going bowling," Chloe announces. She shuffles out of the kitchen.

"Yes," Thomas's mother says. "Saturday at ten. Thomas belongs to a group at St. Mark's United Methodist Church, downtown. He goes there every Saturday. There's usually an activity at the church and then they go somewhere: out to lunch, roller-skating, you name it," she says cheerfully. "This Saturday is bowling Saturday!"

"So . . . do parents attend?" I ask.

"Oh no! This is a time for the young adults to get together and have fun. I go to a women's Bible study at the church. You're welcome to join me. They're all really nice at St. Mark's."

"What I'm asking," I say, ignoring the Bible study invitation, "is . . . what kind of supervision is there? Who drives? Who will be bowling with them? Chloe doesn't go out alone." I hesitate, wondering if Margaret has met Chloe. "She has Down syndrome. My Chloe."

"No need to worry. It's well-chaperoned," Margaret says. The Down syndrome doesn't seem to faze her. "Just good, clean fun."

Chloe walks back into the kitchen. She's wearing her coat over her pajamas and carrying her canvas library bag. The one with her phone number written inside in permanent marker. I walk over to her and shake my head. "Not tonight, Chloe. You're not going bowling tonight. It's almost bedtime. The bowling alley is closed."

"I'm going bowling," Chloe insists. "Me and Thomas."

"Sorry," I say into the phone. "Chloe's so excited about going that she's put her coat on." I turn away from my daughter, who I can tell, by the look on her face, is ready to throw a temper tantrum. "You were saying . . . the chaperones."

"Nice people from church! Volunteers. And the associate pastor."

I know I can't allow the fact that it's a church group sponsoring the outing to affect my decision as to whether or not to let Chloe go. This has to be about Chloe, not about my own personal prejudices. But I'm not sure how to ask if this group is specifically for mentally challenged adults—what experience they've had with special-needs people like Chloe.

I turn back to look at Chloe. She's trying to zip her coat. She really wants to go. How can I say no? Still, how can I say yes? I don't know these people who would be taking her. My job, since her birth, has been to protect her. Because she can't protect herself.

"Chloe's not used to this sort of thing. Going out without me," I explain. "Do you think it would be okay if I go with her? With them?"

"I don't see why not," Margaret says, not sounding keen on the idea.

"Great. So ten o'clock on Saturday at St. Mark's?"

"In the community hall!" She's so damned cheery. "That's where they meet."

"Great. Thanks. We'll see you . . . Thomas, then."

"Thomas will see Chloe tomorrow, won't he?" Margaret says.

The doorbell rings. It's got to be Mark-the-Plumber. "That he will." I nod and force a smile. I want to like Margaret, I do. But there's something in her tone of voice—she's way too positive. Or maybe it's the way her son hugged my daughter today. "Thanks, Margaret."

"You have a blessed evening!" Margaret tells me.

I hang up as I head for the door.

"I want to talk to Thomas." Chloe follows me, still in her coat, still carrying her canvas bag. It says "Go For It @ Your Public Library!" She got it free two years ago when we went to a book fair at the library. Chloe loves books. Picture books. She has a whole shelf of them in her bedroom. Her canvas bag has become a security blanket of sorts. She carries it everywhere.

The doorbell rings again.

"I want to talk to Thomas! Thomas called me!" Chloe's voice is taking on an edge.

"Hang on a minute, Chloe," I tell her, keeping my voice calm. I learned long ago that losing my temper with my daughter gets me nowhere. The less control I exhibit, the less control she exhibits. I hope she's not going to have a meltdown in front of the plumber. When Chloe loses it, sometimes spit and fists are involved.

Mark is standing in the vestibule. He's wearing jeans, an L.L.Bean jacket, and a ball cap. He's carrying a toolbox. When he sees me through the door, he waves. Mark isn't much taller than I am. He's not really my type. I've always been a white-collar kind of girl, but he's nice-looking. And he's been super nice to me since he moved into our neighborhood in September.

"Hi," I say, unlocking and opening the door.

Jin comes up the steps behind him; she has a Wednesday evening class. She's got her cell phone to her ear. She's wearing a bright pink down jacket and a knit cap with earflaps. Although we're the same age, she looks so young and hip. I look like my grandmother when I go to class. I wonder if I should buy one of those hats with the earflaps.

Jin eyes Mark as she puts her key in the doorknob next door. "Another leak?"

I step out of the way to let him in. "Thanks for coming, Mark. This late in the day. Feel free to charge me extra."

"It's no problem to come." He drags one foot and then the other over the mat at the door, wiping his boots before stepping into the foyer. "Of course I'm not going to charge you extra."

"I want to talk to Thomas!" Chloe shouts.

I hesitate, taking a breath. *Sorry*, I mouth to Mark. I turn to face Chloe. "We can call Thomas back, if you want, but not if you're rude to me, Chloe. We don't shout at each other, right?"

Mark looks up at the dripping ceiling. "I'll just go upstairs," he says, pointing to the staircase.

"Sure. Thanks." I look at Chloe as he heads up the stairs.

Chloe's face is bright red. She stomps her foot. The movement is so childish that she could be two and not twenty-five. She shouts at me, "I want to talk to—"

"That's enough, Chloe," I say firmly, barely raising my voice.

"I want to go bowling! I want to talk to Thomas." She's half-screeching, half-boo-hooing.

"You can talk to Thomas if you calm down." I head for the kitchen. I've found that not giving Chloe too much attention when she acts like this helps. "And we can talk about bowling."

"I hate you!" Chloe shouts. "I hate you and I love Thomas."

Her outburst surprises me so much that I turn around. This is not my sweet Chloe. Even in her worst meltdown, she's never spoken to me this way. She *hates* me? I didn't know she even knew the word.

"I hate you," she repeats, stomping up the steps. She's still wearing her coat over her pj's. Still carrying her library bag.

I hear her bedroom door slam a minute later.

I shut my bedroom door closed. Really hard. I'm really mad.

I want to go bowling *now*. I want to talk to Thomas. I have to talk to Thomas.

He says I can go bowling with him.

I hang my bag on the bed. That's where it goes. On the bedpost.

I lay on my back on my bed and I put my feet on the wall by the board head.

I'm so mad at my mom. Mad, mad, mad. I kick the wall. She's a dummy head. A dummy head. A . . . a meanie head!

She doesn't understand. I love apple juice and I love Thomas. I have to talk to him because I have to go bowling. I don't like bowling. It's hard to roll the big ball down the hall. But I like bowling with Thomas because he likes to bowl.

I'm mad, mad, mad, and I cry and I kick.

Mom doesn't understand. She doesn't!

* * *

I'm still standing in the foyer when Mark comes down the stairs. He's left his coat upstairs with his toolbox, but he's still wearing the ball cap. His shirt is flannel. Plaid. Randall would never be caught dead in a blue flannel shirt.

I kind of like it.

"What do you think?" I ask hopefully.

"The bathroom sink this time. My guess." He crosses his fingers and holds them up. "I'm going to shut the main water off. I'll have to cut a small hole in the wall behind the sink. I'll fix the leak tonight, and get your water back on, but I should come back and add shut-off valves and an access panel."

"I know, the plumbing in the whole house needs to be brought into the twenty-first century. Guess we'll do it one sink at a time." I step on the towel on the floor in the foyer and move it around to mop up more water. I hear a steady banging. It's Chloe. She's lying on her bed with both feet on the wall. Pounding. I know, from experience, that she'll grow bored with it, or tired out, within a few minutes.

Still, I'm embarrassed. My adult daughter is throwing a toddler temper tantrum. I know I shouldn't be embarrassed, but I also know we can't help how we feel. Maybe it's because Mark doesn't know Chloe. Doesn't know us. I hope he doesn't think I'm a bad mother.

"Sorry about that," I say, pointing up toward the source of the racket. Chloe's small, but she's strong. She can really stomp when she wants to. "Chloe . . . sometimes she has a hard time dealing with emotions."

"You don't have to explain." He holds up his hand. "My kid brother Abe had Down's. When we were kids growing up"—he shakes his head—"Abe used to throw the biggest fits over the smallest things. Does Chloe throw things? Abe threw things. At the walls. At us. A book, a banana, anything he could get a hold of."

He's smiling. I'm smiling. "At least she doesn't throw things,"

I say, actually feeling fortunate. "Does your brother live with your parents, or is he in a group home?"

Mark looks away for a second, then meets my gaze. "Abe passed away last year. He had a congenital heart defect."

I'm suddenly light-headed. "I'm so sorry," I say when I find my voice.

His words put my life in perspective. Suddenly, I realize how very small this thing about Chloe going bowling is. How insignificant the temper tantrum she's throwing right now is.

I'm surprised to find tears filling my eyes. I'm not a crier and I wonder where this is coming from. Another symptom of menopause? *As if the hot flashes and forgetfulness weren't enough?* "How old was Abe?"

"Thirty-nine."

We're silent for a moment, but it's not an awkward silence.

Then Mark hooks his thumb over his shoulder. "I'm going to go shut the water off." He heads for the utility room. "Shouldn't be more than an hour."

Mark goes to shut off the water and I go upstairs to tell my daughter, who was thankfully not born with a heart defect, as close to 50 percent of all Down syndrome people are, that she can go bowling with Thomas on Saturday, if she wants. I'll make it happen.

She can go to the moon with him, if she wants. I just want her to be safe and happy. I'm her mother. It's all I've ever wanted.

❧ 5 ❧

Sometimes I think back to that moment . . . when I was standing in the foyer with Mark with the puddle of water on the floor between us. I think about the minutes afterward when I went upstairs and calmed Chloe down. When I helped her take her coat off and tucked her into bed. I remember how her face lit up when I told her she could go bowling with Thomas. That my only concern was her safety and that I would do whatever needed to be done to make sure she could go, and still be safe. I remember sitting beside her on the bed and stroking her hair while she rested her head on my shoulder. She'd always been a physically demonstrative person, Down's people are, but in the months leading up to that point, she'd been struggling to find her independence from me, and had been stingy with her affection. Her hug that night made me want to do anything, everything, in my power to make her happy.

It was one of those turning points in my life, in both our lives. A turning point I didn't recognize. But isn't it usually that way? Only in retrospect do we see the defining moments of our existence.

Sometimes I think, what if I had said *no*? What if I'd redirected her; she was always so easy to redirect. What if I'd offered to take her to Build-A-Bear instead? What if Chloe had never gone bowling that day?

Standing here alone in Chloe's bedroom, I feel the cold glass of the windowpane on my fingertips. I remember the feel of her warm breath on my cheek when she hugged me that night. And for a split second, I feel like it's not just my heart seizing, but my whole body. I remember the tale of Medusa and how her victims turned to stone. The same with the Basilisk in the Harry Potter books. It's a common occurrence in literature. I feel like I'm turning to stone.

I can't do this.

I can't do this.

I've never felt as alone as I feel right now, standing at this window, looking out on my dead lawn.

But Chloe was so happy that day. That Saturday, when we walked into St. Mark's church hall, she was beaming. She was wearing her favorite blue sweatshirt. It had kittens playing with a ball of yarn on the front. She'd waited patiently in front of the dryer for twenty minutes that morning until it was dry enough to wear.

"Thomas! Thomas!"

I close my eyes and I hear her voice. I see her as she was that first bowling day.

She bolts from me at the door and runs to Thomas, her canvas bag dangling from her elbow.

The group gathering in the church hall is a mix of average and obviously mentally handicapped young adults. From the way the group of a dozen or so young people is interacting, I can tell that those running the show are familiar with working with men and women like Chloe and Thomas. I exhale with relief. Chloe will be safe, at least, even if she doesn't have a good time. I see another girl with Down syndrome who looks a year or two younger than Chloe. I think to myself, *Maybe they can be friends.*

I'm surprised that Chloe joins the group so eagerly. She usually takes a while to warm up to any new situation. She doesn't like it if we can't park in the same parking spot at the market.

A man in his early thirties wearing jeans and a red polo shirt sees me in the doorway and walks toward me. His hair is military-short and bristly on top. His shirt is embroidered at the breast pocket with the symbol of the United Methodist Church: flames and a cross.

"Good morning. I'm Cliff Jackson, associate pastor here at St. Mark's." He offers his hand.

I shake it. "Alicia Richards. Chloe's mom." I point to her. Thomas has his hand around her waist and they're talking between themselves. I wonder what they're talking about. Chloe's world is pretty small. What *could* they be talking about?

I drag my gaze from my daughter and the man with his arm around her. And he is just that, a man: one who shaves and stands when he pees. I don't know what that has to do with anything; it's just what goes through my mind as I watch them. I guess what I'm considering is how innocent and childlike Chloe is. She doesn't know anything about *men*. She doesn't even know any men, except for her father. Men have sexual desires. I've always tried to protect Chloe from men out of fear that someone might take advantage of her. But it's "normal" men I've always been careful about. Honestly, it never occurred to me that a mentally handicapped man might be interested in her.

I feel the muscles in my mouth tighten as I force an artificial smile. Why is this so difficult for me? This is typical behavior for a girl Chloe's age. She'd certainly be considered a *late bloomer* by today's standards. Haven't I spent her entire lifetime attempting to make her like everyone else? I should be glad for her . . . should be, but it's all I can manage to keep from grabbing her hand and taking her straight home.

"We're so glad Chloe could join our friends here at LoGs today."

"Logs?" I ask. Even my voice sounds stilted. I can imagine what this pastor must think of me. "The new girl, Chloe," he might say later to his wife or a co-worker. "Very sweet. Well-mannered, a delight to have with us. But that mother . . . Ouch. It's a wonder the daughter is as normal as she is."

"Lambs of God. We call ourselves LoGs," he explains with humor in his voice. "Capital *L*, lowercase *o*, capital *G*, lowercase *s*. Thomas is super excited. He had his mom drop him off half an hour early. He's in charge of turning the lights on and off in the hall when we meet. He wanted to be sure the lights were on when Chloe arrived."

I drag my gaze from Chloe and Thomas to the young pastor standing in front of me.

"Chloe's very excited to be here, too," I say. "It was nice of Thomas to invite her. She . . . she's not used to going anywhere without me. Just to her daycare. I was wondering . . . thinking maybe I should stick around. At least for today," I add quickly.

"Looks like she's doing just fine." He glances at them again, then back at me. "We hope we're offering the opportunity for these young folks to have some independence, but I understand your concern. You're welcome to stay. There's coffee and juice." He points to a table set up on the far side of the hall, near what looks like a kitchen door. "We usually do something here and then head to our destination."

I nod. "And how do you get there?"

"We have a fifteen-passenger van. I drive. I don't have any speeding tickets and the church ran a background check before they hired me, so you don't have to worry about that."

I chuckle with him. "I'm sorry. I don't mean to sound like a paranoid parent, it's just . . ." I let my voice trail into silence, not sure how I should word my fears. It's not that I think this nice young man—or any of the others here—would take advantage of my Chloe. Or abuse her. But it happens.

So I suppose I am a little paranoid. Having someone take advantage of Chloe's innocence is my worst nightmare. But I muster through, pasting on my smiling mask and trying to seem agreeable.

"It's fine." He doesn't seem offended. "I'm not a parent myself yet. Newlywed." He shows me a shiny gold band on his left hand. "But I read the newspapers. Many parents aren't as careful as they should be. People like Chloe are a special gift from God, and we all have to be good caretakers. All of us."

The group begins to move toward two long tables that have been set up for an activity. Thomas leads Chloe by her hand.

"This morning we're making a craft with pieces of broken tile." The pastor checks his wristwatch. "We'll leave here in about an hour to go bowling. We'll have pizza there and be back here for pickup by two. Feel free to tag along. It looks like we've got room for you in the van."

"Chloe would kill me," I confess. "I'll take my own car and follow you over. In the meantime, I'll grab that cup of coffee." I see Chloe waving at me . . . more like waving me off. She made it clear in the car ride over that she didn't want me to stay.

"I'd better give them a hand. Let me know if you need anything."

He walks away and I watch him go. He seems very nice. Very pleasant. And he didn't overuse the words *Jesus* or *God* in the two minutes he stood here and talked to me. I hate the way some people feel as if they need to insert God or Christ's presence into every sentence. "I'm feeling much better today, praise Jesus!" or "Thank God they have strawberry yogurt today!" As if, by using the words often enough, they'll be able to impart their beliefs on the listener. On me, more specifically.

Ignoring Chloe, who's now gesturing wildly for me to leave, I go to the table sporting the big stainless-steel coffeepot. I pour myself a cup and add plenty of milk. As I stir my coffee with one hand, I fish my cell phone out of my bag with the other. I'm hoping maybe I've missed a call from David.

There's no missed call.

I thought David might call this morning because we had a date the previous night. Chloe stayed with Jin, and not only did I go to the movie, I stayed out long enough to have a glass of wine and share an appetizer with David. I had a good time. I thought he did. We kissed before I got out of his car. Actually . . . we made out a little. Thinking about it makes me smile again and then I look up, feeling guilty, afraid someone is looking at me and knows my secret.

I glance in Chloe's direction. She's taken a chair beside Thomas at the craft table. A young woman in pigtails is giving instructions on how to glue the mosaic tiles on a small, hinged cardboard box. Chloe's still conversing with Thomas; it looks like she's the one doing most of the talking. He's mostly just bobbing his head up and down enthusiastically.

Carrying my cup of coffee, I go through the swinging doors, into the hallway to give Chloe a little space. Holding my phone in my hand, I debate whether or not I should call David. I mean, why not? Why should the man be expected to make all the advances in a relationship? Wasn't that being sexist?

But what if he didn't have a good time? What if he doesn't think we really hit it off and he didn't call me because he doesn't want to go out again?

But he kissed me. He wouldn't have initiated the kissing if he hadn't liked me a little . . . would he? The thought that he hadn't liked the way I kiss lingers in the corner of my mind.

Or maybe it's just the whole package he doesn't like. Maybe he's another one of these guys who secretly yearns to date someone young enough to be his daughter. Even with my extra weight, my figure isn't bad, but no one's going to take me for thirty.

I groan. I hate feeling this way. Like I'm in the eighth grade and have my first crush.

Maybe a text?

I look at the phone again. That would give him an out, wouldn't it? If he didn't like me, he could just text back something noncommittal.

I find a chair in the hallway and have a seat. I text David.

Had fun last night

Thanks

Talk to you soon?

I wonder if it's too pushy. I send it before I chicken out. Then I check my e-mail. Several of my students have questions, want to turn an assignment in late, or want to complain about their grades. Before I know it, an hour has passed and *the lambs* are pouring into the hallway. Everyone is laughing and talking.

I feel a moment of panic when I don't see Chloe. The pastor must recognize the look on my face because he holds the door open, pointing inside the hall. "She's right there. She's helping Thomas shut off all the lights."

I peek inside. Sure enough, Chloe's on the other side of the hall, watching as Thomas carefully flips one switch after another on a panel on the wall. The overhead lights go off one after the other. When they're all off, Thomas turns to Chloe, towering over her.

"L . . . lights, off!" Thomas declares. Then he offers his hand.

My daughter takes this man's hand and together they walk across the hall and out the double doors where I wait. The only acknowledgment I get from Chloe is a frown of displeasure at the sight of my continued presence, and then her gaze is on Thomas again.

"And you never heard from him all day?" Jin asks. She snatches up the bottle of wine on the coffee table between us. She's on one couch, I'm on the other. It's Saturday night. Another exciting Saturday night in the Richardses' household.

The living room is so big that I ended up buying two couches. Brown leather. Even though the house is Victorian, I didn't decorate it in Victorian style—too much lace and ornate froufrou to suit me. My style is more Pottery Barn meets T.J.Maxx. The leather couches were an expensive purchase, but I'm still tickled with them after five years.

Jin pours more wine into my glass. It's a pinot noir. I don't know a lot about wine; Randall was always that department head. He liked to talk about the *bouquet* and such. He always ordered my wine for me at a restaurant, or bought the bottles for home at the grocery store. He said I didn't know what I liked. He always spent too much money on wine; it was nothing for him to spend fifty dollars on a single bottle. I don't know whom he was trying to impress. Certainly not me. The waitress? The clerk at the store?

Now I buy my own wine and I choose it by the picture on the label. And I know what I like. I like this bottle of pinot. It has a picture of a wolf howling at the moon on it. It was twelve bucks.

I let Jin fill my glass. Chloe's upstairs, already in bed, watching a movie on my iPad. I'm thinking about getting her an iPad for her birthday in March. There are some simple apps to download and it would be nice to make her movies so portable.

"Not a word from him," I tell Jin. "He didn't even answer my text."

I can laugh now. I wasn't laughing about it earlier when I called her to come over. Jin is between girlfriends; when she's single, we often get together evenings to commiserate. Saturday nights have become our *date night*.

Jin pours herself more wine and grabs a cracker off a plate. Chloe had wanted fish sticks and macaroni and cheese for dinner. I hate fish sticks and my waistline hates macaroni and cheese. I made a fruit, cheese and cracker plate, to share with Jin.

"But he kissed you good-bye?" Jin tucks her cute little brown, bare feet beneath her. She is one of those women who always has a pedicure, and walks around barefoot just to shame the rest of us.

I'm wearing shearling slippers over dry, ugly winter feet. My feet aren't as sexy as hers, but mine are warm. "Yes, he kissed me." I take a sip of the wine, which is cool and soothing on my tongue. "And not just a peck on the cheek," I tell my friend.

"With tongue?" she asks.

I feel my cheeks grow warm. I'm embarrassed to be fifty years old and having this conversation. But it's also a little fun. And freeing. "With tongue," I dare.

"And?" she asks.

"And?" I say.

She throws half a cracker at me. "Was it good?"

I catch it and pop it in my mouth. "Yeah." I think about it for a minute. "It was . . . nice."

"Nice? Just *nice?*" She groans and sits back on the couch, pulling a quilt over her skinny legs. "Be glad he didn't call."

"But I like him."

"If he's a bad kisser, you've got no future." Jin gives a wave and takes a drink from her glass.

"I didn't say he was bad." I'm still a little embarrassed to be talking about such a thing, even just with Jin. I even feel a little guilty to be kissing and telling. I like David. He *is* nice.

But Jin isn't buying it. She's frowning. "Did he get you all hot and bothered?"

When I don't answer, she shakes her head. "You deserve better, Ally."

I glance at the fire in the fireplace. It's a beautiful fireplace, framed in oak, with a marble mantle. Jin has a matching one in her living room. The two rooms, before we split the house in half, had been twin parlors.

I wish I had romantic reasons to light a fire.

For years after Randall left, after I kicked him out on his tweed ass, I wasn't interested in finding another partner. I wasn't even interested in dating. My every waking hour revolved around Chloe and my job at the university. In my ex's department. But things have gotten easier as Chloe has gotten older, and the fact of the matter is . . . I'm lonely.

I glance at Jin and smile. "Like you have room to talk. What about Mandolin? That crazy musician you were dating who named herself after an instrument?"

"She wasn't crazy," Jin defended. "She had . . . issues."

I roll my eyes. "Don't we all? But she was crazy. The way she always lined up your shoes in your closet while you were sleeping?"

"And don't forget the condiments." Jin pointed and laughed before taking another sip of wine.

"In descending alphabetical order in your refrigerator door." I point back at her. "And that's not crazy?"

Jin shrugs. "So she had a little OCD. I certainly do. Don't all women our age?"

I give her a look. "But she only ate certain color foods on certain days. Come on."

Jin laughs. "I should have known better. I should have walked away the minute she told me her name."

I laugh with her. "Okay. What about the one who called you after every date to tell you why she didn't like you? Then she'd invite you out again."

"Jasmine," Jin recalled. "Jasmine was a great kisser."

"But she didn't like you and she told you so on a regular basis."

Jin shook her head, laughing. "I think we're going to need another bottle of wine."

I grab a cracker and a piece of cheese. "Admit it. Abby was the most normal woman you ever dated."

"Abby. Abigail. My little Adams."

It was a personal joke between them . . .

Jin sighs and gazes at the fire.

Jin and Abby had been together fifteen years when they split. Abby is Huan's other mother. She's an attorney. She lives in Baltimore now. They'd broken up for all the reasons that heterosexual couples do after that long of a relationship. Jin felt neglected.

Abby felt Jin didn't appreciate the financial security she offered the family in exchange for her long hours at the office. Their parenting styles were different. What it came down to was that their relationship had lost its spark; they were bored with each other. The breakup had been amiable, and though Huan lived with Jin, he saw Abby all the time.

I study Jin's face for a moment. She seems sad at my mention of Abby. Wistful. I sometimes think that the two of them still aren't done. I think Jin still loves her, though Jin would be the last one to admit it.

"So, have you talked to her recently?"

"Who?" Jin's still in a far-off place.

"You know *who*. Abby."

"As a matter of fact, I have. Yesterday."

I wait.

"We're still friends." Jin takes a defensive tone. "I called her about our life insurance policies. There was some kind of option on them. You know me, I don't understand that kind of stuff." She looks into her glass of wine. "So we talked."

"About more than just life insurance policies?" I smile slyly when I say it.

"We were talking about you and David. Not about me." She shrugs. "I say that if he doesn't call you, it's his loss."

I glance at my phone lying on the coffee table in front of me. The only text I've gotten today is an advertisement from my cell phone carrier. My only call was a wrong number.

"You think I should text him again . . . in case he didn't get it?"

"No." Jin empties the last of the wine into her glass. "I think you need to get us another." She shakes the bottle at me.

I'm just getting up when my phone rings. My house phone. I look at Jin.

She raises her eyebrows.

I frown. "It's not him."

"It might be him."

I snatch the phone off the end table. I have caller ID, but it doesn't work on this phone. I need to replace it. "It's not him," I say. "It's not him because he only has my cell number." I hit the TALK button. It's probably a wrong number. "Hello?"

"C . . . Can I . . . I talk . . . talk to K . . . Koey?" a male voice booms.

✎ 6 ✎

Mom knocks on my bedroom door and comes in. "The phone is for you," she says. She doesn't sound happy. I don't like it when Mom isn't happy. It makes me sad.

I'm in my bed in my pj's. They're warm and snuggly and they have flowers on them. Blue. Me and my kitty are watching *Aladdin* on Mom's iPad. I like *Aladdin*. "Prince Ali turned out to be Ali Ababwa." I can sing the words.

I look at her, surprise on my face because I'm surprised. No one calls me on the phone. "Who's talking on the phone?" I say. I try to make the movie stop singing. Mom showed me how to make them be quiet. I touch the button, but they keep singing.

"I think it's Thomas," my mom whispers. I don't know why she's whispering. Is it a secret?

But when she says his name I feel funny in my belly. But a good funny. Not like when I eat too much candy and I have to throw up. I like his name. I say it over and over again when I'm by myself. *Thomas. Thomas.* I whisper it now. "Thomas."

Mom walks over to my bed. Kitty Spots jumps off my bed and runs away. I call her that because she has spots on her fur. She runs out the door. Mom holds the phone out to me. I take it, but

I don't talk to Thomas. I want Mom to leave. I want to talk to Thomas by myself. I don't want to share him.

"I'm gonna talk to Thomas," I tell my mom. "You leave."

She looks sad for a minute, but she makes Aladdin stop singing and then she goes out of my room. But she doesn't close my door.

"Thomas." I say his name to him on the phone.

"K . . . Koey," Thomas says. He says my name wrong, but it doesn't make me mad. I like Thomas. A lot. I love him. Me and him, we're going to get married. He told me.

"This is . . . is T . . . Thomas," Thomas says on the phone.

I laugh. "I know," I tell him. I don't know why I laugh again, but I do. "You called me."

I get out of my bed. Mom's in the hallway. I look at her. She's a nosy head. I close the door.

I don't know what I'm supposed to say on the phone to Thomas. I guess he doesn't know what to say either, because he doesn't talk. He just says "K . . . Koey," again.

Then I hear his mom talk. Then Thomas talks.

"We . . . w . . . went bowling, you . . . you a . . . and me," he says. He has a hard time saying words, but it's okay. I don't laugh. It's not funny when you can't say something. A boy laughed at Thomas at the bowling alley when he tried to get us a soda, but Pastor Cliff talked to him quiet and the boy didn't laugh anymore.

"We went bowling," I tell Thomas. I remember when we went bowling and I say, "It was fun. We roll the ball. It's really heavy. Pow!" I pretend I'm rolling the bowling ball in my bedroom. That's silly because I'm wearing my pj's. I don't go to the bowling alley in my pj's! Thomas makes me feel silly. Good silly.

I didn't like bowling before. My dad took me. He read his newspaper and told me to bowl by myself. My dad doesn't like me very much. That makes me sad, but I don't tell Mom because she will be sad. Dad takes me to dinner at Chick Filly. I love

Chick Filly, except when he gets me the salad so I don't get fat. I don't like the salad. I like the chicken nuggets and the French fries and lemonade. And milk shake.

"K . . . Koey," Thomas says.

"I like bowling," I tell him. "We can go bowling again. The lambs can take us." I liked riding in the van with the lambs. They didn't look like sheep to me. Lambs are baby sheep. I have a book about farm animals and there's a picture of sheep. I can't read, but Mom reads me the book. I wonder if Thomas will read me my book. He says he can read.

"I c . . . called you on . . . on f . . . fa f . . . phone," Thomas says. "I wanted to t . . . tell you some . . . somefing."

I sit on my bed. "What?"

He laughs like he doesn't want to say it. "You're m . . . my . . . g . . . girlfriend."

He told me when we went bowling that he was my boyfriend. I was his girlfriend. I don't know exactly what that means. On TV it means you kiss on the lips. Huan kisses his girlfriend on the lips at his house when his mom isn't there. He puts his hand in her shirt. I'm not supposed to tell. Huan is my friend but not my boyfriend.

I wonder if Thomas wants to kiss me on my lips. When I think about it, I think maybe I want to kiss his lips. That makes me giggle more.

"Tell your mom," I tell him. "I'm your girlfriend. Chloe Richards-Monroe is your girlfriend. That's my name. Chloe Richards-Monroe."

"K . . . Koey Richards is my . . . m . . . my girlfriend," he says.

I laugh and he laughs and I wish he came to my house. Then we could watch *Aladdin* on my bed. "You should come watch *Aladdin* at my house, Thomas. On my bed," I tell him.

"Wh . . . what's *Aladdin*?" he asks me.

"The movie, silly head." I call him silly head and he laughs.

Then I hear his voice but I don't hear his words. I think he's talking to his mom. He calls her mama. Thomas loves his mama. She loves him. But she's not his girlfriend. Your mom can't be your girlfriend. He told me when we went bowling.

"Mama s . . . says I . . . I can't watch *A . . . Aladdin* on . . . on your bed. If . . . if I come to . . . to your house, I . . . I have to sit on f . . . fa . . . the c . . . couch. Nice boys sit . . . sit on f . . . fa couch. But not . . . t . . . tonight. She says not . . . not tonight."

"Wednesday?" I ask.

"W . . . Wednesday," he says. "Now I have . . . have to take . . . a . . . a sh . . . shower."

"Bye," I tell him. Then I push the button on the phone and then I push the button on the iPad. *Aladdin* comes on again. I hope Thomas will like *Aladdin*. On Wednesday.

"So he's calling her, now?" Jin asks me when I come down the stairs and into the living room, sans phone.

I nod, taking my seat across from her. I reach for my wine.

Jin frowns and creases appear on her forehead. "What do they talk about?"

I can see that, in my absence, she retrieved another bottle of wine from the rack in my kitchen. She's opened it to let it breathe. She's had refrigerator rights for years, which have become wine rack rights. Which isn't a problem because she buys wine for the rack more often than I do. Jin doesn't like to drink alone.

I sip my wine. "I don't know what they talk about. Whatever it is, she doesn't want me to hear. She closed her door. Suddenly at the age of twenty-five she wants privacy."

"You shouldn't be angry with her." Jin shrugs a slender shoulder. "It's only natural." Her tone is gentle, and I think to myself that she must be a great partner. I feel bad for her that she doesn't have someone right now. Me, I guess I'm kind of a loner, but Jin likes being half of a couple. I know she doesn't like being single.

"I'm not angry," I argue.

"And you shouldn't be hurt, either."

I open my mouth to say I'm not hurt, but instead I finish the last of the wine in the bottom of my glass. I *am* hurt and I don't know why.

Again, I feel like a terrible mother. This is what I've wanted for Chloe for so long—for her to have a life beyond me. I've always wanted her to have friends. So what if it's a boy? There's nothing wrong with that. Thomas can be her friend without being her boyfriend. Chloe doesn't understand what a boyfriend is. I wonder how I can explain it to her.

Jin pours wine from the new bottle into my glass. "People with Down syndrome have boyfriends and girlfriends, don't they?" she asks.

I wonder, not for the first time, if Jin is clairvoyant. I don't believe in such things, but I wonder how she sometimes knows what I'm thinking. I swirl my wine and watch it swish around the glass, thinking this should be my last one tonight. Otherwise, I'll have a headache in the morning. "I . . . I don't know." I look up at her. "I suppose they do."

"Why wouldn't they?" She pours herself more wine. "Chloe loves you. She loves me and Huan. Why couldn't she love a man?"

I don't answer.

She's quiet for a moment. The fire pops, and it seems as if the room bursts with the fresh scent of the cherry. I bought a whole cord of cherry wood and had it delivered just before Thanksgiving. It was more expensive than a regular load of mixed hard and soft woods, but it was worth every penny. The smell is glorious.

"When Chloe was born," I say slowly, "I was so afraid she would never talk, never tie her own shoes, never be potty trained. I read things like that. People said those things."

Jin sits back, tucking her legs under her and pulling the quilt over her legs again. She's in for the long haul. She's listening.

"Do you know that fifty years ago, doctors were still telling parents to institutionalize children born with Down syndrome?" I ask. I draw my finger around the rim of my wineglass. "My pediatrician didn't say such a thing, of course. He told me that Down syndrome children brought great joy to their parents. He said there was no limit to the possibilities of what Chloe might learn, what she might do." My eyes fill with tears and I feel silly. I thought I had already shed all the tears I had for Chloe, years ago. "I just want what's best for her."

"She's not going to be harmed by going to a church youth group or by going bowling with a boy," Jin says quietly. "He won't hurt her." She pauses. "Well . . . he might. But a broken heart is something we all experience at some point in our lives." Her gaze meets mine. "You have. I have. It's one of the things that makes us human, Ally."

We're both quiet for a moment; it's a comfortable silence.

"And who knows," Jin continues. "Maybe she'll fall in love."

I smile, close-lipped, and take another sip. The wine is drier than the other bottle and tingles on the tip of my tongue.

That is what we want for our children, isn't it? To love and be loved? But I don't know if Chloe is capable of loving a man in a romantic way. There are so many things she doesn't understand. Like sarcasm. Like why, after all these years, Randall can still hurt my feelings. "She doesn't even know what a boyfriend is," I say dismissively.

Jin gives me a look.

"She doesn't."

"Have you talked to her about relationships between men and women? About sex?"

"Not really. I mean . . . she knows where babies come from. Sort of. She gets the whole period thing." I reach for my cell phone on the coffee table. I can't imagine talking about sex with Chloe. It took me almost three years to teach her how to use a tampon. I wouldn't know where to begin on the subject of sex. I hold up my phone. "No call. No text. From David." I set the phone down again. "Maybe he's just super-busy."

"Maybe." Jin sounds hopeful.

I'm not. This has happened before. It's why I don't date much. The losers are the only ones who call back. Guys like David, nice guys . . . they want younger women. Women with fewer responsibilities. Women who are more fun.

Obviously, there's nothing I can do about the responsibility part, but I promise myself that the next time a nice guy asks me out, I'll be more fun.

Just as soon as I figure out how.

David doesn't call or text Sunday, either. But Thomas calls again. Twice. Both times, Chloe takes the phone to a different room from the one I'm in. She's so happy that he's called that I can't help but be happy for her.

After she hangs up the second time, I have her bring her dirty laundry from her bedroom to the laundry room. We're working on learning how to sort lights and darks. I'm hoping she can, eventually, wash her own clothes. Maybe even mine.

We stand side-by-side. "How's Thomas?" I ask. "Dark clothes in this basket, light clothes in that one. Whites here." I indicate three laundry baskets that I've lined up on the floor for her.

The laundry room is on the second floor, next to the bathroom. Originally, it had been a tiny bedroom or parlor or something. When Chloe was a baby, we brought the washer and dryer out of the basement so I could do laundry without having to drag baskets of clothes and Chloe up and down two flights of stairs.

"He went to church, but no lambs. No lambs today," Chloe says, shaking her head emphatically. She pulls the first item of clothing from her tall wicker basket. It's a pair of dark blue pants. She throws them in the lights basket.

I pull them out. "Darks go here." I toss them into the first basket. "He's calling often."

She looks at me. Blinks. I know that face.

"*Often*. A lot. He's called many times," I explain.

She throws a navy blue sock in the middle basket. I pluck it out and drop it on top of her pants. "Darks here, lights here, whites there," I explain again patiently. I take a pair of dirty jeans from my basket and throw them on top of Chloe's. Then I toss a pair of khaki pants into the middle basket. "See, lights in the middle." I grab a pair of white panties next and toss them in the whites basket, just so Chloe has an example in each basket.

"Thomas called me," Chloe says proudly. She holds up a dark blue sweatshirt and is about to drop it into the middle basket.

I guide her hand so it's over the first basket before she lets go of the sweatshirt. "So . . . what do you talk about, you and Thomas?"

She smiles, almost shyly. "Thomas likes dogs. He had a dog in his other house, but then they came here. Mar-y-land," she pronounces carefully. It comes out Mair-we-land. "The dog had to live in another house. Me and Thomas are going to get a dog when we get married."

"Thomas and I." I ignore the *married* part. "Did you tell him about your cat? About Spots?"

"He likes dogs. Not cats." She holds a light blue T-shirt in her arms, debating which basket to put it in.

I point to the one in the middle.

The phone rings.

"Thomas!" Chloe digs into her dirty clothes again and giggles.

"You just talked to Thomas," I say. "How many times a day is he going to call?" My tone is teasing and Chloe laughs. Chloe's always had a sense of humor.

I walk down the hall to grab the phone from beside my bed. Surprise, surprise, it's Thomas's number. "Hello, Thomas," I say, heading out of my bedroom.

"Hello?" comes a woman's voice. "This is Margaret, Thomas's mother."

"Oh, hello, Margaret." I try not to sound surprised, even though I am. I retrace my steps down the hall to the laundry room. "How are you, Margaret?"

"We had a lovely morning at church, Thomas and I!" I can hear her smiling and I wonder why I can't smile all the time like her. I bet if *she'd* gone out with David, he would have called *her* back. I bet Margaret is a lot more fun than I am.

In the laundry room, I find that Chloe has added a black sock to the whites basket. "What can I do for you, Margaret?" I throw the sock in the correct basket. Chloe learns best by watching. I know that if I just keep sorting laundry in front of her, eventually she'll get it.

"I was calling about Chloe's invitation."

"Chloe's invitation?" I realize I've just repeated what she said and I feel foolish. I'm an English professor, for heaven's sake. Where is my command of the English language? I snap out of it. I slide the phone away from my mouth. "Chloe, honey, did you invite Thomas . . . somewhere?"

Chloe continues to sort clothes: a pink sock in the darks, white panties in the darks, the other pink sock in the whites. What are the odds she would get every single article of clothing wrong?

"Thomas is coming to watch *Aladdin*. Not in my bed." Chloe doesn't look at me. She stares into the laundry basket at her feet. It's the way she focuses on a task. "On the couch. Wednesday."

"Sorry," I say into the phone. I'm not sure what Chloe's talking about concerning her bed and Thomas. "Chloe didn't tell me she had invited Thomas over. But it's fine. Not a problem," I add quickly.

"Does Wednesday suit?" Margaret asks me. Still smiling. I can hear it in her voice.

I consider explaining Chloe's whole Wednesday thing, but Wednesday actually works. If Chloe and Thomas are going to be friends, it only makes sense that she should invite him over. This way, I can get to know him better. And keep an eye on them.

"That would be great. Will Thomas be at Minnie's Wednesday afternoon? I could pick them both up after my last class," I tell Margaret. "I teach at Stone. Four thirty?" I continue. "Thomas is welcome to have dinner with us. They can watch the movie and have dinner and then you could come by and pick him up. Eight, maybe?" It feels so strange to be saying this.

"I'm sure Thomas would enjoy that!" Margaret says.

"Great." I grab the pink socks and peach-colored underwear Chloe has distributed evenly in the three baskets and put them all in the middle basket. "If you don't mind, just let Minnie know he'll be coming home with us."

"Oh, Thomas can tell her. He's a big boy, aren't you, Tommy?"

"Big b . . . boy," I hear Thomas repeat. His speech is so gruff and guttural. I wonder if he's had speech therapy. He sounds so . . . *retarded* is the only word that comes to mind and I feel my cheeks grow warm. That's not a word that's used anymore. Certainly not a word I would use. I'm ashamed of myself. I know better.

"Well," I say, feeling awkward. Any time Chloe's schedule changes, I tell Minnie myself. I can't imagine relying on Chloe. "We'll see Thomas . . . and you, Wednesday."

"See you then!"

"Wednesday," Chloe says, throwing a black T-shirt in the whites basket. "Thomas and me are going to watch *Aladdin* on Wednesday."

She's grinning from ear to ear.

⚘ 7 ⚘

Four phone calls from Thomas later, and none from David, not so much as a text, and Thomas is plopped on our couch to watch *Aladdin* with Chloe. On Wednesday.

Chloe is standing in front of the TV armoire beside the fireplace. "I can do it," she tells me, taking the remote from my hand. She points it at the TV and pushes a button with great flourish.

It took her so long to get dressed this morning that I was late to class. Just like any young girl getting ready to go on a first date, she tried on and discarded multiple outfits, all involving sweatshirts with graphic prints of animals. In the end, she chose a light blue one with a white polar bear on the front.

I glance at the TV, which is not responding. "You have to tell the TV that you want to use the DVD player," I tell her patiently.

Thomas is sitting on the couch in a Mr. Rogers–type navy cardigan; his hair is slicked to one side and glued down with a serious helping of hair gel. Today he's wearing new wire-framed glasses, which make him seem even older than thirty—information I gleaned from a conversation with Miss Minnie this morning. He moved here with his parents from Ohio three months ago. His father was laid off and found a new job with a local tool and die company.

Fancy that . . . an intact family with a handicapped child. It's such a rarity, they should put the Eldens in *People* magazine or at least give them their own reality show. Mr. Elden certainly wasn't cut from the same bolt of cloth as Randall. When Randall realized what a challenge raising Chloe would be, he hadn't been able to run fast enough.

I taste my bitterness in my mouth and swallow against it. This wasn't who I wanted to be. It was better for Chloe that Randall had gone when he had, before she'd known enough to understand that while he still paid child support, he'd abandoned her. And what kind of life would we have had with him if he'd stayed? Would I have had to be checking his pockets every night for students' numbers and eavesdropping on his phone calls?

I'm better off without him, I tell myself. Chloe is better off. I have to believe that, don't I?

I look back at Thomas. He's wiggling in his seat and clasping his hands in his lap, obviously nervous to be here.

Chloe hits several random buttons on the remote, sending the TV shooting off into a cable television alternate universe. I'm not annoyed that Chloe can't operate the remote (I had to read the instruction manual myself three times), only that she won't let me help. We do this dance at least twice a week.

"You have to hit the little black button on the right. There," I say, daring to put my finger on the remote in her hand. I step back quickly as she snatches it away from me.

Chloe holds her tongue between her teeth so that it protrudes from her lips, in obvious concentration. The TV screen changes from scrambled black-and-white images to a screen showing various input options.

"You have to use the arrow key."

"I know!" She glances at Thomas, then back at the TV. "I can do it!" She hits several buttons, none of them the arrow key, and the screen shoots off into space again.

Now the TV is waiting for instructions from the Wii. We don't have a Wii.

"First the black button," I say quietly.

She sets her jaw, obviously annoyed with my interference. She hits the black button.

"Perfect. Now the arrow key." Again, I reach over and touch it.

Again, she pulls the remote back, but this time, she hits the arrow key. It only takes her two tries to get it to stop on the correct video input.

"Now hit the ENTER key," I say.

She hesitates.

I reach over and press the button. The video pops on the TV. "There you go. I'll be in the dining room grading papers if you need me. There are Cokes in the fridge." As I walk out of the living room, I catch a quick glimpse of Chloe as she sits down on the couch so close to Thomas that she's practically in his lap.

"This is *Aladdin*," she tells him. "You'll like *Aladdin*."

"I l . . . like *Aladdin*," he echoes.

It's an early indication of how their relationship will develop. In the coming weeks and months I learn that Chloe likes bossing people around. She's always had it in her, apparently. She'd finally found someone she *could* boss. And, Thomas, it seems, likes being bossed around.

"Pretzels on the counter," I call as I walk into the dining room.

"Thanks!" Chloe hollers, only it comes out more like "fanks." Diphthongs are tricky.

"F . . . fanks, D . . . Dr. Richards!" Thomas repeats in his guttural tone.

I sit down at the end of the dining room table and look at the piles of students' papers. I've got hours of grading to do; I reach for my reading glasses but on impulse, I pick up my cell phone . . . just in case David called.

I check the screen. He hasn't. Maybe his cell self-destructed and he lost all his numbers. Right. And maybe the tooth fairy will bring me a new car tomorrow, one without transmission problems.

I hold the phone in my hand. Chloe's singing the first words of the opening song of *Aladdin*. I know the words by heart. I know all the Disney songs.

"Oh, I come from a land, from a faraway place," Chloe is singing at the top of her lungs. She can't carry a tune, but she doesn't care. She sings her heart out. My Chloe, with her intellectual disabilities, is bold in ways I never will be. She enjoys life in ways I don't seem to be able to. She takes chances. Thomas is a perfect example.

I look at the phone again. Then think to myself, *What the hell? Why not?*

I dial David. I expect to get his recorded message. I'm contemplating what I should say. Do I pretend it's not odd that he hasn't called me since our date five days ago? Do I just flat-out ask him why he didn't call? Do I ask him if my chubby waist is a turnoff?

"Hello?" David says.

I freeze. I know my eyes must be dilating. Do I hang up?

Of course not. It's his cell phone. The caller ID popped up. He *knows* it's me calling . . .

"David . . . hi," I say brightly. I feel like an idiot. If he didn't want to call, he certainly didn't want me to call him. "I was just calling to say . . ." I hesitate. "You didn't have a good time the other night, did you?" I say with a sigh.

"No, no, it's not that. I did. I just . . ."

The silence between us is physically painful.

"I just think . . . we're not right for each other," he finally manages. "I'm sorry."

Surprisingly, his words don't make me feel all that awful. I laugh. "It's okay," I say . . . and I realize as the words come out of my mouth that it really is . . . okay. "I just wanted to call. And see." I pause and then go on. "Truthfully, David, a woman my age doesn't have the time to sit around and wait for a man to call. You have a good day."

"You, too," he says, not sounding as if he knows exactly what just happened.

Congratulations, I tell myself. You've hit a new low in the world of dating.

I should be mortified, but I'm not. Why did I expect this to turn out any differently than all the other dates I've had in the past decade? It wasn't as if David was my dream man. He was . . . adequate. How low had I fallen to have been willing to settle for adequate?

I slide the phone onto the dining room table, put on my reading glasses, and begin grading a pile of essays on the features of Romanticism in Keats. As I read, I hum the catchy song, "Arabian Nights," from the movie playing in the living room. Instead of being bummed by David's rejection, I feel . . . exhilarated. Not by the idea that he didn't like me, but by the idea that he could say so and I wouldn't be devastated. I tried to have a relationship with him, and I failed. Chloe fails every day. She keeps trying. I need a little bit of her spirit in me, I decide. And tonight's the night to start.

After the movie and wading through twenty-five essays, Chloe, Thomas, and I have dinner: salad, homemade baked ziti, and bread. When Chloe sets the table—she always sets the table—she enlists Thomas's help. She shows him where to place the forks and knives on each side of the plates. When he puts a fork on the right side of a plate, she carefully moves it to the left. As I carry the casserole dish of hot ziti to the table, the two of them are laughing about something. It makes me smile to see her so happy.

The three of us take our chairs at the kitchen table and Thomas folds his hands in prayer and squeezes his eyes shut.

"What are you doing?" Chloe demands, taking a piece of bread out of the bread basket and trying to hand the basket to him.

"P . . . praying," he booms, eyes still shut. "Thank You, J . . . Jesus, for this foo . . . food!" He's so loud. Louder than Chloe, whom I'm always telling to turn down the volume. "Amen!"

Chloe looks at me and I'm not sure what to say. We never say grace at our table. I'm not sure why. I always did, growing up. Actually, my family didn't *say* grace. In the Quaker tradition of my mother, also a born Quaker, we observed a moment of silence to give thanks privately. I think about her and how much she would have enjoyed having dinner with us tonight. I know she would have understood the significance of tonight, and would have been proud of Chloe.

"Mom," Chloe says. Her hands are folded in a prayer death-grip. "Can we pray?"

Thomas opens his eyes. They're both looking at me.

Chloe doesn't know what praying means. Or much about who God is. I've brought her up in a household of intellect. Or so I've told myself. I clasp my hands. "When I was a little girl, we didn't speak out loud. We closed our eyes"—I close mine—"and thanked God for our food and for each other. Silently."

"You talk in your head but not in your lips?" Chloe asks.

I nod and smile, my eyes still closed.

Then I'm quiet for a moment, we're all quiet, and I'm surprised at how good it feels, this silence. I open my eyes to see Thomas holding the bread basket and staring at me. Chloe still has her hands clasped, her eyes squeezed shut. I wonder what she's thinking.

Thomas and I regard each other for a moment. Then he bites off a big hunk of bread. His chewing is sloppy. Chloe opens her eyes and grabs his plate, giving him a heaping serving of ziti.

I actually enjoy dinner, maybe just because the change is nice. I ask Thomas some questions about his recent move. Chloe keeps interrupting and answering for Thomas.

"His dad got a new job!" Chloe practically shouts across the table to me. "In Mary-land."

"So it's just you and your mom and dad, Thomas? Do you have brothers and sisters?" I ask.

"I . . . I have t . . . two sisters," he tells me, painfully trying to pronounce each word correctly. He blinks when he talks. "They . . . they live in . . . in Hi-O! R . . . Rooffy and K . . . K . . . Kaf-ar-in. Girls. Sisters are girls."

"We're going to Hi-O to see his sisters," Chloe tells me. "Me and Thomas. On Wednesday."

I nod. I've learned long ago that sometimes it's better to just let Chloe say what she's thinking and not always put her on the defensive. She forgets half of the stuff she says, anyway.

We're finishing up sherbet for dessert when the doorbell rings. I glance at the clock on the stove. It's 7:55.

"It's your mom," Chloe says, bringing her face inches from Thomas's.

"It's my . . . my m . . . mom," he repeats, managing to wedge his spoon between the two of them, practically knocking Chloe in the nose with it, to take another bite.

"I'll get it!" Chloe almost knocks her chair over getting to her feet.

Thomas stands, his spoon still in his mouth.

"It's okay. Chloe can let your mom in. Finish your sherbet," I tell him, waving him down.

He hovers over his chair as Chloe runs out of the kitchen.

I follow Chloe's lead. "Sit down, Thomas. Finish your sherbet."

He sits, seeming relieved to be told what to do.

I hear Chloe at the front door.

"Check to see who it is before you open the door," I call. Her first impulse is to let anyone and everyone in. We're working on that. Thanksgiving week, she led the FedEx guy upstairs to find me. Luckily, I had closed the bathroom door.

"It's Thomas's mom!" Chloe shouts.

I hear her open the door, and then I hear Chloe and Margaret exchanging greetings. Chloe leads Margaret to the kitchen.

"Hi. We're just finishing up," I say cheerfully as I stand.

Margaret is wearing an ankle-length skirt or dress under her wool coat; the skirt looks homemade. Her hair is long and thin and graying and pulled back in a ponytail. She's wearing no jewelry except for a gold wedding band, no makeup. I guess she's at least ten years older than me. I doubt she was ever attractive, but age and gravity haven't been good to her. She's not really heavy, just . . . lumpy.

I make a silent vow to dig my pilates DVDs out and actually start using them.

"I'm Alicia." I shake her hand. "It's nice to meet you, Margaret."

"Nice to meet you." Her hand is warm.

"Thomas, would you like some more sherbet?" I ask.

He's licking his spoon.

Chloe takes her chair beside him to finish off the last bite in her bowl. "No more ice cream. Ice cream makes Thomas fat." She pats her own belly.

Margaret and I look at each other and chuckle.

"Chloe, you shouldn't answer for Thomas," I say.

"Oh, he might as well get used to it," Margaret tells me jovially. "Someday he'll have a wife telling him what to do, won't he?" She laughs.

A *wife?* I smile, wondering if she's serious. I've only spent a little time with Thomas, but my mom/educator experience tells me that Thomas is not as high-functioning as Chloe. I grab a couple of dirty plates off the table and carry them to the sink. "We're glad you could come, Thomas."

"Darling, wipe your mouth," his mother instructs, motioning.

He starts to use the back of his hand, but Chloe pushes a napkin into his hand. "Use a napkin," she instructs. "Always wipe your mouth with a napkin."

"F . . . fank you, d . . . darling . . . darling," he says, swiping the napkin across his lips.

His use of the same endearment his mother just used doesn't go unnoticed by me. He's obviously just mimicking.

When Thomas gets up, I see little bits of napkin sticking to his five o'clock shadow. Chloe reaches up to pick the pieces off his face. I find the intimate moment disturbing.

Chloe really likes this boy, I think to myself as I run hot water over the plates. The idea that she doesn't like him *just as a friend* hovers in my mind and I don't know what to do with it.

"We should go, Thomas," Margaret says.

I dry my hands on a dish towel and walk them to the front door. "We're so glad you could come, Thomas."

"Glad you could come," Chloe says, hopping up and down on the balls of her feet. She throws her arms around Thomas, and Margaret takes a step back.

"Oh my! Oh my goodness," Margaret says, sounding flustered.

"Chloe's a hugger," I explain, reaching for Thomas's parka on the coatrack. "Chloe," I say. I'm going to tell her to take a step back. Maybe Thomas doesn't like to be hugged. (Of course I already know that's not true; I've already seen several lingering hugs.) But before I get the words out, Chloe plants a big, wet kiss on Thomas's mouth.

Now I'm the one who's flustered. I hold Thomas's coat against my chest. The moment turns even more uncomfortable when Thomas kisses her back. Mouth open. I actually feel my face get hot.

"Thomas, darling." Margaret grabs his hand, her voice sweet and singsongy. "Remember, we talked about mouth kissing?"

I must have been holding my breath because I exhale in relief. Margaret's going to handle this. I don't have to.

"Private moments, Thomas. Right? Kissing is for private moments." She tugs, and my daughter and this mentally retarded man break suction.

Retarded. There's that word again. This time I'm too upset by the mini make-out session in my front hall to be disturbed by my mental word choice again.

At that moment, Jin appears in the doorway that opens into the vestibule. "Sorry! Didn't know you had company. Just wanted to let you know that my kitchen faucet is spewing water again. I'm Jin. I rent the duplex next door from Alicia." She comes in. She's barefoot in Victoria's Secret sweatpants and a tight pink wifebeater. No bra.

Margaret, in her homemade skirt, shrinks back, her hand still on her son's. I can tell by the look on her face that she doesn't approve of Jin's choice of ensemble. And she must have gaydar because I can also tell by the look on her face that she likes lesbians in wifebeaters even less than the tank tops themselves. Maybe she's frightened of Asians.

"This is Margaret," I introduce with a nervous laugh. "Chloe's friend Thomas's mother."

"This is Thomas, Aunt Jin," Chloe introduces. Her cheeks are pink. "He's a good kisser," she says. "On the mouth." She pats her lips.

Jin looks at me and arches her eyebrows. I can just imagine all the things she wants to say. "Nice to meet you both," she calls with a wave. "Talk to you later, Ally."

Jin disappears next door as I hand Thomas his coat.

"Come back tomorrow," Chloe is saying, bouncing on her feet again. "Wednesday."

Margaret is helping her son into his coat. "Thank you again for having Thomas."

I hold the door open to usher them out. Chloe follows them.

"Honey, it's cold out," I warn. "Come back inside."

Chloe waves furiously at Thomas as they exit through the outer door of the vestibule Jin and I share.

"Bye!" Chloe calls.

"B . . . bye, K . . . Koey," Thomas answers.

Chloe closes the door behind them and bounces back into the house and heads for the kitchen. I just stand there. Jin must be on the other side of her door, waiting for them to go, because the minute their car door slams, she steps out into the vestibule.

"Chloe's Thomas is cute."

I cut my eyes at her. "He's intellectually disabled."

She offers a quick smile as she cuts from her door to mine. "I got news. So is your daughter. Is that spaghetti I smell? Did you save some for me? All I had for dinner was a cold bean burrito. I think it was like a week old."

I follow her, closing the door behind me. I talk in a stage whisper. "Jin, they kissed when they said good-bye. *On the lips.*"

Jin is headed for the kitchen. "So Chloe told me," she calls over her shoulder. "My turn to call the hunky plumber, or yours?"

8

Thomas kissed me with his big lips on my lips. It tickled and it felt funny. Warm and squishy. He tasted like my mom's ziti, but it wasn't yucky. It tickled my belly, which was weird because he didn't touch my belly, just my lips.

I stand on my tiptoes and look at my face in the bathroom mirror. I do it a lot. Sometimes I make faces, but not tonight.

When I look at my face I look the same, but I feel different. Like when Thomas came to Minnie's the first time.

I liked it when Thomas kissed me. It felt good. Not like when Mom kisses me good. Different good. Like in my private parts good.

I swish my mouth with water, then I spit. Then I drink more water, but I don't swallow it. I spit more. I look at my teeth. Clean. I wash my toothbrush: wash, wash, wash. Then I turn off the water and shake, shake my toothbrush. I put it in the Dumbo toothbrush holder. It goes in the hole by Dumbo's trunk. Never by his tail.

I make straight my towel on my towel rack and then I get a wipe out of the tub of wipes under the sink and I clean my sink. I always clean my sink before I go to bed. I don't like spit in my sink. If your spit has toothpaste in it, it makes your sink all white and dirty. I throw the dirty wipe in my princess trash can and I shut off my bathroom light. I always shut the light off. Electricity costs money. That's what my mom says. I don't know how much. Maybe like as much as a million-jillion dollars.

I get in my bed and I get the book I'm going to read. I don't really read, but I remember most of the words because Mom can read. She's a teacher at college. Different college than Miss Minnie's. Mom has to read so she can read papers people give her. I mostly look at the pictures in books.

I wiggle under the covers and lay on my pillow. I read some pages of my book, but it's not a good book tonight. Sometimes it's a good book. It's the one about the bird that gets lost from its mother. It asks a bulldozer, "Are you my mother?" That's funny and it makes me laugh. Birds don't have bulldozer moms. They have bird moms.

But the book doesn't make me laugh tonight. I try to think about the bird that can't find his mother, but I can't because I'm thinking about Thomas.

When we were watching *Aladdin*, I had to keep telling him who Prince Ali and Princess Jasmine were. And the bad guy, Jafar. Jafar's scary but not as scary as Scar. Scar's in *Lion King*. Thomas never did watch *Lion King*, either. Him and his mom watch Veggie Tales. They're stupid head but I didn't tell him because that would make him sad. When he comes to watch *Lion King* at my house, I will tell him who Simba is.

Tonight Thomas kept asking me what a genie is. When I told him it was a guy in a lamp, he said I was very smart.

No one ever told me I was very smart before.

I close the book because I'm not reading it.

I keep thinking about Thomas saying I'm smart. I'm not smart. I'm a dummy head because I can't read *Are You My Mother?* for real. Thomas can read. He's smarter than me.

At the bowling alley, he said we had to have one dollar and

twenty-five cents to get a soda. He had money in his pocket. We didn't know how much one dollar and twenty-five cents was, but Thomas is smart because he could read that sign.

He gave the girl two hundred dollars and she gave us money pennies back and gave us a Coke. We shared.

Thomas keeps saying I'm his girlfriend and he's my boyfriend. He said he bought me a Coke so now I'm really his girlfriend. I don't think if he bought me a Coke I'm his girlfriend. I'm his girlfriend because he kissed me like Hercules kisses Meg. Meg is Hercules's girlfriend. And Ariel kisses Eric. In *Little Mermaid*.

I close my eyes and I think about Thomas's mouth when it touched my mouth.

I think Mom is mad that me and Thomas kissed. I'm sorry I made her mad. I don't want to make her mad.

But I want to kiss Thomas again on his lips. Maybe on Wednesday.

That night, the minute Chloe goes up to bed, and Jin goes back to her place, I sit down with my laptop. I'm disturbed by Chloe's physical display of affection toward Thomas. She's always been a hugger. Down syndrome people tend to be physically affectionate, but I've never seen her behave this way. Where did she learn to kiss like that?

We always kiss on the cheek. She and I. I don't think Randall kisses her anymore, but when she was younger, he kissed her cheek, always her cheek. How can she know about kissing on the lips and what it means?

I do a Google search on intimacy between mentally challenged adults. It's not as easy to find information as I thought it would be. I find very little using the word *intimacy*, but when I dare type in *sex*, I get more hits than I care to look at.

I wonder if Margaret has gone home and Googled the same topic. Is this the first time she's encountered this with Thomas? Or has he kissed other girls before . . . maybe in Ohio? Maybe they do that sort of thing in Dayton. Around here, it's just not done. It's not even talked about in the parent support group I attend.

I read.

Apparently, until recently, very few studies have been done on intimacy and the mentally disabled. Because people like Chloe were once institutionalized and housed by gender, there was very little interaction between males and females; there was no research on the subject. Until recently, society hadn't really considered sexuality among the mentally challenged.

I read an article about sexual abuse of the mentally disabled. There's an article about Down syndrome women being particularly at risk because of their tendencies toward physical affection.

It makes me angry. I don't read the whole article. If I'm overprotective, this is why. It's right here, in black and white.

I read about an eight-week sex education class for mentally handicapped young adults being taught at a center in California.

I've taught Chloe about bad touching and good touching, but not sex, per se. I've explained to her how Jin holding her hand is good touching, but a man touching her butt at the grocery store is bad touching. I've tried to make her understand that anything that makes her feel uncomfortable is bad touching and that she needs to tell me about it.

But I don't think she understands. I'm sure she doesn't.

I read for more than an hour. I read about society's recent shift in beliefs, how mentally challenged adults are being encouraged, by their parents and caregivers, to have relationships. Supported in sexual relationships. I find several references to an HBO documentary about two Down syndrome adults who marry and live with the woman's parents. I write down the title to check later to see if I can see it On Demand.

My reading leaves me more upset than I was before I sat down. I don't know what to do. My first impulse is to put an end to the relationship before anything bad happens.

Do I tell Chloe she can't see Thomas anymore? Do I not let him come here, or let her go anywhere with him? Could I just make sure they're never alone? Should I take her out of Minnie's or change her schedule with Minnie?

But Chloe likes Thomas. He's her first real friend. She likes everyone at Minnie's, but no one has ever called her to do things outside of Miss Minnie's. I suspect that, like Chloe, they don't have a life beyond Miss Minnie's, except for their families. Thomas is a friend Chloe can meet on equal ground, unlike Huan, whom she calls her friend but who isn't really. Not any more than the bagger at the grocery store or the clerk at the post office is her friend. And Chloe's obviously thrilled to have Thomas for a friend. How can I take that away from her? How can I not want my daughter to be happy? If she were normal, I'd be encouraging her to seek a healthy relationship.

If she were *average* is what I mean. We don't say *normal* in mentally challenged caregiver circles. It's not politically correct. This *is* normal for Chloe, and men and women like her. Political correctness has not, however, prevented me from thinking it.

I stare at the computer screen, thinking how different my life might be if Randall and I hadn't discontinued that first pregnancy. I never use the word *abort*. Just like I never use the word *regret* when I think of it. Regrets never do anyone any good. We can learn only from our mistakes.

But you can't help where your mind goes sometimes.

If I'd carried our first child to term, he or she would have graduated college. I think about it all the time, my thoughts sometimes bordering on obsession. I go over the same questions again and again in my mind. Would she have gone to Princeton as Randall had dreamed? Would she be married and working in the academia field?

It's easy to let my mind wander over the possibilities. Without the stress of a disabled child, maybe Randall and I would still be together.

But if I'd had that first baby, would we have ever had a second? Would we have ever had Chloe? I always come to this question, eventually.

And I always know, in my heart, the answer. Knowing Randall, had I delivered our first child, Chloe would have never been born. Randall would never have agreed to a second child. We're academics, after all. We don't *do* children. We teach them.

I can't imagine giving Chloe up for Randall. Chloe is, by far, the best thing that has ever happened to me. Ever will happen.

And this is how I repaid her for coming into my life, for *making* my life? I screwed up her chromosomes?

I close my eyes. This is silly. Why do I do this to myself? This is *not* my fault. Chloe's Down's is *not* my fault. I know that logically. Scientifically.

So why does it still *feel* like it's my fault? After all these years, why do I still feel this way? Because I did it. I gave birth to a *damaged* child.

If we lived in some societies, we would both be ostracized. My husband would have divorced me, and my in-laws would consider Chloe and me pariahs. Really ... not so different from Main Street America. Oh, everyone is polite about it, but I see their looks, and sometimes I can almost hear them thinking, *I wonder what she did to have a child like that.* Most pity me, but I don't want their pity. What I want is acceptance ... acceptance for both of us. Acceptance I know we'll never get.

My fingers hover over the keyboard. I feel lost. Like I can't find my way home. I can't read any more articles about people like Chloe being in love or having sex.

I barely realize what I'm typing, until the words come up. I bring up the Friends' Meeting House in a town twenty minutes from here. I don't know what makes me think of it, or look it up.

I haven't been to a Quaker Meeting in twenty-six years.

I stopped going after Randall and I were married. After we were married, we were so busy. And my mom was dead. I didn't have to go for her sake anymore.

But I remember going a couple of times before Chloe was born, when my stomach was huge. To this very same Meeting House in Oak's Bend.

The truth is, I really stopped going *after* Chloe was born. When she was born with Down syndrome. I abandoned my faith because I felt it had abandoned me. I felt that God had abandoned me and Chloe. Or maybe He never existed at all?

How is that for academic thinking?

I'm surprised that my eyes have filled with tears. I'm not a crier. Never was, but any tears I had inside me have been cried out. I cried for Chloe, for myself, yes, even for Randall in the days after she was born. It seemed as if I did nothing *but* cry in those first weeks and months after we brought Chloe home from the hospital.

The thing was, despite the sentence, Trisomy 21, Chloe was a beautiful baby. The way she looked up at me with those big blue eyes of hers, eyes that would stay blue. The way she cooed and batted her little fists. She loved me from the moment she came into the world, a nonjudgmental love that I had never experienced before.

And she was such a good baby. Despite the nurse's warnings that Down's babies have trouble suckling, Chloe took to my breast right away. She slept when she was supposed to sleep and she rarely cried. Chloe was always happy, always wanting to please me. Her physical development was slow, but eventually she did all the things babies were supposed to do.

She made *me* happy.

I stare at the picture of the quaint nineteenth-century Meeting House on the computer screen, with its cedar shakes and big, plain windows. Inside, I know there are old benches facing each other. No crosses on the walls, no adornments.

There are some Friends' Meeting Houses where there's a service with a sermon and singing. This Friends' Meeting practices the tradition of silent worship; attendees sit in contemplative quiet in the hopes of experiencing the presence of God.

I think about sitting on one of the benches, and I remember the sense of peace I had felt there once upon a time.

The phone rings, startling me. The house phone. I glance at

my cell phone as I reach for the other phone on the coffee table. It's nine fifty-five. Who could be calling this late?

I look at the caller-ID. "Mark?" I say into the phone.

"Sorry I'm just getting back to you."

For a moment, I draw a blank. I don't remember calling the plumber. Not since last week. I haven't gotten last week's bill yet.

"Jin's kitchen faucet," he reminds me.

"Right," I say quickly. "Sorry, things have been crazy here tonight." I rub my temple. "Jin called you."

"I didn't get an answer at her place. I was going to come by tomorrow morning, if that's okay."

"Tomorrow . . . that's fine. Great."

He's quiet for a second. "You okay, Alicia?"

His tone of voice catches me off guard and my eyes actually tear up again. No one but Jin ever asks if I'm okay. Not my colleagues, certainly not Randall. He never asked about my emotional well-being, even when we were married. I know Mark is just my plumber, but I'm somehow comforted by the concern in his voice.

"Just a long day. Some things going on with Chloe."

"Kids," he says with understanding in his voice. "I have two. They live with my ex-wife, in Chestertown."

I never thought about the fact that Mark had probably been married, probably had kids. He's younger than me, but only by a few years, I would guess. "Boys or girls?" I ask.

"One of each. Twins. Emma, she's the oldest by six minutes, and Elon. They're sixteen."

I smile because I hear him smile. "Twins," I say. I had always thought about what it would be like to have twins. Of course, Randall and I had never even contemplated having another child after Chloe. He had a vasectomy when she was three months old. Randall and I were responsible parents. We would have never dared taken our chances in conceiving another child.

I realize that I've allowed an awkward pause between us. "So . . . I'll see you in the morning?"

"See you in the morning."

I hang up and look at the computer screen. An ad for a well-known online dating service pops up on the screen. Half off tonight. I click the box that launches me onto the site . . . just for the hell of it.

I look at the cost. With the half-off coupon, it's $14.99 for a month. It goes down to $12.99, if I sign up for six months.

Would it really take six months for them to find me a date? I could find my own date in six months. I read some of the testimonials.

Ah . . . these people are looking for a spouse. I don't need a husband. I would never do that to Chloe—bring a man into the house. But surely there must be men looking for companionship without marriage.

I nibble on my lower lip. *Fifteen bucks*, I tell myself.

I hear a tap at my front door. I know who it is. It's the only person who scratches at my door at ten at night. Jin's back.

I shuffle to the door in sweatpants, sweatshirt, and shearling slippers.

"Sorry," Jin says as I unlock the door. "I know it's late but you're not in bed."

I raise my arms and let them fall. "Not in bed." I wave her in. Ours is the most comfortable relationship I've ever had. The easiest. The kindest. Without Jin, I'd be lost. "I'm just surfing the Net." I close my laptop when we walk into the living room. I know Jin would be supportive of the idea of me Internet dating, but I don't want to discuss it with her. Not right now, at least.

"So, what's up?" I can tell by the look on her face that something is. She's still wearing the pink wifebeater and yoga pants, but at least she's thrown a sweatshirt over them. Of course, it's one of those off-the-shoulder sweatshirts, the kind skinny people dance in. I gave up feeling frumpy around her years ago. I just don't have the energy.

I sit. She sits across from me.

"Chloe in bed?" she asks.

I nod. "I can't believe she kissed Thomas," I blurt out.

"So he *is* her boyfriend."

"Never mind." I hold up my hand. "I can't talk about this tonight. If I think about it anymore, my head is going to explode." I pull a throw pillow onto my lap. "You didn't just come over to say hi after you ate all the pasta?"

She looks at her hands in her lap. She's one of those people who, even at our age, can still sit Indian-style comfortably on a couch.

I wait.

She groans and hangs her head. "Abby called my cell. That's why I didn't pick up when Mark called."

"He'll be here tomorrow morning."

She nods, then hesitates long enough for me to think I might have to wheedle the Abby information out of her, but then she goes on. "I didn't actually talk to her." Jin nibbles on her lower lip. "She left a message. She wants to come this weekend."

"I thought Huan was going to the Metropolitan Art Museum in New York with friends this weekend."

Jin picks at the hem of her yoga pants. "That's why she wants to come this weekend. To see me. Without Huan."

"Why?"

Jin shrugs, but doesn't look at me. "What if it's bad? What if she has cancer or something?"

"I doubt that's it." I open my laptop and casually close the windows on the dating service and the Google searches. I'll think about couples.com later.

Now Jin is picking at the polish on her big toenail. "You think she's getting married again?"

I slide one foot under me. That's about as flexible as I get. "I thought you said that Huan said that she broke up with that corporate lawyer, like, three months ago."

"She did," Jin says. "But maybe they got back together and

they're getting married and she wants to tell me face-to-face." She opens and closes her arms. "I want to be happy for her, but I can't. How could she be happy with this woman when she couldn't be happy with me?"

I'm surprised by the emotion in Jin's voice. She's really upset.

"You don't know that she's getting married." I power down my computer. "That's as crazy as guessing she might have cancer. There's no evidence that either is true."

"What do I do?" Jin asks, meeting my gaze, again.

What do I do? I think. *About Thomas. About Chloe and Thomas.* "I guess we just wait and see."

﹁ 9 ﹂

Was that next week a defining week in my life? In Chloe's?
I always thought I could identify significant moments in
my life as they happened. In the past, it had been relatively easy:
high school graduation, college graduation, my mother's death,
going home with Randall that night, my subsequent pregnancies,
getting my doctorate. I suppose I knew that Chloe meeting
Thomas *could* have been a defining moment. She was infatuated
with him from that first day, but that week, two weeks after
Chloe met him, that was a defining time in both my life and hers.
His, too, I suppose, but I couldn't think about Thomas or how he
was feeling. How could I? I couldn't even deal with my own feelings, and certainly not Chloe's.

I think that week defined my future because I could have put
a stop to it then. Maybe if I had put an end to it then, everything
would be different now. But how could I have possibly known
that? And if I had known, would I have had the guts to do things
differently? Would I really have been able to put the kibosh on
Chloe's relationship with Thomas? Did I have the right? And
would my attempt to do so have made things worse?

I lean my forehead on the cold glass at the window. Alone

again. But when I close my eyes, when I let go of the present and the emptiness around me, I hear Chloe.

I hear her screaming.

A temper tantrum.

Right on the steps of Miss Minnie's. Approaching her twenty-sixth year and my daughter is stamping her feet, thrashing her arms, and screaming like a two-year-old. It was the week after Thomas's first visit to our house.

"No! No, I want Thomas! I want Thomas to come!" She's reaching for the door, grabbing the doorknob, trying to pry the door open as I attempt to lead her away.

"Thomas isn't coming home with us today," I say calmly, picking her canvas bag up off the wet stoop.

"Thomas is coming! We have to watch a movie. We watch a movie on Wednesday!" she shrieks, clawing at the door.

Chloe is short, but she outweighs me. I'm trying to find a dignified way to drag her away from the door, toward the car, but I can't get her to budge. First I pull her, then I get behind her to give her a push. She's sobbing. Drooling.

The curtain in the front window moves and three faces appear. Alexandra is there; she's severely autistic. And Ann; general retardation, but high-functioning. Ann's parents are actually considering sending her to a group home in the Annapolis area. Susan talks all the time about working at McDonald's; the girl probably could work there if she had a simple job. Above their heads, Thomas materializes.

"K . . . Koey!" he shouts. He presses his mouth to the glass and makes it wet. "Koey!"

"Thomas!" Chloe sees him in the window and lets go of the doorknob so suddenly that I almost fall.

She moves quicker than I think I've ever seen her move. Before I can right myself, she's running down the wheelchair ramp, ducking under the rail, and leaping into the flower bed under the window. "Thomas!" she cries desperately. "I want to watch the movie! We have to watch the movie!"

I straighten my coat, slipping the library bag over my shoulder. The air is growing crisp. It smells like snow.

"Chloe, Thomas can't come with us. Not today. We didn't get his mother's permission to take him home with us." I walk part-way down the wheelchair ramp and eye the flower bed. It rained the night before, then froze, then thawed in the noonday sun. The flower bed is a quagmire.

I'm wearing my new knee-high leather boots and a skirt. I really don't want to get my boots muddy, and I certainly don't want to trample Minnie's bushes and plants. I'm a college professor, for God's sake. My behavior should be at least semi-dignified. What if one of my students sees me? I run into them all the time: in the grocery store, at the post office, at the coffee shop. I learned the hard way to never leave my house in my glasses, wearing baggy sweatpants and one of Chloe's kitten sweatshirts.

I glance over my shoulder. No cars driving by, no pedestrians. I don't see anyone in the neighborhood watching, but anyone who heard the commotion would certainly peek out their door.

"Please, Chloe?" I say calmly. "Can you just get in the car and we can talk about this at home?"

"I can't get in the car!" Chloe moans. She is pressing both of her hands to the glass. Her sneakers are muddy, her coat spattered with mud. "Thomas, come out! Thomas!"

"K . . . Koey," he echoes. He's not crying, but I can see tears in his eyes. He's upset. Chloe is upsetting him. He pushes his way between Alexandra and Ann and hovers, his big bulky self filling the window.

Chloe makes a fist and strikes the glass.

I duck under the rail of the wheelchair ramp and jump down into the flower bed. I'll have to pay for the plants my daughter is trampling. I put my arm around her shoulders and gently lower her hand. Chloe's super-strong. I'm afraid if she keeps hitting the window, she'll break the glass and hurt herself.

She's done that before . . . hurt herself. There was the broken arm when she jumped out of Randall's car before he came to a full stop, when she was twelve. Then three trips to the emergency room for stitches due to: a kitchen knife mishap, a temper tantrum in the bathroom involving the mirror, and a jar of pickles she tried to open herself in the picnic aisle of the grocery store. I don't want to add a plate-glass window injury to the list.

"Chloe, please," I say forcefully. "You know you can't have what you want by acting this way."

She looks at me, her face bright red, her cheeks wet with tears, snot running from her nose to her lips. I bet Thomas wouldn't want to kiss her right now. I pull a tissue from my coat pocket. "You need to come with me, and we'll talk about having Thomas come over to watch a movie another night."

She turns her head to look at me at last and I wipe her nose with the tissue, the same way I did when she was a child. And she still is a child in many ways, but in her face, I see an adult. Maybe an adult trying to escape her child's mind. The thought brings a lump up in my throat and my eyes blur. I love her so much. I just want her to be safe and happy.

"Thomas can come watch a movie?" she blubbers.

"Not today."

"Wednesday?" she asks, sniffling.

Today is Wednesday. Thomas came to our house last Wednesday and Saturday Chloe spent half the day with him with the LoGs. They went to an arcade and I followed the church van there and sat in the parking lot. Like a stalker. I didn't witness any more lip-kissing, but I didn't go into the arcade. Because if I didn't see it, maybe I could pretend it wasn't happening? Because nowhere on the Internet when I Googled "sex and Down syndrome" did anyone tell me what I should do to protect Chloe. To let her have a life, but still protect her.

That's all I really want. It's what every mother wants, isn't it?

I think about my own mom and I wonder what she would do in my place. But she's been dead so long. So many of my memories of her and of my childhood and teenage years have faded. I desperately wish she was here now to tell me what to do with my own daughter.

I pull Chloe into my arms. She fights me for a second, but then relaxes a little. She doesn't hug me, but at least she lets me hug her. When she was little, this was, sometimes, the way I calmed her when she had one of her temper tantrums. I didn't exactly restrain her, but I wrapped her in my arms. She feels so good close to me. I know she's getting my coat all snotty, but I don't care.

Chloe's whole body shudders. "I want to see *Aladdin* again. With Thomas," she mumbles. The girl doesn't give in easily, I'll give her that.

I stroke her hair, thinking I need to talk to someone, but who? Who can give me advice? Who can help me reason my way through this? Randall? I hold back a bitter laugh. When has he ever been helpful in making decisions about Chloe?

Maybe our family therapist, Dr. Tamara?

Is it time to talk to Margaret?

I don't want to talk to Margaret. I don't want my daughter to be with her son, her big, stuttering son whose glasses are always perched crookedly on his nose.

I kiss the top of Chloe's head. "Wave good-bye to Thomas and let's go home."

"He can come?" She takes a great shuddering breath and looks up at me with her hooded blue eyes. Blue eyes that can melt my heart. "Thomas can come on Wednesday? So we can watch *Aladdin* . . . and . . . and *The Little Mermaid*?"

"We'll talk to his mother."

"He has a TV." Chloe allows me to lead her out of the flower bed. The four inside watch from the window. I want to turn around and holler to them that the show is over, but I keep walking. I wonder if Minnie has witnessed the whole incident from another window.

"I'm sure he does," I say, giving her a reassuring squeeze. We walk down Minnie's driveway and head for the curb.

"But not good movies," Chloe says. She's still taking big, shuddering breaths. "He doesn't have good movies. I can go to his house and take good movies. His mom, she can pick us up."

"We'll see, Chloe." I fumble for the keys in my pocket and press the UNLOCK button on the fob. The Honda beeps.

"I can go?" Standing on the sidewalk, she looks up at me.

I can't imagine letting my daughter go with strangers. I mean they're *practically* strangers, Thomas and his mother . . . and his father. I don't know his father. What if he's some kind of pervert who likes girls with IQs below fifty? It's a terrible thing to think, but how would I know? How does anyone know until their child is molested or raped?

I know I let her go with the church group, but letting Chloe go to Thomas's house, that would be different, wouldn't it? Groups are safer. And I've been right there if Chloe needs me—a parking lot away.

I don't know what to do. I don't know what to do.

We make a quick stop at the grocery store and arrive home without further incident. I let Chloe choose what we have for dinner: fish sticks, mozzarella sticks, and French fries. The white food menu. All unhealthy, all contributing to both of our expanding waistlines, but I let her put the items in the grocery cart anyway.

We both have to leave our shoes at the front door because they're so muddy. While I unload the groceries in my stocking feet, Chloe goes upstairs to change her clothes. Apparently, she and Thomas had apple juice again today and she spilled it all over her new sweatshirt, the blue one with the kitten and the pink ball of string on it—Chloe has four or five kitten sweatshirts. I can't keep them straight, but she can.

As I turn on the oven, the phone rings. It's Minnie, according to the caller ID. I hesitate, phone in my hand. Minnie rarely calls. No . . . Minnie *never* calls. I exhale.

"Hello?"

"Alicia, hi. It's Minerva."

"Minnie . . . hi." I stack the fish stick box and the mozzarella stick box on the counter beside the stove. "I'm really sorry about Chloe's behavior today," I say, deciding I should be proactive. "I don't know what got into her. This thing with Thomas—"

"Actually, that's what I wanted to talk to you about," she interrupts.

I like Minnie, but she's all business. In the beginning, I liked her because she *was* all business. She helped me handle Chloe and the problem of what to do with her without a great deal of emotion. Without making me feel as if I was making a heart-wrenching decision.

"I'll be calling Thomas's mother next."

I rest my hand on the freezer door. This doesn't sound good. I wait.

"I had a chat with Chloe and Thomas today, but I think it's best if you talk with her, too," Minnie says. "I think this is one of those instances where we need to back each other up."

I open the freezer and put a half gallon of butter pecan ice cream in, wondering what the hell my daughter's done. "Absolutely."

"Did she tell you?" Minnie asks.

I close the freezer. "No. What did she do?"

"She and Thomas locked themselves in the bathroom," Minnie tells me, making no attempt to soften the blow. "Together."

"They *locked* themselves in *the bathroom*? Why did they do that?" I can't imagine Chloe using the toilet in front of Thomas. Chloe is fairly modest. She doesn't even pee in front of me anymore. Of course she sees no reason why she can't barrel into the bathroom when *I'm* using the toilet . . . or bringing the FedEx man in for a quick look-see. "Were they . . . using the toilet together?" I ask, frowning.

"No. When they let me in, everyone still had their pants on."

"Well, that's good to hear." I almost chuckle at my sarcasm, but I know I shouldn't be a smart-ass right now. I don't want to anger or offend Minnie. Minnie's one of the most important people in my life right now. Maybe even ahead of the plumber.

"I think they were kissing," Minnie says.

I blink. "Kissing like . . . good-bye?" I try not to recall the two of them at my front door in a lip-lock.

"No. Not good-bye kissing. It was lunchtime."

"Ah . . ."

"I apologize. We have a one-person-in-the-bathroom-at-a-time rule, even with the girls," Minnie goes on, "but I was in the kitchen making lunch. I can see I'm going to have to be more vigilant with them . . . my home is not a place for making out."

Making out? Chloe was *making out* with him? "Oh no, of course not." I grab a cookie sheet from the cabinet and dump the whole box of mozzarella sticks on it. "I . . . I'll speak to Chloe about this. She shouldn't be . . . obviously . . ." I'm an English professor but I find myself having a difficult time speaking my native language. ". . . Making out . . . that's . . . totally inappropriate." I slide the baking sheet into the oven. "Certainly nothing I'd ever encourage."

"Alicia"—Minnie's tone softens—"this is only natural, you know. She likes Thomas, and he likes her. They're adults, with the same feelings and desires we have. They just need to figure out when physical displays of affection are appropriate and when they're not."

It's not ever *appropriate!* I want to shout at her. I don't want that man's tongue in my daughter's mouth. I don't want Chloe having *feelings and desires*. I certainly don't want Thomas having feelings and desires for my innocent little girl. "I . . . I'll certainly talk with Chloe," I manage to tell Minnie.

"Go easy on her," Minnie says kindly. "This is her first boyfriend. We all know what that's like. It's a very exciting time."

She says it as if it's the most natural and normal of things. I want to respond, but I don't know what to say. Obviously, Minnie thinks it's okay that Chloe and Thomas are kissing; she just doesn't want them doing it in *her* bathroom.

I take a deep breath and exhale. "Thank you for calling, Minnie. I'll certainly speak with Chloe." I lower the phone to my side. I hear Minnie's voice—some form of good-bye—but I don't hear what she's saying.

I hang the phone up as Chloe shuffles into the kitchen. She's changed into flannel pajamas with fluffy kittens all over them and is wearing her baby blue chenille robe. Old houses are always drafty.

"Did Thomas call me?" Chloe asks, her face bright. All evidence of her tears is gone. "Is the phone Thomas? I heard the phone. It rrrr-ringed," she says, carefully pronouncing the *r*.

"It *rang*," I say. "And no, it wasn't Thomas. But I need to talk to you about Thomas."

She shuffles to the refrigerator, opens it, and pulls out the carton of milk, then the plastic squirt bottle of chocolate syrup. She's not supposed to have chocolate milk for dinner, but I don't want to muddy the water. And honestly, I've got more important things to be concerned about than Chloe's chocolate consumption.

"Thomas calls me. I'm going to his house to watch *Little Mermaid*." She gets a glass out of the cupboard. "And *Aladdin*. At his house."

"Chloe, that was Miss Minnie who called. Were you in the bathroom with Thomas at Miss Minnie's today?"

She turns her back to me—her way of ignoring the conversation. She thinks if she ignores me, the subject matter will magically disappear. Which means . . . she's guilty. I feel my heart tumble a little further.

But did I really think Minnie had made the whole thing up?

"Chloe?"

She pours three-quarters of a glass of milk and then tips the bottle of syrup and gives it a squirt.

"What were you doing in the bathroom with Thomas . . . with the door locked?"

She gives the chocolate bottle another squeeze.

"Were you kissing Thomas?"

More chocolate.

I reach over and gently take the bottle from her. "Chloe, I need you to tell me what happened in the bathroom today with Thomas."

"You're gonna be mad." She shakes her head, keeping her eyes downcast, and opens the utensil drawer and takes out a spoon. She keeps shaking her head. "Mad. Don't tell. Don't tell." She puts her finger to her lips. "A secret," she whispers.

I raise my voice. "Thomas told you not to tell?" Now my heart is beating faster. This is just what I was afraid of. This man taking advantage of my daughter because she doesn't know any better. "Chloe, what did Thomas tell you not to tell me?"

She slides the drawer closed and drops the spoon into her glass. The metal spoon clinks on the sides as she stirs. "Don't tell. Don't tell." Then she giggles into the glass of milk. "I told Thomas my mom will be mad about kissing." Satisfied by the number of times she's stirred the milk, she puts the spoon in the sink and carries her glass to the table. I follow her.

"You want chocolate milk?" she asks me as she sets her glass down in front of her place at the table. "I can make you chocolate milk. It's good." She takes a big slurp.

"No, thank you. I don't want chocolate milk." I look at her round face and beautiful almond-shaped eyes. I use the *mommy voice.* "Chloe, whose idea was the kissing? Thomas's?"

She smiles and puts her finger to her lips again. "A secret."

"Not a secret! Absolutely not." I follow her to the cabinet where she takes out two paper napkins. "We don't keep secrets. Right? No secrets between you and me."

She folds one of the napkins carefully in half. Now she won't look at me.

"Did Thomas tell you not to tell that he kissed you in the bathroom?" I ask firmly.

She shakes her head and then carefully puts the napkin down at my seat. She's still not looking at me.

"Chloe, please don't lie to me. If Thomas told you not to tell, you're not in trouble." Now I'm shaking my head. "Kissing is not a nice secret."

She begins folding her own napkin. She looks up at me, moving her mouth from side to side, thinking. Despite her stubborn streak, Chloe wants to please people. She wants to please me. "I told," she whispers.

"You told what?"

She looks down at the napkin. "I told Thomas not to tell about the kissing," she says, half-whispering. Her eyes immediately tear up. "That's why I told him not to tell. Because you would get mad at me."

I guess I should be relieved. If it was Chloe's idea not to tell, Thomas isn't a predator. "Did Thomas lock the bathroom door?"

She sets the napkin in its place and then lines it up just right. "I told him, 'Lock the door, Thomas. Pri-vas-see. Kissing.'" She dares a giggle and I know very well we're not talking about kissing a cheek.

"Chloe, honey." I sit down, pressing my hands to the oak table. "You're not supposed to be kissing Thomas in Minnie's bathroom. You're not supposed to be kissing Thomas at all."

"Because we're not married." Chloe is still trying to line the napkin up just right.

"Because you're not married," I agree, thinking that's as good an explanation as any.

Chloe nods with me. "Because we're not married," she repeats. It comes out *mar-wied.*

I smile. "I'm glad you understand. It's okay to be friends with Thomas, but you can't kiss him."

"That's what I told Thomas." Chloe plops into her chair and begins to stir her chocolate milk again. "We have to get married."

10

The next morning, I'm waiting for Randall at his office door, two cups of coffee in my hands, when he arrives. I stopped at the coffee shop and got them, his with cream, but no sugar, mine with plenty of artificial sweetener and enough half-and-half to make it a latte.

He doesn't look pleased to see me.

I'm wearing my new black boots that I cleaned up the night before, and a calf-length skirt. The boots, even with their small heels, somehow make me feel stronger. More powerful. They gave me the confidence I needed to march down the hall this morning to Randall's office.

"We need to talk," I say.

"I have class in an hour. I have papers to grade."

"I'm not in the mood for your nonsense this morning. You and I both know your TAs grade your papers, Randall. I wouldn't imagine you've actually read a student's paper in years." I step up behind him as he slips his key in the door. "So I don't want to hear your excuses. I need to talk to you about Chloe."

He unlocks the door and walks in, briefcase in hand. It's not until he sheds his coat and sits down behind the big cherry desk that I get a good look at his face. I'm startled by the unexpected realization that Randall is looking older these days. For years, the gray in his beard and dark brown hair was distinguishing, but now . . . it just makes him look old. He turned sixty-six in January. The sixties are supposed to be the new fifties, but Randall's not going to be a poster child for the idea.

I frown, sliding his cup of coffee across the desk toward him. "Are you all right, Randall? You look . . . tired."

He rubs his temples. "Things at home . . . there have been . . . some . . . difficulties."

I take a sip of my coffee. It's perfect: just the right temperature, just the right sweetness and creaminess. "The usual cycles in a marriage, or difficulties like you're cheating on your wife with one of your students and she caught you?" I ask.

Randall looks up. "Alicia, that's uncalled for," he deadpans. "I think you should look into seeing a therapist. It's unhealthy to still be carrying so much anger after all these years."

I exhale. "I see a therapist."

"You see a *family* therapist. For you and Chloe." As he speaks, he moves objects around on his desk. Randall has some OCD tendencies. I'm sure he arranged his letter opener, day diary, and leather cup of pencils last night before he left the office, but now, he moves them out of place and then back into place. Jin insists we all develop small neuroses with age, but Randall's had his for years. "I mean for yourself," he says.

I think about reminding him that I have a right to my deep-seated anger, as do wives number one and three. He cheated on Elaine with me, then on me with Ann, and then on Ann with Kelly; we were all grad students. But I didn't come here to point out his shortcomings . . . or have him point out mine. I came here to talk about Chloe.

"Chloe's met a young man."

Randall looks at me for the first time this morning. "Has she now?" He reaches for the coffee I set on his desk. "A mentally challenged young man?"

"No, Randall," I say tartly. "A brain surgeon has asked our daughter out."

His bushy eyebrows with their little gray spiky hairs knit together, and he takes a sip of the coffee. He used to tweeze them; he needs to tweeze them.

I exhale, taking one of the two leather chairs positioned just so in front of his desk. I don't usually sit in his office when he's sitting because I feel like I have an edge with him if I remain standing. Today that doesn't seem all that important. I'm not here to win an argument. I'm here because I genuinely want to hear what he thinks. And I know it's my duty as Chloe's mother to give her father's input some consideration.

"I'm sorry. You're right. That was definitely expressing deeply seated anger I still hold for you." I take another sip of coffee. "Chloe met a young man at Minnie's. Thomas is new. He moved here from Ohio with his family. He doesn't have Down's. I think he falls under the general retardation category. Chloe really likes him."

"How nice for Chloe."

"She didn't mention him to you?"

They've had three Chick-fil-A outings since she first met Thomas. I'm surprised she hasn't said anything to her father. At the grocery store the night before, she told the woman passing out samples of cheese all about Thomas and the Thomas the Tank Engine socks he had worn to Minnie's that day.

Randall smiles, but it's not a real smile. It's tight at the corners of his lips. A perfunctory smile. "I'm so pleased Chloe's found a friend. Aren't you're happy for her, Alicia? I know she's been hoping to make friends."

"I'm afraid he's more than a friend. They locked themselves in the bathroom at Minnie's and were making out. Chloe decided it should be a secret, because she knew I'd be angry if I found out."

"You do appear to be angry," Randall points out. The *making out* part doesn't seem to have registered.

I'm tempted to take his coffee back. "You're missing the point, Randall. I'm concerned. If this boy could convince Chloe that kissing is okay, who knows what could be next?"

"But you said it was Chloe's idea to keep the incident a secret. Maybe the kissing was Chloe's idea, as well."

I set my coffee on his desk. "Randall, I don't care whose idea it was. My concern is that Chloe is locking herself in the bathroom and kissing this man. My concern is that she might allow inappropriate touching."

"What does the therapist say?"

"We have an appointment Friday."

He sets his coffee on his desk and tents his fingers, letting a long pause settle between us. Randall does this—pauses for long periods of time. He thinks it makes him appear more cerebral. There was a time when I thought it did. Now it just annoys the crap out of me.

But I play his game. I wait.

"Alicia, it's only natural that Chloe be exploring her sexuality at this point in her life. She's a young woman with dreams and desires like all women her age. You were married and had a child by the time you were twenty-six."

"She has an IQ of 48, Randall." I'm getting loud. There's no point in getting loud. There was probably no point in coming here or wasting my money on his cup of coffee, either. I know Randall will have no advice to give me. He never does. I take another sip of coffee.

He waits to respond. "Can you tell me your concerns in relation to Chloe's awakening sexuality?"

I look up at him. "I'm concerned that your daughter doesn't understand what kissing means or where these *feelings* she has might lead."

"Have you talked to her about sex?"

"No, I haven't talked to her about . . . *sex*, Randall. She can't put batteries in a flashlight; she can't remember the difference between red and yellow. She still calls your wife by your previous wife's name."

"I think she does that on purpose," he says.

I almost laugh out loud. She probably does. "You understand what I'm saying. You know Chloe. I think sexuality is a subject beyond her comprehension."

He adjusts the lid on his coffee. "And I disagree. I think you should talk with her therapist first, but I think we need to accept that our daughter is maturing and she needs to be taught the aspects of adult sexuality."

"So, when are you going to explain to your daughter the finer points of male genitalia in relationship to her female genitalia? When are you going to tell her where Thomas would like to put his penis?"

Randall closes his eyes, then opens them, looking at me as if I'm an idiot for even suggesting such a thing. I wish he'd holler. Maybe throw something. But Randall never loses control. Ever. This is his way of demeaning us, demoralizing us, his women. It's his way of raising himself high on a pedestal above us.

I get to my feet. "I didn't think so." I make it all the way to his door before he speaks.

"You're too controlling," he says, in his stuffy voice from behind his stuffy desk. "You're not allowing her to grow up. You're not allowing her to spread her wings."

"That's not it." I defend myself, turning to face him. "I want her to be happy. I'm willing to let her spread her wings," I say. "But it's my job, Randall, to make sure she doesn't fly too close to the sun." I walk out the door, leaving Randall to contemplate my reference to Icarus.

But in my haste to make my literary exit, I leave my coffee, too.

"I hear what you're saying, Dr. Tamara," I say, leaning back in the comfortable leather chair. "But I think I *have* encouraged

Chloe's independence. She's attending the church group on Saturdays. That's a big step . . . for both of us."

"But, Alicia, you're sitting in the parking lot."

I study him for a moment. Dr. Anthony Tamara is a small, slender man with dark hair and serious eyes behind wire-framed glasses. He has skinny wrists. I don't know why, but they've always annoyed me. I don't like men with skinny wrists.

Dr. Tamara reminds me of a male version of Dr. Malfi, the psychiatrist on *The Sopranos*. I can't decide if Jennifer Malfi is just one of the few other psychiatrists I know, or if it's the Italian psychiatrist connection. Although, technically, Dr. Tamara isn't a psychiatrist; he has a doctorate in family psychology, specializing in parents of special needs children. I'm not sure Dr. Tamara has been all that helpful over the years, but Chloe and I have visited him monthly because I felt it was the right thing for me to do. It was my duty, as a parent, to see that Chloe got counseling.

Chloe's out in the waiting room; the receptionist is keeping an eye on her. I can hear Chloe singing. I brought my iPad for her to watch a movie because I knew Dr. Tamara would want to see me alone. Chloe's using earbuds, but she forgets that just because the receptionist can't hear *The Lion King*, that doesn't mean Mrs. Marples can't hear Chloe singing "Hakuna Matata."

"Alicia?" Dr. Tamara says. "Do you think you're truly offering Chloe independence when you drop her off at the church and then follow the van she's riding in to the arcade?"

"My job, as her mother"—I touch my hand to my heart—"is to protect Chloe. My most important job, as her mother, as the one who brought her into this world, is to keep her safe."

"You said yourself that the pastor and the volunteers at the church have experience with mentally challenged young adults. Didn't you?"

I nod. "True."

"So why not let them have the responsibility for Chloe's safety for a few hours . . . the way you do with Minnie?"

I look at my nails. "And you think I should let her go to Thomas's house alone, too?"

"I think that if her relationship with Thomas continues to progress, that would be the next logical step. You said Margaret gave you no reason to believe she would put Chloe's safety at risk."

I clench my hands into fists and slowly relax them. "This just goes against everything I've done all these years. I've kept her close to me to protect her."

"And perhaps to protect yourself?"

I look at him.

"You don't have time for a relationship because work and Chloe take up all of your time."

"I have a *relationship* with Jin," I defend. "An excellent relationship."

"I meant a *romantic* relationship."

I think about the online dating idea. I *would* like to find a nice guy, just to have someone to go to the movies with. To have someone who cares about me . . . who wants to spend time with me. Is it really time to try it? "How am I using Chloe as a way to keep from having a relationship with a man?"

"You tell me."

I groan. I hate this about therapy. I don't want to come up with my own conclusions. I want him to tell me what to do! Just once, I don't want to make all the life-and-death decisions by myself. Okay, so maybe whether or not to let Chloe go for pizza without me isn't a life-or-death decision, but it certainly feels that way.

I look at Dr. Tamara. "I spend so much time, so much energy on Chloe that I don't have time for a romantic relationship," I say.

He smiles. "Maybe it's time for both of you to have a boyfriend."

Again I groan. I look away. "You don't have children," I say. "You don't understand what this is like. To know she'll never be able to live alone. Know she should never even cross the street alone."

"I think I do understand. I see many families like yours, Alicia. Dealing with the same issues."

I look back at him. "You think I'm being overprotective. You think I should let Chloe date."

"I think that if she has the desire, she might have the ability. I think you should let her explore relationships with people beyond you, her father, and Jin. I think you can help her find the tools to be able to have a relationship with Thomas. With other men."

Other men? There will be *others?* I don't want to contemplate that idea for even a second. Thomas is enough to worry about.

"The mentally challenged are doing far more, becoming far more than what we thought possible in previous generations. The mentally challenged are holding down jobs, dating, living independently or semi-independently, even having families," he goes on. "There's no reason why they can't do what those of average mentality can do. They just have to do it differently. They just need the support and guidance of their loved ones."

I feel as if my brain is about to explode. I can't think about this anymore. Not today.

"So my advice to you," Dr. Tamara is saying as I try to listen again, "is to talk to Chloe about acceptable and unacceptable behavior in public. And about private time. About what's appropriate when she and Thomas are alone."

"You mean talk to her about sex?"

"If and when you think it's appropriate."

I don't want to think about Thomas touching Chloe intimately. I can't. "I have strong feelings about sex between unmarried couples," I say. And that's true. Sort of. If I hadn't had sex with Randall while he was still married to Elaine, I wouldn't have gotten pregnant. If I hadn't gotten pregnant by a married man, then I wouldn't have had the abortion. I'd say that's a pretty good argument against sex outside of marriage.

"Then tell Chloe that," he says. "But really, ultimately, sex is a personal decision. You and I have the right to decide how we'll share our bodies . . . and so does Chloe."

Suddenly I feel exhausted. Depleted. I *really* can't think about this anymore. Not today. "You've given me a lot to think about," I say, getting to my feet.

"I know it's overwhelming, but give yourself some time. Give Chloe some time. Treat her as you would any young girl in her first relationship. There's no reason there can't be boundaries. I'm not saying there shouldn't be. I'm just saying it's time that you consider the idea that Chloe is growing up . . . to be the beautiful, amazing woman you always wanted her to be."

I nod because I'm not sure I have any words left in me today. Between the conversation with Randall, and the conversation with my co-worker's sister, who works in an adult living facility for mentally handicapped adults (she proceeded to tell me that the residents did better when they had a *special someone*), and now Dr. Tamara, I'm just talked out. I'm reasoned out. And I'm certainly emotionally wrung out.

"If you'd like to schedule some extra sessions, to get you and Chloe over this bump in the road," Dr. Tamara says, rising to his feet to walk me to the door, "just let Jeanie know. And Alicia . . ." He rests his hand on my shoulder.

I look at his skinny wrist.

"*Relax*," he says.

❦ 11 ❧

Relax. Relax. That's what I keep telling myself. I try to relax. Friday night, Chloe and I make cookies from scratch: chocolate chip. Very relaxing. We talk about her upcoming birthday. We talk a little bit about the word *intimacy*. The talk goes better than I expect, although there's a lot of giggling on her part. I don't bring up any of the physical aspects of a relationship between a man and a woman, beyond kissing, but we do talk about the word *appropriate* and what it means. I explain to her that it's not *appropriate* for her and Thomas to kiss in Minnie's bathroom. I'm not sure that she understands what I'm trying to tell her, but at least she agrees to not do it anymore.

And I *relax* a little. Maybe Chloe's relationship with Thomas is going to be a good thing. Maybe I really can relax, as Dr. Tamara suggested.

I'm reading on the couch in my pajamas Saturday night when my cell phone rings, startling me. It's nine thirty-five. Jin. Abby was supposed to be coming for their mysterious talk, then Abby had to postpone, at the last minute. I'd assumed Jin and I would have our standing date, but then she said she had a *thing*, so she'd go to that. I assumed it was an art *thing*. She's always attending some art thing: a show, a cocktail party, a meet-and-greet the artist.

"Hey," I say into the phone.

"Ally?"

She sounds like she's crying. I sit up and all the relaxation evaporates from my body. Her art *things* didn't usually involve crying. "You okay?"

I hear a sniffle. She's definitely crying. "I think she's getting married."

I almost ask *who?* Luckily, I catch myself. I get up off the couch and begin to pace in front of the fireplace. "Wait. Abby told you she's getting married? I thought you weren't seeing her tonight." I grip my phone. "Does Huan know?"

"Abby was so nice when she called. She said she had been so looking forward to seeing me." Jin was talking fast . . . and beginning to cry again. "She said she was sorry she had to postpone our date . . . not a date. You know what I mean."

"Jin, where are you?"

She takes a shuddering breath. "Abby's."

I can feel the frown lines on my forehead tighten. "She's with you?"

"No. I'm in my car sitting in front of Abby's house. She . . . she's inside. With . . . with *her*."

"With the ex?" I ask.

"Elise," Jin says bitterly. "Huan never liked her. She was snarky with him behind Abby's back, but then all sweet and nice in front of her. Oh Ally, what am I going to do? She can't marry her." Now she's sobbing. "She can't marry that snarky woman."

I glance at the staircase. I can see a pale light coming from above and hear the faint sound of Ellen DeGeneres's voice in *Finding Nemo*. I did a bad thing today. I lied to my daughter and told her *Finding Nemo* was a Disney movie. Which isn't a total lie because Disney owns Pixar, right? I saw the DVD in Walmart and I was sick to death of the same old Disney movies.

"I still love Abby," Jin blubbers. "I didn't think I did. I don't want to, but I do. I love her. I can't live without her, Ally."

"Jin. You haven't gone to the door or anything, have you?" I ask, headed up the stairs.

She takes a shuddering breath. "I should go in. I should confront the bitch."

"No. No, you should sit right there in the car. You don't know why she's there. It could have nothing to do with them getting married. It could be something for work."

"It's not work. I'm going to the door. I'm going in."

"You can't go in there. Not like this."

"I have to talk to her," Jin says, bordering on hysteria. "I have to talk some sense into her. We have a son. We have a life."

I hurry up the stairs. I'm already in my pajamas so I'll have to change back into jeans. "Listen to me—"

"Ally—"

"Jin," I say sharply. "Listen to me. Don't get out of the car. Just sit there. Just wait for me. I'm coming." I reach the top of the staircase.

"You're coming?" she says, sounding nothing like herself. Sounding lost. I've never heard Jin like this. She's always been so . . . *sensible* about her relationships. Even after they ended.

I cover the phone with my hand and stick my head through the doorway of Chloe's bedroom. She's lying on her bed in sweatpants and a sweatshirt: tiger cub on a branch with the words *Hang Tough*. "Chloe! Want to go for a ride?"

She looks at me. "I'm watching *Nemo*." She points at my iPad screen. The father clownfish, Marlin, is talking to a big turtle.

I smile slyly at my daughter. "Let's go for a ride and get ice cream!"

"Ice cream!" Chloe scoots off the bed and grabs her canvas library bag from her bedpost.

I head down the hall toward my bedroom and raise the phone. "Jin, sit right there. Don't move. We're on our way."

*   *   *

I have to stop for the ice cream before we get to Abby's home in Queenstown, just east of the Chesapeake Bay Bridge. It's not easy to find a place selling ice cream at 10 p.m. in February on the Eastern Shore of Maryland. We find a gas station. I get a cup of coffee, Chloe gets a jumbo Nutty Buddy. I call Jin twice on our way. She's staying put. *Good girl.*

I know where Abby's house is because Jin made me ride over to take some things there right after they split up. Over the years, I've been here with her a couple of times to drop Huan off or pick him up. It's been a while, but I find the house without any problem.

Jin's still sitting in her Prius. Directly across the street from Abby's quaint white bungalow. I park in front of her and cut my lights. Chloe's fallen asleep in the backseat, cuddled in the blanket she brought along. I smile at the smear of chocolate ice cream dried on her cheek. I get out and lock my car. I get into Jin's Prius on the passenger's side. She's just sitting there, hands in her lap, staring straight ahead.

"Hey," I say gently.

"She's gone. She left."

It's chilly inside Jin's car. I'm glad I'm still wearing my coat. "Abby or Elise?"

"Elise," she says softly. "She left."

"Which means they're probably not getting married."

She looks at me. "I want to go in. Should I go in? Should I just ask her why she cancelled on me so she could see Elise?"

I shake my head. "Not tonight. Not like this. Tonight, you should come home with me. We'll have a glass of wine. You can stay over."

"My car."

I shrug. "We'll move it to the outlet parking lot and come back for it tomorrow."

"You don't think I should go to the door . . . or maybe call?"

"And say what?" I reach out and squeeze her hand. It's cold. "That you're stalking her?"

"I'm not stalking her."

I'm quiet for a minute. "You kind of are."

"What would I do without you?" Jin closes her eyes. "Thanks for coming for me and keeping me from making a fool of myself."

"Anytime."

Abby called Jin the next day. Turns out Abby was making the final break with her lawyer ex-girlfriend because she wanted to revisit her relationship with Jin. Abby and Jin began talking to each other regularly on the phone.

The days on my iCal go by so quickly that sometimes I lose track. Chloe's birthday comes and goes; I get her a personal DVD player instead of an iPad. I start leaving Chloe with the LoGs on Saturday mornings at St. Mark's. Thomas comes to our house every Wednesday to watch a Disney movie and have dinner with us. Spring arrives and the LoGs' ventures change from pizza parlors and arcades to the zoo and parks. My semester classes end, including the one I've been teaching for Sue Chou. I agree to teach only one class in the classroom for each of the summer sessions, and two online classes. It will be a light summer schedule for me, giving me more time to focus on Chloe. Which she doesn't seem to be all that thrilled about.

It's June when the families from St. Mark's LoGs are invited to a picnic at a local park and I find myself sitting in a parking space next to a Dumpster. I drove here alone because Chloe wanted to ride in the church van . . . with Thomas. My window is down; I can hear children's laughter coming from a swing set nearby. I feel the heat of the June sun on my face.

Margaret will be here. And Thomas's father, Danny. I'm dreading this picnic. You would think I would enjoy spending time with families who go through the same trials and tribulations I do, dealing with a mentally handicapped child. But I don't. They don't make me feel better. They make me feel worse and I don't know why.

I think I'm dreading having to talk with Margaret and Danny because I know the subject of Chloe going over to their house is going to come up. So far, I've been able to handle Thomas and Chloe, putting the Eldens off, always having an excuse up my sleeve as to why Chloe can't go to *his* house this Wednesday. My busy teaching schedule has been a great crutch, but the semester is over and now it's summer and my schedule is less time-consuming. I offered to let Chloe cut back on her hours at Miss Minnie's because I could be home with her more, but she refused. Another fit at Minnie's. She loves Miss Minnie's even more than before because now Thomas is there. They're both going full-time, five days a week, at their request. And both have been bugging me to let Chloe go to Thomas's for dinner and a movie.

Jin says it's time for me to let Chloe go to Thomas's. It's been five months and the romance is still going strong. As far as I can tell, the kissing hasn't progressed to anything more, though Chloe and Thomas always seem to be touching each other. Jin says my annoyance with the touching is a reflection of my own need to be touched. She doesn't come right out and say I'm jealous of my daughter and her boyfriend, but I know that's what she's thinking.

I signed up for the online dating. I've e-mailed back and forth with a couple of guys. Two weeks ago, I met *John* for coffee. He was okay, but after twenty minutes, the conversation became forced. I just couldn't get past the idea that in his profile he said he was five-foot-eleven, when in reality, he was closer to five-five. I didn't care that he was shorter than I was. I just cared that he had lied. Why would a guy lie about how tall he was? And if he'd lie about something so inconsequential, what else would he lie about? I didn't see John again.

Tonight I'm meeting *Theodore* for a drink at a local pub. He seems like a nice guy. He owns a landscaping business in the next town north of Port Chapel. But I know it won't work out. What do I have in common with a landscaper? I don't think of myself as an elitist snob like Randall, but I'm probably more of one than I care to admit. Me and a landscaper, a carpenter, a gym teacher? I just don't see it working out. I want to cancel my date, but Jin says I can't. She says I have to *put myself out there* if I'm going to find someone special. I'm not sure I should be taking dating advice from her, though. She's been sneaking around behind her son's back, talking to her ex, her son's other mommy.

"Alicia! So good to see you!"

Margaret and her husband have pulled into the parking space beside me. I get out of my car. "Margaret." I push my sunglasses up on the bridge of my nose and smile.

Margaret climbs out of the passenger side of her blue minivan. She's wearing a long, flowered skirt that looks like all the other flowered skirts she wears. Her mostly gray hair is in the usual bun, and despite the eighty-degree weather, she's wearing a long-sleeved T-shirt with clouds and a Bible quote on it. It reminds me of Chloe's kitten shirts. I know I'm not particularly fashionable, but I feel like a runway model in my khaki capris, tank top, and leather flip-flops.

Margaret is wearing black shoes that have Velcro straps across the top—just like Thomas's. I get why *he* wears them. He has problems with manual dexterity. His fine motor skills are poor. It's interesting that Chloe's are pretty good. As much as I hate to admit it, Thomas and Chloe make a good team. Chloe seems more physically capable of doing things, while Thomas can read a little. He's able to read simple directions, like on the slice-and-bake cookie package. Between the two of them, and a thousand questions to me from Chloe, they can bake cookies together in my kitchen now.

I eye Margaret's shoes. One of the Velcro tabs has curled up and won't stick, probably due to the red fuzz poking out of the

Velcro fibers. I've only met Thomas's father a couple of times, and then just to wave a hello, but I know he wears the same shoes. They must get a discount.

I realize how mean my thoughts are. Maybe not mean, but certainly unnecessarily critical. The Eldens are nice people. I think of them as *crazy Christians*, but that's an unfair evaluation. They're different than I am. They're not well-educated, well-spoken, or well-read, but they're nice people. And they're nice to my Chloe, I remind myself again. Does any of the other stuff really matter?

This time, my smile is genuine as I pop my trunk to retrieve a cooler of deviled eggs. "Chloe's been looking forward to this picnic all week," I say.

"Thomas, too!" Margaret generally speaks in exclamations. It drove me crazy at first, but I'm getting used to it. "We brought a fluffy Jell-O salad. Our Thomas loves fluffy salad!"

Green fluffy Jell-O salad with marshmallows grosses me out, but I don't say so. Thomas had never had couscous or hummus until he came to our house. It's only right that Thomas and his family introduce Chloe to fluffy Jell-O salad.

"Danny, get the salad! And my diet soda." She looks at me. "I've got *the sugar*."

Thomas's father comes around the van. Sure enough, he's wearing the same Velcro shoes . . . and plaid shorts and a hibiscus-flowered shirt. He's short and bald on his crown. I've wondered where Thomas got his height, but never asked. I never ask anything beyond "How are you today?" I don't want to be friends with the Eldens. I don't know why, but I don't want Chloe to be friends with them, either.

As if I could stop her.

That's how I feel lately, as if my daughter is a train barreling down the tracks and I can't set the brakes. A month ago, she asked for some new clothes because she wanted to look pretty for Thomas. For her boyfriend. She wouldn't listen to me when I told her she was already beautiful without the new T-shirts with kittens and puppies on them.

Then, last week, she asked me about getting her some makeup. Susan, at Miss Minnie's, wears makeup. I bought Chloe some mascara and lip gloss, but I know sparkly blue eye shadow is in our future. For Chloe's whole life, I've been her major influence, her *only* influence. Now, suddenly, she's taking advice from TV commercials and mentally handicapped girls.

Danny nods to me. To my knowledge, he doesn't speak. At least, he's never spoken to me. He just smiles and nods. I know he's not deaf, though, because Margaret is always ordering him around and he does as she tells him. It seems like a strange relationship to me, but who am I to judge? Look at Randall and me. When was that ever *not* strange?

We head toward the pavilion, me carrying my cooler and two chairs in bags. The Eldens follow behind me. Margaret talks nonstop. She keeps up Danny's end of the conversation. Mine, too.

"I think it's so nice that the church planned this picnic for the kids! I have such fond memories of the church picnics of my childhood. I wonder where the kids are?"

Margaret always refers to Thomas and Chloe as *the kids*. I sort of get it; they're children, at least mentally. But Thomas shaves and Chloe menstruates. They're not kids.

"Thank goodness there's shade! Danny, look, there's shade under the pavilion," Margaret calls over her shoulder. "I'm so glad there's shade! Thomas burns easily. I made him put suntan lotion on this morning before he left for church, but he burns. Like his mother!"

Someone has already taped plastic tablecloths to several tables under the pavilion marked with a poster board sign that reads *St. Mark's*. A young woman in red pigtails whom I recognize from somewhere is lining casserole dishes up on one of the tables. A young man with a goatee is manning an enormous cinder-block grill just beyond the pavilion. The smell of burgers wafts in the air.

"Dr. Richards," the girl says. She holds out her arms for the small cooler I'm carrying. "I didn't know you would be here." She must be able to tell from the look on my face that I can't place her.

"Jennifer Smith," she says. "I took your E212 Romanticism class last fall. I sat in the back of the class, on the right."

"I'm sorry," I apologize. "I'm not good with names, but I usually remember my students' papers."

"It's okay. I never talked in class. My final paper was on how the ancient North was re-created for contemporary national, political, and literary purposes."

Margaret reaches my side and is fussing with her husband about how he packed the fluffy Jell-O salad in the ice.

"I *do* remember you, Jennifer. It was a good final paper." I grimace. "Please tell me I gave you an A?"

The student smiles as she pulls the deviled eggs out of my cooler. "I got a 93 on the paper and an A- in the class, which I was thrilled with." It's her turn to make a face. "Bio major. British literature, not my thing."

I laugh with her. I can tell Jennifer is a bright kid, and for just a second I imagine she's mine, my daughter, and we're discussing the Romanticism movement in British literature in the nineteenth century. With the red hair and the blue eyes, she could *be* my daughter.

"Mom!" I hear Chloe's voice from far behind me and I'm instantly annoyed with myself. Chloe's my daughter and I love her. I wouldn't give her up for anything in the world, not even for ten biology students named Jennifer.

Jennifer slides my now-empty cooler across the table toward me. "I love Chloe. Funny girl."

"You know Chloe from . . . St. Mark's?" I ask. *Chloe is funny?* That's never been a word I would use to describe her. I wonder how she's funny at church. Is it things she says? Does she make faces? Do silly things? How did I not know that Chloe is funny when she's with other people?

"Uh-huh. I had a rough schedule this spring so I didn't get to help out much at church, but now that the semester is over, I have more free time. Chloe's cool."

"Mom!" Chloe hollers. I can tell she's running.

I turn to wave at her, to see her sprinting across the grass toward me. She runs awkwardly, her short limbs pumping hard for the distance she covers. "I won! We practiced the egg roll and I won the practice!" she tells me.

"Mom!" Thomas hollers from behind Chloe. He's running, too. Lumbering gracelessly, large limbs flailing.

"And Thomas, too," Jennifer is saying. "I think it's cool that Chloe has a boyfriend."

I turn back to Jennifer. "You do?"

"Sure." She grins, accepting Margaret's enormous plastic bowl of Jell-O salad. "Everybody at church does. Everybody at school thinks you're cool, too. The way you let Chloe wear her hair and wear sneakers and stuff like everyone else. You know, like she's normal." She makes a face. "Sorry. That wasn't very politically correct, was it? You know what I was trying to say."

"The students think I'm cool?" I can't hide my surprise. I didn't know my students thought I was cool. I don't know why I care, but I do, and I'm tickled.

"Mom!" Chloe runs right into me and I have to put my arms around her to keep her from knocking me over.

"Chloe!" I laugh, because she's so excited. So happy.

"I won the race," she tells me, out of breath. "It was just practice, but I won!"

"K . . . Koey, she w . . . won!" Thomas shouts from behind her.

"Thomas, you're so loud." Margaret covers her ears. "My Thomas, he's always been so loud!" she announces to no one in particular. "Danny, take the cooler back to the car. I don't want to lose my good cooler."

"Hey, Chloe," Jennifer says. "You won? That's great."

"Just practice." Chloe looks up at me, her face filled with joy. "But that means I'll really win, right?"

"I don't know. I hope so," I tell her. Then I see that families are starting to take their seats on the benches at the picnic tables. The assistant pastor is standing at one end, apparently waiting to make an announcement. "I guess we'd better find a place to sit, Chloe." I glance over at my student. "It was nice talking with you, Jennifer."

"You, too, Dr. Richards."

"We should sit," I tell Chloe, gently herding her toward the tables.

"With Thomas!" She bounces up and down on the toes of her sneakers. "We have to sit with Thomas."

"C . . . 'Cause K . . . Koey is m . . . my g . . . girlfriend," Thomas volunteers, grabbing my daughter's hand.

Margaret meets my gaze. "It's so nice that they've found each other, our Thomas and your Chloe."

I smile but I look away. Jin says I need to talk to Margaret, that we need to discuss Chloe and Thomas's relationship and where it's going, but I can't bring myself to do it. Over the last few weeks, I've come to the conclusion that Margaret doesn't realize her son is mentally disabled. She's in some incredible land of denial.

A place I wish I could go, if only for a visit.

We dine on burgers, salads, and green fluffy Jell-O salad. Thankfully, Chloe eats all of the Jell-O salad on my plate. Then we play picnic games: a three-legged race, rolling a hard-boiled egg race, a sack race. Tug-of-war. Chloe loves every minute of it. She jumps and claps and screams with glee, even when a boy with Down syndrome beats her in the hard-boiled egg race.

After the games, a young man comes to talk to us about the Special Olympics. A mentally handicapped girl stands in front of the group, grinning as she tells us she plays softball on a team for the Special Olympics and how her team is traveling to Delaware this summer to compete regionally. Chloe nudges me several times during the presentation to tell me she wants to participate. Of course no matter what activity is mentioned, badminton, figure skating, even power lifting, she's on board with it.

When it grows dark, the hot coals are raked together on the outdoor grill and everyone toasts marshmallows to make s'mores. I chat with a few parents, a few LoGs, but I don't enter into any serious conversation with anyone, really. There's one single guy there about my age. His son, Pedro, was invited by one of the other LoGs. Doug and I chat, but he's just going through a divorce from Pedro's mom and all he talks about is her. I can tell that even if Chrissy's done with the marriage, Doug's not, and I quickly conclude that even if he was interested in going out with me, I should not walk away; I should run.

It gets chilly as the sun goes down, and I wait for my turn to roast my marshmallow over the coals. A few feet away from me, Thomas pulls his Penn State Football sweatshirt off and gives it to Chloe. My first impulse is to call to her and remind her that her sweatshirt is in our car, but it's such a sweet moment. I keep my mouth shut, and I watch as Chloe tugs the sweatshirt over her head and Thomas arranges it for her. He kisses her on the mouth and they laugh because, apparently, she has marshmallow on her lips and he can taste it.

"Ah, young love," Margaret says from behind me . . . with a sigh, rather than the usual exclamation point.

It was another important milestone in my life and Chloe's, but again, I didn't see it. Chloe wore Thomas's sweatshirt for days before I convinced her to return it.

Summer passes too quickly. I begin to let Chloe go to Thomas's occasionally. There's no way Danny Elden is a pervert;

he's just a nice, quiet little man with a bossy wife. The plumbing in my house continues to be the bane of my existence. I think I see more of Mark-the-Plumber that summer than I see of Theo, whom I began dating the week of the LoGs picnic. Chloe's relationship with Thomas shows no signs of fizzling out, and before I know it, it's September again and my fall classes are starting.

❧ 12 ❧

"Four . . . five. . . . I need a dress," Chloe says. She's counting out apples she and Thomas picked in the local orchard this afternoon with Margaret. "A pretty dress, one. And a cat costume, eight!"

"You skipped six and seven." I'm standing at the kitchen counter beside her, rolling out the piecrust dough. I didn't make it from scratch, but at least I bought the kind in the grocery store that you have to roll out and actually put in your own pie pan. "We need eight apples. Try again. Why do you need a dress? And you already have a cat costume. From last Halloween."

Chloe puts the apples back in the bag and begins to count again. "One, two, three—but it's a *black* cat. I want to be a *white* cat. Five, six, eight."

I reach over in front of her. "One, two, three, *four*, five, six, *seven*, eight," I say, counting out the Granny Smith apples in front of her. "Now you count. What do you need the dress for? You never wear dresses."

"One, three, four . . ." She giggles. "For the dance, silly head!"

"One, two, three." I recount the apples in front of her. "What dance?"

"LoGs dance. I have to wear a dress." She pirouettes with an apple in each hand. To anyone else, she might have seemed awkward, her movements jerky, but to me, she's beautiful. Graceful.

"Miss Margaret says girls wear a pretty dress," Chloe continues. "Thomas is going to be my *date*. Me and him, he's my *date*. Five, seven, eight—"

"One, two, three, four, five, six, seven, eight apples." I count them out with one floury hand. I move the paper bag to the other side of the counter. I take a breath, feeling more impatient about the dress than the counting.

Thomas is changing her. He's changing my little girl. Or is my little girl just growing up? Would she want a dress for the dance, even if Thomas hadn't asked her to be his date? I keep making this all about Thomas. If it wasn't Thomas, would it be a different boy?

I look at her, feeling a mixture of happiness and sadness; happiness for her, but sadness for myself. There's probably some truth to what Dr. Tamara, Randall, Minnie, Jin, *everyone* continues to say about me being overprotective. Chloe really has demonstrated that she can continue to learn and continue to grow, when I give her room.

What no one brings up, what no one seems to want to discuss with me is, where is Chloe's limit? At what point will I go from being the parent who encourages her child to be all she can be, to the parent allowing her to walk too close to the edge of a cliff?

I press my lips together, smile, and say, "Try counting just four apples, first. You're good with four."

"I'm good with four," Chloe repeats proudly. This time, she successfully counts out four apples.

"Now count four more." Satisfied with the almost circular shape of my piecrust, I reach for my red ceramic pie plate. "And that makes eight."

Chloe counts out four more apples. "That makes eight!" She jumps up and down, clapping. She does another pirouette, hands high above her head. She's somehow managed to get a dusting of flour on her cheek and her hair has come loose from her droopy ponytail. She's gorgeous.

I still remember her jumping up and down in the kitchen. Pirouetting. She was so happy that day about the apples, about going to the dance with Thomas, about a kitten Halloween costume. If only I could have frozen that moment in time. I remember how good I felt, watching her dance in the kitchen. For once I wasn't worried about anything imminent. I wasn't scared. I took pleasure that day in the simple task of baking a pie with my daughter. Of being with her and enjoying her beautiful smile. I remember the smell of the pie baking: the sweet of the fruit, the spiciness of the cinnamon and nutmeg.

Chloe and I were happy that day. Happy with each other, happy with the world. Why couldn't things have just stayed that way? Chloe was happy with her relationship with Thomas and I was . . . *content* with it. Thinking back, I see now that life was pretty good. My dating life was down the tubes again and I'd put on three pounds instead of losing the fifteen . . . but I was . . . happy.

Chloe went to the dance at church with Thomas that fall, in a pretty blue dress. Of course it was blue. Luckily, we couldn't find a blue dress with kittens on it in Chloe's size.

It was Chloe's first dance. There were other firsts that fall. In November, I walked through the doors of a Friends' Meeting House for the first time in more than two decades. I can't say that I immediately felt at home there, because I didn't, but it felt . . . like there might be something there for me.

Quakers worship in different ways in different parts of the country and the world. Some have services very similar to Methodists or Baptists, or any other Protestant faith, with ministers, hymns, and the recognition of particular religious holidays. This two-hundred-and-fifty-year-old Friends congregation, however, was *old school*. There was no hierarchy in the church: no

ministers, no lay speakers. It was non-liturgical, so they cele-
brated no holidays. What set it apart the most from other Protestant services, however, was that it was conducted, for the most
part, in silence. *Friends* gather in expectant waiting. They clear
their minds and wait for a whisper of God's word.

The hour of near silence was hard for me. I was used to noise,
the noise of others, my own noise, noise that was making me
silent inside. Maybe the noise was holding back the anger I felt
toward God for making my Chloe . . . what? Less than she could
have been? Less than the child Randall wanted?

I only went once that fall; it was a Sunday morning when
Chloe had begged to go to St. Mark's with Thomas and his family. I wasn't invited. Not that I would have gone. But somewhere
between driving her to St. Mark's and driving home, I turned the
car around and headed north. I arrived at the Meeting House a
little late, and when it was over, I slipped out as quietly and in-
conspicuously as possible. I can't say that, that winter, I was
dying to go back . . . but I can say that I thought a lot about it in
the following months. I thought about the sense of peace I felt at
one point. It only lasted a fraction of a second, but over the next
months that fraction of a second teased me. Tantalized me.

Christmas came and went. I cut back on how much I spent on
Chloe, but she didn't notice. Randall began teaching fewer
classes and contributing less money to Chloe's *upkeep*, as he liked
to call it. Like she was a piece of livestock . . . or a pet. I made
enough money to pay the mortgage, to buy groceries and other
necessities, but there was no possibility of any big-ticket items
under the Christmas tree. You'd think a tenured professor in a
private liberal arts college would make big bucks. You'd be
wrong.

Things seemed to stay the same that winter: my classes, my
students, Jin's friendship. But they didn't, really. They changed.
Life is that way. Things change even when you feel like you're
standing still. One of my students committed suicide. My first.

She was in my Brit Lit Two class. A nice girl. Quiet. My students said she killed herself over a boyfriend. I couldn't imagine being her mother. The pain she must have felt. Losing a daughter over a boy? It made me cry just to think about it.

That winter, Jin was not only talking to Abby, but seeing her a couple of times a month. And keeping it from Huan. I knew they were taking things slowly, but I noticed that Jin seemed happier. I also noticed that she wasn't dating anyone else.

In January came Chloe's and Thomas's *anniversary*. I should have declined the invitation to Thomas's house for the celebratory dinner, but Chloe was so excited.

Dinner is fine. We have pork chops and macaroni and cheese and peas and carrots. I think the menu is a little heavy on the carbs for Margaret, who is a type 2 diabetic, but it's right up Chloe's alley. She's never liked leafy green vegetables, and I'm always trying to make them more palatable to her with cheese or ranch dressing.

We talk about the LoGs' upcoming field trip to go snow tubing in Pennsylvania. Margaret and I are both going. We talk about how to make chocolate chip pancakes, and about the snow in the forecast. The evening is fine. It's fine.

"And now for anniversary cake!" Margaret announces, carrying a big cookie sheet with a white homemade cake on top into the dining room. "Can you get paper plates, Danny? In the pantry."

Danny obediently rises from the chair at the head of the table and goes into the kitchen. He hasn't said a word all evening, but he's pleasant enough. He smiles a lot.

"Cake!" Chloe cheers.

"Cake, K . . . Koey!" Thomas echoes.

"Does it got candles?"

"I don't think it *has* candles," I tell Chloe gently. "Anniversary cakes don't usually have candles."

"I have candles if Chloe wants candles!" Margaret insists. She sets the cake on the table between my daughter and her son and goes to the china cabinet to dig through a drawer. She pulls out chopsticks, matches, a tea candle, a pack of cards; the drawer seems bottomless.

My attention strays. The Eldens live in a three-bedroom pre-fab house in a cozy neighborhood on the east side of town. Their dining room is separate from the kitchen, but it's very small and I feel like there's too much furniture in the room. The décor is very busy. It reminds me of one of Margaret's skirts. There's flowered wallpaper and flowered place mats and bouquets of plastic flowers in vases. There are family portraits hung on all the walls, framed in thick, ornate gold-colored frames. Lots of pictures of Thomas grinning. The room makes me feel a little claustrophobic, but Chloe obviously feels comfortable here.

Thomas and Chloe are beaming at the white sheet cake. He's in a Thomas the Tank Engine sweatshirt; she's wearing puppies tonight.

Happy Anniversary, Chloe and Thomas! the cake from Walmart says in blue icing. *Many More!*

"I know I have candles here somewhere!" Margaret is saying. She's still pulling things out of the drawer.

Danny comes back into the dining room carrying Thomas the Tank Engine paper plates, the kind you get for a kids' party.

Thomas spots them. "M . . . my p . . . p . . . plates," he sings. "M . . . my s . . . s . . . special plates."

"Your special plates, honey." Chloe pats his hand.

Chloe uses those kinds of endearments now. She and Thomas call each other *honey* and *sweetie* and *baby*. It bothers me. It grates on my nerves, especially when he calls her *baby*. Because she's *my* baby.

But she's so happy. How can I begrudge her this happiness?

"Aha! I told you I had candles!" Margaret triumphantly holds up a little box of multicolored birthday candles. She brings the candles and the matches to the table, leaving all the stuff she pulled out of the drawer of the china cabinet on the edge of the dining table. A part of me actually envies her at that moment. I can't imagine feeling the freedom to just leave a pile of junk on the counter with guests in my home. Am I really that controlling? That controlled? I make a mental note to try to be more spontaneous, less fastidious. I've always told myself that I run my household the way I do because it's easier for Chloe. I told myself that structure is what *she* needs, what *she* craves. Would Dr. Tamara agree, or would he say that I am, again, using Chloe as a crutch?

"Hold hands!" Margaret insists as she sticks several candles in the cake. "Hold hands and be ready to make a wish."

Chloe and Thomas grab hands, holding on to each other as if they've just been set adrift in a life raft on the ocean. Margaret lights the candles. Danny peels five plates off the pile.

"Make a wish! A special wish!"

Chloe closes her eyes so hard that she scrunches her face. "Close your eyes, Thomas," she tells him.

Only then does Thomas close his eyes.

"Don't say your wish out loud!" Margaret warns. "Whisper it to yourself!"

I see Chloe's lips moving. Her eyes are still shut. Thomas's eyes are shut, too, but he seems to better understand what making a *silent* wish means.

"Now blow out your candles!"

Chloe's and Thomas's eyes fly open, and they both lean over the cake. They blow hard. Chloe knows how to blow out candles. No spit. Thomas makes a raspberry sound and I try not to be grossed out.

Margaret claps.

Thomas claps. "I m . . . made the wish, M . . . Mama! I . . . I m . . . made the w . . . w . . . wish! I wished m . . . me and K . . . Koey g . . . get married!"

There's something about the way Thomas says it that makes me think he and Margaret have discussed the *M* word. For some reason, when I look up, I look not at Thomas, or Chloe, or even

Margaret. It's Danny's gaze I meet for the briefest moment and when I do, I see the same fear in his eyes that I feel in my heart.

I had fun at my ann-versary with Thomas. I don't think Mom had fun. I don't think she liked the cake. Maybe she don't like white cake if it's got colored sprinkles in it.

I don't look at Mom's face when we drive home in the car. She don't look at me, either. I know why. It's not because of the white cake.

Thomas said his wish. He made his wish because we blew out candles on our cake. Then he told.

I love Thomas. He's my boyfriend, and he does what I tell him because I'm his girlfriend. He's my honey and that's what you do if you're someone's honey. He says we can get married. Belle and the Beast get married. I think Jasmine and Prince Ali get married, too. Boyfriends get married to girlfriends. They can sleep in a bed together. They can kiss whenever they want and they can touch boobies.

Thomas said his mom told him he can't touch my boobies anymore unless we get married. He touched my boobies when we watched *101 Dalmatians* at his house. She came in the living room to bring us sodas and her face got red. I think maybe she cried. She made Thomas go in the kitchen and talk to her. She told me to put my shirt on and fix my bra. It was the blue one with the yellow polka dots.

Thomas was crying when he came back in the living room. I think he was sad because he likes my boobies. His mom didn't come in the living room but his dad did. Now his dad watches Disney movies with us, too. I don't think he likes them. He always sleeps when they're on.

I look at my mom again. People say I look like her but she's pretty. Even when she's sad. She looks sad, now.

I don't want her to be sad. But I want to marry Thomas. I want to be married like Belle and the Beast. You dance if you get married.

I don't tell Mom I want to get married. Not tonight. I decide me and Thomas, we'll talk about it. That's what you do. You talk to your honey.

We will talk about getting married. Then I will tell Mom. On Wednesday.

❦ 13 ❧

Okay, I'll admit it. I took the coward's way out that night. I didn't ask Thomas about what he meant when he said he wished for he and Chloe to get married. I didn't ask Margaret if she and Thomas had discussed marriage. I avoided meeting Danny's gaze the rest of the night. I ate cake, I helped clean up the dishes, and I made small talk, but I said nothing about the proverbial eight-hundred-pound gorilla in the room.

I said nothing to Chloe.

I said nothing, as if the idea would just go away. Like it had when she first brought up getting married a year ago, when she met Thomas. It's a trick I learned from her. If she broke a water glass, she wouldn't clean it up and throw the pieces away, she'd just leave it there on the floor, as if she thought it would magically go away. As if I would, *magically*, not notice the broken pieces of glass all over the floor. And if I asked her to do something she didn't want to do, like take a shower, or pick up the markers she left all over the kitchen counter, she'd just ignore me.

I was hoping for magic. I thought that if I ignored Thomas and his wish, he would forget about it. I hoped we'd all forget until it was as if the words had never been spoken.

I misjudged Thomas. I still didn't know him well, so that's

understandable, but how did I misjudge Chloe so badly? I know my daughter. I know how stubborn she can be, how determined, once she gets something in her head.

It's a March morning, a few weeks after Chloe's twenty-sixth birthday. We're still in our pj's. The kitchen is warm and cozy, and I've made cinnamon oatmeal with raisins for us. I'm enjoying my second cup of coffee, reading my paper, when Chloe, with a mouth full of oatmeal, speaks.

"Mom?"

I don't look up from the paper. "Yes?"

"I wanted to tell you." She slurps her hot chocolate, washing down the oatmeal. She's speaking very clearly these days, enunciating well. It takes her longer to say something, though, because she's concentrating so hard. "Mom?"

"Tell me." I sip my coffee; it's just the right temperature, the right sweetness, the right creaminess. There's nothing like the perfect cup of coffee.

"I want to tell you. Me and Thomas. We're getting married."

I lower the paper. My heart is beating a little fast for eight thirty in the morning. "Who says you're getting married?"

My daughter meets my gaze. She licks the marshmallow off her spoon. "Thomas says."

I feel a sense of immediate relief. "Oh. Well, Thomas says lots of things that aren't true, sweetheart. Remember how he told you that he was going to get sled dogs and a train and the dogs were going to pull the train through the snow?"

"Dogs can't pull a train," she says.

"Indeed, they can't." My impulse is to raise the paper again and let it go at that, but something keeps me from doing it. Something about the look in her eyes tells me that the conversation is not over. Not for Chloe, at least.

She spoons more oatmeal into her mouth. "*I* say we're getting married." Her emphasis is on *I*.

For a moment, I don't know how to respond. She rarely speaks this way to me. With *tone*. Chloe likes to please me. She's a pleaser. Most Down syndrome people are. "You . . . *you* want to marry Thomas?"

"He's my boyfriend."

I conceded that point months ago. My daughter has a boyfriend. It's healthy. She's twenty-six. It's okay for a twenty-six-year-old woman, even one with limitations, to have a boyfriend. I'm a modern woman. A modern mother. I'm willing to say it's okay for Chloe to have a boyfriend.

"He *is* your boyfriend," I say. "But boyfriends and girlfriends don't necessarily get married."

Of course, if couples stay together, they *do* marry . . . or at least cohabitate. Average couples. But Chloe and Thomas are not average. For all of Chloe's advances, there's still no way she could handle independent living. Perfect example:

Last week, she cut her finger with a paring knife while trying to open a bag of chocolate chips. When she saw the tiny dot of blood, she started screaming. She didn't blot it with a towel or run it under the faucet; she started screaming. From upstairs, I heard her screams. From the sound, I thought she might have cut her hand off. She's cut herself before. She's seen *me* cut myself far worse. We've talked about what to do in such an *emergency*. She just got overwhelmed. It happens sometimes. Tiny stumbling blocks become major events for Chloe for no good reason. But what if she'd had a true emergency? Would she be able to handle herself? I'm afraid she wouldn't.

And as far as Thomas being independent? Margaret dresses him. She shaves him. I know the life we lead as mothers of mentally challenged children. She probably helps him with other, more personal, things in the bathroom. Margaret has just now begun to allow Thomas to walk from their front door to the curb to get their newspaper—and she watches from the window. Thomas looks more normal than Chloe, but from what I've observed in the last year, he probably has a lower IQ than she does. Though he's able to read a little, he's not able to think through simple tasks like how to get his pants right side out or how to fit pretzel sticks into a Ziploc bag. He's very impulsive and he has rituals that if he can't complete, he'll have a meltdown. Literally. He'll crumple into a sobbing mess on the floor. Margaret's son isn't any more capable of independent living than my daughter is.

I lay down my newspaper. "Chloe, I don't know that getting married to Thomas is a good idea," I say carefully.

She scrapes her bowl with her spoon. She's not listening to me. "I love him. He's my honey. I'm his baby." She giggles.

She's been saying this for months and I've been dismissing it. About loving Thomas. How can she possibly understand the complicated concept of love between a man and a woman? I can't think of a way to explain that, though. I take a different tack. "Married people live in their own house. They don't live with their parents. They go to work. You and Thomas don't go to work."

She thinks for a moment. "We go to Miss Minnie's."

I nod. "But that's not work, Chloe. No one gives you money to go to Miss Minnie's. I give Miss Minnie money so you can go there. I work so I can pay for Miss Minnie's and for our house. So we can buy groceries."

"You buy movies," she points out. "*Nemo* broke and you bought me a new *Nemo*." She thinks for a second. "The box is different," she adds.

"Right. I bought you a new *Finding Nemo* with money from my job at the university."

She licks her spoon and then looks at me with utter seriousness. "I can't get a job because I got Down's."

The way she says it breaks my heart. I nod. "We've talked about this, right? We all have things we *can* do and things we *can't* do. I don't think you could go to work, Chloe."

"I can't teach college. I'm not smart."

I press my lips together before I speak, to control the emotion in my voice. "You couldn't teach college."

Again, she thinks. My daughter, with her limited capacity for thinking, thinks hard. "Thomas," she declares. "*He* could work. He could buy movies."

"Thomas can't go to work. Remember, Miss Margaret said he worked at the library in Ohio, but he didn't like it and he left the library by himself, one day, and the police had to find him?"

"He didn't like the library." She frowns and thrusts out her lower lip. "They were *meanie heads*. They said he had to put books on the cart. I like the library. I get books and I put them in my bag." She stands up, taking her bowl with her.

"Hon," I say gently. "I don't think either of you could work."

"We don't have to work!"

"Chloe, have you talked to someone about this? Did someone say you and Thomas should get married?" I wonder if Margaret put them up to it. Margaret, who pretends her son isn't mentally challenged.

"*We* say. Me and Thomas. We're getting married. We're big enough." She shuffles in her slippers to the kitchen sink and begins to rinse her bowl. "We're allowed," she says, starting to take on a stubborn tone.

I'm not sure how to respond. Luckily, I'm saved by a knock on the back door. I'm halfway to the mudroom before I realize who it must be. I see Mark's smiling face through the window in the door. He comes in the back door now. He's become a back door friend.

"You forgot I was coming," he says when I open the door. "I can come back."

I look down at my flannel pj's. The top and bottom match. They're clean. They're actually kind of cute. And I brushed my hair and my teeth before I came down. I open the door wider and wave him in. "You've seen me look worse than this."

"I did see you that time Chloe stopped up the drain in the tub and the water poured through the ceiling onto your head."

"Maybe you can't come in," I say, but I'm still motioning for him to come in.

"I got that part for the garbage disposal." He sets down his big red toolbox on the floor and wipes his feet. He's constantly in and out, trying to hold my plumbing system together. We've actually joked that I need to put him on retainer.

I head for the kitchen. "Coffee's made."

"I don't want to bother you." He hangs up his coat in the mudroom. It's green corduroy with a fluffy cream-colored lining. It looks good on him. Rugged. It reminds me of something a modern-day cowboy would wear out West.

"You don't want to *bother* me? Mark, we're practically best friends, you're here so often."

He chuckles with me and lets me pour him a cup of coffee. As I slide the mug across the counter, I notice that he didn't shave this morning. He looks good with just a little beard stubble. He's a good-looking guy. I wonder how things are going with the new woman he's been dating: Tracie. From the plumbing supplies store. But I don't ask; at this moment I'm a little jealous that Tracie is dating my handsome, nice-guy plumber. *My* dating life is tanking. I haven't been able to make myself go on another first date in months.

"Good morning, Chloe," Mark says.

Chloe turns around from the sink, her lower lip thrust out. She looks at me and then directly at Mark. She's definitely annoyed with me now. Her eyes are squinty. "Me and Thomas, we're getting married," she announces. Then she marches out of the kitchen. "On Wednesday!" she hollers over her shoulder as she disappears down the hall.

I'm surprised I'm not embarrassed. I prefer keeping family matters private, but I suppose what I said was true. Mark really *has* become a friend. It started out that he was just our friendly neighborhood plumber . . . but now he's a friend. He comes by some mornings without his toolbox. This is the fourth cup of coffee we'll have shared together in the last two weeks.

He sits down on the bar stool at the counter. He raises the mug to his mouth and takes a sip. I suppose if I don't say anything about Chloe's announcement, he's not going to say anything. But how can I not say something?

I walk over to the table and get my mug and come back to the counter. "She's *not* getting married," I say.

He nods.

"I mean . . . how could she? You see her. You know what she can and can't do. She's not capable of being in a relationship with someone, living with someone."

Mark frowns good-naturedly. "Apparently a lot of us aren't."

I don't know why, but I laugh. I'm still laughing when I start to speak, but by the end, my voice is cracking. "She wants to get married. She wants to *get married*. What am I going to do?"

"You think she's serious, or do you think it will blow over?" He takes another sip of coffee. I like the way he talks. He takes his time, thinking. His manner is very casual. Unlike mine. When I hear myself speak, I don't like it. I always sound like I'm in overdrive. It's who I am, but it still makes me cringe sometimes.

Being with Mark makes me slow down a little. I think he makes me a better listener.

"I mean, is this the first time you've heard the idea?" he says.

I exhale and reach for the substitute-sugar bowl. "Noooo." I draw the vowel out. "When she first met him, she told me they were getting married. I don't think she was serious. She just said it in the excitement of the moment, her first boyfriend and all. But then, a few weeks ago, when we were at Thomas's, he made a wish. On the anniversary cake candles." I cut my eyes at him. "He told us his wish was that he and Chloe get married."

Mark makes a face like he's cringing. "So, she might be serious now."

I hear the front door open, then close. Then Jin's footsteps—always as light and silky smooth as a dancer's. I get another coffee mug out. I have the sickest feeling in the pit of my stomach. "She might be serious."

Mark's quiet again. "You talk to his mom?"

"You think I should?"

Jin walks into the kitchen. She's dressed for work, which looks very similar to being dressed to go to the grocery store or the mall. She's wearing jeans, a cute, filmy blouse over a cami, and an artsy scarf I know she dyed herself because she gave me one for Christmas.

Jin stops, looks at me, then Mark, then me again. "What's up?"

I pour coffee for her. When Mark comes for coffee, Jin comes. I swear, I think she smells him. (He smells good, but not like cologne, like . . . soap and guy good.) Or maybe she just sees him through her kitchen window. If she isn't a lesbian, I might be worried that she was trying to home in on my handsome plumber.

Jin accepts the mug I pass to her. She likes hers black. "Does Mark think you should . . . what?" she asks. She parks her skinny bottom on the bar stool next to him.

I want to bang my forehead on the granite countertop. I don't want to talk to Margaret about why Chloe and Thomas aren't getting married. I don't want to talk to Mark and Jin about it. I don't even want to talk to myself about it.

Mark doesn't say anything.

"What?" Jin asks.

I add cream to my second cup of coffee. Lots of cream. "I was asking Mark how long he thought it would be before you admitted you're dating your ex."

Mark looks into his coffee cup, but I can tell he's smiling. On the inside, at least.

Jin looks at me. "You didn't say anything to Huan, did you? I don't want to confuse him. I don't want him to get his hopes up."

Something about the way she says it makes me think Jin doesn't want to get her own hopes up. I make a mental note to revisit this topic when we're alone with a bottle of wine.

I speak quietly, either because I don't want Chloe to hear me, or because I'm still hoping the whole thing will magically go away . . . if I don't say it too loudly. "Chloe told me, then Mark, that she and Thomas are getting married."

When Jin speaks, she takes on a Tiger-practically-God-Mom tone. "You need to call his mother."

"A moment, Alicia?"

I look up from my desk, startled, to see Randall standing in the open doorway of my office. If I'm not with a student or a colleague, I always leave my door open, so students know I'm available. Sometimes I think they find me a little standoffish, so I do what I can to appear more accessible.

"Um . . . sure." I put my pen down and slide the student's paper to the side of my desk. A lot of professors like papers electronically submitted. They like to grade them right on the computer, but I still like to see the essays. I like to write on them with my favorite gel roller pen.

Randall walks in and closes the door behind him.

Suddenly, I feel uncomfortable. "Am I getting fired or something?" I say, only half-joking.

"You're tenured. It would take a lot to fire you. Like a sex scandal or something." He's not joking.

I fight the inexplicable urge to laugh. Me and a sex scandal. Now, *that's* funny. It's been so long since I had sex that I can't even remember—I push the thought from my head and gesture to the chair in front of my desk. It's a comfy leather chair I found at a yard sale years ago.

He tugs at his pants at the knees and sits. An affectation that annoys me. Who *does* that? Men haven't had to pull on their pants in order to sit down in decades. Did he see it in a movie? I always want to ask, but it never seems like the right time. Now is definitely not the right time.

"I'll get right to the point, Alicia."

I'm still not sure if this is a personal or professional visit. I wait.

"There's been talk in the department about your lack of academic publication."

Of all the things I thought Randall might be here to talk about, this subject was the furthest from my mind. I shift closer to my desk, folding my hands on the calendar ink blotter. "Thomas Stone University doesn't require publication by their professors. It's part of our image: small class size, a limited number of teaching assistants, professors teaching their own classes. No research or publishing required. It was one of the things that drew me here to begin with. The same with you."

His face is completely devoid of emotion. What's happened to the passionate man I fell for all those years ago? The man who could talk passionately about the Brontë sisters for hours, then make passionate love to his grad assistant? I have a crazy urge to *do* something: throw my lukewarm mug of coffee at him, hit him between the eyes with my new gel pen. I want to wake him from this sleep he seems to have fallen into, a sleep that's alienated him from all that he once loved, including me and Chloe. Instead, I just sit there and wait for him to respond.

"Publishing is not a requirement of your employment, but times are tough with small, expensive liberal arts colleges in this new economy. We have to find new ways to attract students."

"You want me to write a paper for publication? Maybe a book? How about a textbook? Randall, do you hear yourself?" I'm starting to get warmed up now. "Do you not know the responsibilities I have at home? What it takes for me to take care of your daughter? Your daughter, who wants to kiss boys and go to the mall alone with mentally handicapped girls from church?"

"It's not necessary for you to raise your voice," he says, coming to his feet. "I just wanted to make you aware of what your colleagues are saying."

"Your check is late, *again*," I respond. I know I shouldn't bring personal stuff into this conversation, but I can't help it. How can this not be personal? This man took advantage of me when I was twenty-three years old. I had just lost my mother. I was young and impressionable and he was older and . . . and only semi-separated from his wife. He was a professor, for God's sake! He *shouldn't* have seduced me. I shouldn't have let it happen, but he shouldn't have done it.

As I rise from my chair, looking at him, I realize this is the very first time in my life I've ever wanted to say to him that what he did all those years ago was wrong. It's the first time I've ever really admitted it to myself. All these years, I wanted to believe I had been in control . . . that *I* had teased *him*, tempted him with my youth and academic aptitude. But the truth is, he took advantage of me. And it was wrong. Somehow, working through this thing with Chloe and Thomas, worrying so much about her being taken advantage of, had made me realize that.

"Is there going to be something put in my file?"

"Pardon?"

I look him eye to eye. "As head of the department, will there be some sort of formal . . . reprimand because I haven't published, even though it was clear when I was hired that that wasn't necessary?"

"No . . . no, of course not," he huffs, taking a step back. "I simply wanted you to be aware of what was being said."

I sit down and pick up my gel pen. "Send the check, Randall." I slide the student's paper in front of me and reach for my reading glasses. "If there's a concern about my lack of publication, have the dean contact me." I give him a quick smile. "Have a good day, Randall." And then I lower my gaze and go back to reading a comparison of Keats's poetry to Shelley's.

⟨⟨ 14 ⟩⟩

"I'm so glad you called. Danny said I should call." Margaret chuckles. "I was going to, but I was nervous." She looks at me across the table. "About calling."

We decided to meet for lunch at a little Tex-Mex place on Main Street. It's just a five-minute walk from my office. I have a meeting in an hour with a student applying to be my grad assistant next year. I made the date for lunch knowing Thomas and Chloe would be at Minnie's and knowing I couldn't stay too long. I suppose I'm as nervous about meeting Margaret alone as she is about meeting me.

"Why would you be nervous about calling me, Margaret?" I say, taking a chip from the basket on the table between us. "We talk on the phone all the time." Which is only partially true. We *do* speak on the phone—about who's picking Chloe and Thomas up from Minnie's or when Margaret should come for Thomas—but we don't *talk* talk. No one's feelings or concerns are ever discussed. Nothing more controversial than how late the *kids* can stay is ever addressed. I dip my chip into the green sauce in a little wooden bowl in front of me.

Margaret exhales. She's wearing her hair pulled back tightly at her temples and braided in a single, skinny braid down her back.

Her pink sweatshirt says, "Sing to the Lord!" and has musical notes on it. Her skirt has pink and lavender hibiscus flowers on it; I noticed it when she came inside.

I wait.

She lifts her gaze to meet mine. "I was nervous about calling because I think it's time we talked about the kids' futures." She folds her hands on the table. "Together."

"Their futures together," I repeat. A little trick I learned from our therapist. He does it all the time. I used to hate it, but I've become pretty fond of the conversation technique. It's a good way for me to delay my own words . . . or feelings.

She takes a corn chip, but she doesn't put it in her mouth. "Chloe said she talked to you, but . . ." She stops and starts again. "She wasn't really sure what your response was."

I'm still chewing. "About?" I realize I'm being a jerk. I know exactly what she's talking about. It's the same thing I came here to talk about, but I'm still avoiding it. I came to talk about this but still, I'm afraid.

"About them getting married," Margaret says. She waits for my response. When I don't answer right away, she says, "Did Chloe talk to you about she and Thomas getting married?"

I'm tempted to lie. But I came to talk and talk I must. "She mentioned it." It's my turn to fold my hands. "Margaret, I'm not so sure it's a good idea to encourage this. I . . . I have concerns."

"I think every parent does," Margaret says gently. "But . . . Chloe and Thomas really love each other." She nods, surprising me with the sudden firmness in her tone. "And I think it's time we talk. I think it's time we consider the kids' wishes."

Realizing what she means, I suddenly feel off balance. Like the world is shifting beneath me.

I look out the window, half-expecting the street to be tilting at a crazy angle. It's the first week of April. It's a mild day and there are students everywhere, enjoying the warmer-than-usual temperature. I recognize a girl from one of my classes. She's walking with a tall boy who's wearing a gray knit beanie pulled down over his head, to his eyebrows. They're holding hands, and I can tell by the way they're looking at each other that they're in love. Chloe and Thomas look at each other the same way.

"I . . . I don't know if it's even feasible," I tell Margaret. "I mean . . . just the logistics. Where would they live? Obviously they can't have their own apartment."

"We'd have to talk about that."

No exclamation point. She sounds so calm. I sound calm, but my heart is pounding. I wonder if hers is, too, but I don't think so. I get the idea from what little I know of Margaret that this is what she wants, what she's always wanted for Thomas.

Margaret's smiling when she looks at me. "I always hoped Thomas would meet a nice girl. Chloe's such a sweetheart. We already love her like a daughter."

"Marriage?" I say. "Marriage?"

The waitress appears at our table with two oval plates. She puts chicken tacos on a bed of shredded lettuce in front of me and cheese and onion enchiladas with sides of beans and rice in front of Margaret. It's funny how the mind works. I'm thinking about the absurd idea of Chloe getting married, and at the same time, I'm jealous of a Mexican dish. Margaret's lunch smells and looks so much better than mine. I can't imagine how many calories must be in the huge plate of steamy, cheesy gooeyness, but I want it. I wish I'd had the guts to order it.

Is that the case with Chloe and Thomas, too? Can I not imagine the possibility of Chloe marrying because I don't have the guts? Is Margaret the smarter person here? Is she the better parent?

"You really think they want to get married?" I ask.

"I really do." Margaret unrolls her silverware from a white paper napkin. "And why shouldn't they? I mean, honestly? Two people in love, they should marry. It's what God intended."

I don't know how I feel about the whole *what God intends* so I skip over that and move on to the more tangible. Margaret doesn't say anything about mentally challenged people having the same rights as those of average intelligence. Even if she doesn't recognize Thomas's shortcomings, surely she knows Chloe's. You just have to look at Chloe to know she has Down syndrome. But if Margaret isn't going to go there, I'm not going to go there. Not right now, at least.

I gingerly pick up one dry taco. "And how does Danny feel about the idea?" I stuff some lettuce inside the hard shell to try and make it more appealing.

"He's talked to Thomas and to Chloe. He thinks they understand the seriousness of this kind of commitment." She chuckles. "Well, as well as any of us do before we actually *get* married. Heaven knows, I didn't understand my vows when I made them! Danny was twenty-one. I was twenty."

I bite into my taco. My mind is racing. I don't know what my next move is. I guess I need to go home and Google *marriage and Down syndrome*. I need to make an appointment with Dr. Tamara. I guess I need to talk to Randall. I almost groan out loud.

I take another bite of taco.

Chloe and Thomas married? This is a bad idea. It's *such* a bad idea. It's an impending disaster of catastrophic proportions. Everything in my gut tells me it will be a debacle. But it's just emotions, feelings. I don't have substantiating evidence.

"Alicia, I'm just going to come out and say this, and I hope you won't be offended." Margaret holds her fork poised over her plate. It has a piece of soft corn tortilla, a sliver of onion, and long strings of white cheese hanging off it. "The kids have been together long enough, they've been a *couple* long enough that . . . I think they're beginning to experience certain *feelings*. Physical feelings for each other. Which . . . is only natural. It's what God intended. *Within marriage.* Which is why I think we need to listen to what they're saying."

I realize halfway through her speech that she's talking about sex. She's telling me her son wants to have sex with my daughter. It makes me . . . uncomfortable . . . to think of them naked in bed. To think of them touching each other. I won't allow my mind to go any further.

But once again, I admire Margaret. I don't want to, but I do. I admire her for her guts and for her conviction. Religious or whatever.

I look at her plate. I admire her for her choice in lunch, too.

"So, where did you leave it?" Jin asks me.

It's Friday night. Chloe went to Thomas's for dinner after her day at Minnie's, and I picked her up at eight. She's in the kitchen making chocolate milk. She's singing a song from *The Princess and the Frog*. It's her new favorite movie. She's off-key and she can't remember the words correctly, but she sounds so happy. The happiness in her voice makes me want to cry. I could never make her this happy. It's Thomas who makes her feel this way, Thomas the big oaf with his glasses that never sit straight on his face and his ridiculous size double-X Thomas the Tank Engine T-shirts . . . and his sweet, lopsided grin.

"I don't know where we left it."

Jin tucks her bare feet up under her and pours us both large glasses of pinot grigio. She's wearing one of those crazy sweaters that has the long corners front and back. She's done some creative thing, tying the front corners and putting the knot at the nape of her neck. I tried one of them on recently in a department store. No matter how I tied it, it looked like a big, bulky, sloppy mess on me.

"What do you mean, you don't know where you left it?" Jin asks.

I fill my cheeks with air and exhale, blowing it out slowly. "I don't know." I lower my voice. "Margaret thinks they're in love."

Jin shrugs. "So do I. Don't you?"

"Margaret thinks they have certain *physical feelings* for each other." I use her words.

Jin shrugs again. "That's pretty normal, isn't it? I mean,

Chloe's twenty-seven. Thomas is, what? Thirty-one? People who are in love want to have sex, Ally."

"Keep your voice down," I say. I take my glass, swirl the wine, and bring the rim to my lips, but I don't drink. "Margaret thinks they should get married because of these *feelings*."

"She thinks they should get married so they can have sex?"

I cut my eyes at Jin and then cock my head to indicate Chloe in the kitchen. There's no way Chloe's listening, though. She's singing so loudly that she couldn't hear us if we were jet engines.

Jin raises her glass as if in a toast. "Sounds like as good a reason to me as any to get married. Maybe if Abby and I had gotten married when we wanted to have sex, and made that permanent commitment, we'd still be together."

"Same-sex marriage wasn't legal in those days," I point out.

Jin frowns. I thought she was going to be on my side on this thing. She isn't. I can see it in her face. She's trying to be supportive, but she thinks I'm being overprotective. She thinks I'm keeping Chloe from being as normal as she could be. She thinks I should let my daughter marry that retarded guy. She doesn't understand what it's like to be me. To be Chloe's mom. She can't possibly. Her son's freakin' brilliant.

I sip my wine.

"You're angry," she says.

"I'm scared." I dare to look up at her over the rim of my wineglass. "What if she really, really wants to get married, Jin?"

"What if that's what will make her really, really happy?"

"The sheer logistics of a marriage," I point out, using my best Dr. Richards voice. "Where would they live? *How* would they live?"

Dr. Tamara tents his fingers in midair in front of him. "They have plenty of options. The world is changing how it looks on its mentally challenged citizens. There are assisted-living apartments, residential homes—"

"Absolutely not. Chloe couldn't function in a place like that.

You and I have talked about this before. Chloe belongs with me. I'm her mother. She'll always live with me."

"Long-term, that may not be feasible. As you and I have discussed. Parents grow old," he continues. "They become ill. They die. But let's deal with one issue at a time. You don't think Chloe and Thomas should marry because you don't know where or how they would live? You just said Chloe belongs with you. There's no reason why she and her husband couldn't live with you, is there? Or with his parents?"

"Chloe wouldn't like living with the Eldens. You know how she is about her things. About how she likes to keep her bathroom. She's very fastidious. The Eldens are . . . not as fastidious. I'm not saying their house is dirty or anything, but Chloe likes order."

"So maybe they could live with you. Do you think his parents would be open to that option?"

"I . . . I don't know. Thomas . . . he has rituals. I'm not sure I would know how to accommodate him."

"I think you could learn."

I look past him, to the bookshelf on the far wall. I'm tired. I'm not sleeping well. I have another forty-two papers to read for my Brit Lit 1789 to the Present class. "It's not just the *living options*," I say.

"Okay. What *are* your concerns?"

I look at him. I've got that weird *have I fallen down the rabbit hole?* feeling. Here, of all places, you wouldn't think I would have to say this. "My primary concern is that my daughter has Down syndrome. That she is a beautiful, amazing woman who has limitations. Severe limitations that could prevent her from being someone's wife."

"Do you think her cognitive limitations extend to her ability to love and be loved?"

"Yes!"

His face never changes . . . which is somehow worse than him negatively reacting to my politically incorrect comment.

"No," I say softly. I fiddle with the cuff of my sleeve. "I guess not. I don't know. *Obviously*, I don't know." I gesture wildly with my hands. "If I knew, I wouldn't be agonizing over this. She loves me . . . sometimes I think more deeply than I love her. She's nonjudgmental. She's kind. She's giving. She loves so simply that there's no complications to her love."

"Do you think she could be those things with a husband?"

I avoid eye contact with him. "Certainly. Why not, right?" I raise my hands and let them fall. "It's just that . . ."

"It's just that . . ." Dr. Tamara repeats.

"Marriage is incredibly hard between two people of average intelligence. And you know it." I say that because I know he's recently divorced.

He's quiet for a moment. I swear, I spend half of our sessions in silence, waiting for him to speak.

"Do you think your divorce, your inability to remain in your own marriage, is influencing your view on Chloe getting married?"

"Of course it is!" I hate the sound of my voice: tense, exasperated, barely in control of my emotions. "Of course my failed marriage makes me question Chloe's ability to have a successful marriage," I say, taking my volume down a notch. "Randall and I were two smart, independent people who didn't have to be reminded to use toilet paper. We loved each other. At least to begin with. And *still*, we couldn't make it work."

"Chloe and Thomas lead a simpler life. One I think we all envy sometimes. I know I do," he says. "What if they're better suited to marriage than we are?"

I think on that for a moment and then look at him with his perfectly creased trousers and skinny wrists. "I talked to Randall yesterday about this. Briefly."

"And?"

"And . . . he says that he thinks Chloe is much happier since she met Thomas. When they meet for dinner on Tuesdays, Thomas is all she talks about now, apparently. Randall thinks we have no choice but to let her get married if she wants to." I think about the conversation we had in the hall outside his office. "He and his wife have separated."

"Have they?" He subtly checks the big clock on the wall behind me. "And how do you feel about that?"

"How do I *feel?* Honestly, I don't care. Not a bit. I feel . . . absolutely nothing."

"No sense of satisfaction? Maybe just the tiniest bit? Because you said this marriage wouldn't last."

"Nothing," I repeat. "I feel absolutely nothing. I've got all of my feelings wrapped up in Chloe. I've got nothing left for Randall."

Again, the silence.

I think, then I speak again. "Actually, that's not entirely true. When I was talking to Randall yesterday, I found myself . . . feeling sorry for him."

"Did you? And what do you think prompted that response?" Dr. Tamara tents his fingers again, and I wonder if he learned that in one of the recent conferences he attended. It's a new gesture. He's given up tugging on his earlobe and replaced it with this finger-tenting thing. I can't decide which one annoys me more.

"I don't want to talk about Randall or how I *feel* about him or the fact that he's ruined another marriage with his infidelities," I say, with no maliciousness in my voice. "I want to talk about Chloe. About what I should do about her wanting to marry Thomas." I hold up my hand. "And I know we don't usually do things this way, but Anthony, I need you to tell me what to do. I don't want to talk it through, think it through, I don't want to do any more Internet research." I find myself striking my palm with my fist. "I just want someone to tell me what to do. Do I let Chloe marry Thomas?"

I know I must be looking at him like a kid looks at her father. There's an almost pathetic tone to my voice. "Just tell me what to do," I repeat softly.

Dr. Tamara smiles. "You know I can't do that, Alicia."

I sit there and stare at him . . . until he starts to look uncomfortable. It's like we're playing some kind of bizarre game of Chicken.

He tents his fingers. "Let's bring Chloe in and see what she has to say. Shall we?"

We don't get cheeseburgers and fries on our way home from Dr. Tamara's. I want cheeseburgers and fries. Mom says it's not good healthy. I'm mad at Mom.

I wouldn't get in the front of the car. In my seat. I got in back because I don't want to look at her mean, stupid head.

I'm really mad. I kick the back of the seat.

Mom told Dr. Tamara I love Thomas. I'm mad she told. I don't like Dr. Tamara. I don't like his nosy head questions. He's always asking me stupid things. I want to tell him to mind his own bead-wax.

"Chloe, please don't kick the seat," Mom says.

I stop because I don't want to make her more mad.

I want to make Mom more happy. I wonder why she doesn't want to make me happy. I love Thomas. If she let me and Thomas get married, I'd be real happy.

15

I didn't say yes right away. I told Chloe that *maybe* she could get married. Someday. I told her it was too soon to decide. That she and Thomas had only been dating a year. But the months passed too quickly. One minute it was January and Thomas and Chloe were blowing out candles on their anniversary cake, the next, it was mid-August. My classes would be starting again soon and Chloe and Thomas had been together a year and a half.

I took them to the zoo in Washington, D.C., as sort of an "end of the summer" outing. We drove to the New Carrollton Metro station and took the train in. Thomas was very excited. He'd never been on a subway train.

"Sit next to me! Sit here," Chloe insists as we board the Metro car. She has a new tube of lip balm, cherry flavored, and she's rubbing it on her lips.

An end-of-the-line station, it's a good place for Thomas's first exposure because we had a few minutes to get settled before the train moved. Like Chloe, Thomas is slow to adjust to new experiences, even ones he's looking forward to. Luckily, Chloe has been on the Metro several times a year since she was six or seven, so she's a veteran. She knows how to insert her ticket and walk through the turnstile, and she's an ace on the escalator.

Chloe plops down in a window seat and slaps the seat beside her. "Sit here, Thomas. Mom, you sit there." She points to the seat behind her. It's that way with her now. I've been permanently downgraded to the backseat of her life.

"H . . . here?" Thomas asks.

A young couple squeezes past him in the aisle.

"Sit here, Thomas," Chloe repeats with authority. She points with her tube of lip balm to my designated seat. "Mom!"

"Who put you in charge, Miss Bossy?" I ask, sitting down.

"Who p . . . put you in ch . . . ch . . . charge, Miss B . . . Bossy?" Thomas repeats in his gruff, guttural voice.

A woman with two little boys who had taken seats opposite us stares at Thomas and protectively pulls her youngest son onto her lap. She tugs at the other boy's hand.

"Thomas?" I say.

He looks at me and I press my finger to my lips.

"Too loud, Thomas," Chloe insists. "Inside voice!"

Thomas hovers over the seat beside Chloe, but doesn't sit. She pulls him closer so he's no longer in the aisle, but he just stands there. He's wearing a floppy, orange bucket hat. It's going to be a hot day, so it was good that Margaret sent him with a hat, but I can't help wondering if it wouldn't have been better for him to have a hat that would help him blend in. He's already different from most young men his age; does she have to exacerbate the problem by making him look so different, too?

I've always taken such care to help Chloe look like other girls her age. I know I can't hide the classic physical characteristics of Down's: the eye folds, the round face, the small ears. I don't even know that I want to. But I still think it's important that I dress her the way I would dress a daughter of average intelligence. Of course, at her age, what girl is still allowing her mother to lay her clothes out on the bed in the morning? I guess it's the principle of the thing.

Thomas is also wearing a green Thomas the Tank Engine tank

top, the kind with the big armholes . . . and plaid orange and purple shorts. I had learned from Chloe that the reason Thomas has so many Thomas shirts (I couldn't imagine who made them in his size) is that his mother made them for him from plain T-shirts and some sort of iron-on graphic kit from the craft store. Thomas has put on weight since we met him, so between his height and his girth and the outfit, it's hard for people to not stare at him.

But who am I to judge his mother's fashion choices?

I glance at my daughter, who has Thomas's hand and is pulling him down, making him sit. I laid out a cute pair of navy shorts, sandals, and a blue and white spaghetti-strapped top for Chloe. She put on the shorts, but is wearing an old Ohio State T-shirt that belongs to Thomas. Margaret gave it to her to wear one day when Chloe spilled Coke all over her own shirt. It's huge on her and goes past her knees. This is the third day in a row she's worn it. Without washing it. There's a red Popsicle stain on the front and it doesn't smell all that fresh, but I couldn't get her to give it up this morning. Eventually, I gave in because we were going to be late picking up Thomas. Her only concession had been to wear the tank top under it. Maybe if she gets hot enough, she'll take it off and I can stuff it in my backpack. Then, at least, I can wash it before I give it back to her.

What's disturbing about the whole T-shirt thing, more disturbing than the Popsicle stain, is the reason Chloe gave me for not wanting it washed.

"Mom! It smells like Thomas," she told me last night when I tried to get her to surrender it.

She'd rubbed her cheek against the sleeve. "It smells good. Like Thomas," she'd said.

All the logic in the world couldn't change the fact that my daughter really *was* in love with this man. And they were still talking about getting married. Margaret had been good. She hadn't called any more powwows on the subject, but she'd mentioned it a couple of times over the last few months. She'd also made a point of suggesting *the kids* shouldn't be left alone. She said that she or her husband had always made sure their daughters had chaperones when they were dating and the same rules applied to Thomas. It wasn't like Thomas and Chloe were driving to the movie theater and making out in the car. But I agreed they would be chaperoned at my house. From what Chloe had to say, the Eldens were far more vigilant than I was, though. I never left the property, of course, but I did work in the yard, talk on the phone, even pop over to see Jin sometimes.

Things were heating up with her and Abby. Huan caught them having lunch together in Chestertown. There was talk of giving it another try, so there was always something interesting going on at Jin's. I think I'm beginning to live vicariously through her love life. The fact that her partner is a woman doesn't matter to me. I like hearing about the romantic dinners, about the little gifts they give each other, about the late-night phone calls that go on for hours. I've been on exactly three dates this summer. In two of the cases, I told the guy not to bother to call me. The one guy I *wanted* to see again, promised to call and never did.

The train pulls away from the station with a lurch and Thomas and Chloe clutch each other and burst out laughing. He leans down and touches her nose with his. "B . . . baby," he croons.

"My honey," she responds, her voice all gooey and sweet.

"N . . . knock, knock," Thomas says.

"Who's there?" Chloe responds diligently. No matter how many knock-knock jokes he tells in a day, she still plays along. This is the fourth I've heard since we picked him up at his house this morning.

"Chugga, ch . . . chugga."

"That's not words," Chloe argues.

"Ch . . . chugga, chugga," Thomas repeats. "Y . . . you h . . . have to s . . . say 'ch . . . chugga, chugga, wh . . . who'!"

Chloe makes a face. "Chugga, chugga *who?*"

"N . . . knock, n . . . knock," he says again.

"Who's there?" Chloe repeats again.

"Ch . . . chugga s . . . says the . . . t . . . tank t . . . train engine!" Thomas laughs.

Chloe looks out the window. "No more knock-knock, Thomas. Look out the window, now."

He does as he's told and I look away from them. I watch out the window as we pick up speed and the suburbs of D.C. whiz by. Seeing Chloe and Thomas this way makes me smile, but it makes me sad, too. I can't say I'm jealous of Chloe. There's no animosity. I guess I'm just sad that I have no one in my life to make me feel the way Thomas makes her feel.

Is that jealousy?

Seeing them like this also worries me. No matter how badly I wanted to ignore the idea of them marrying . . . it isn't going away. Thomas isn't going anywhere.

We have a good day at the zoo; no temper tantrums from Chloe, no *accidents* with Thomas. (He carries a spare pair of underwear and shorts with him, just in case he gets excited and waits too long to *go*.) Chloe and Thomas seem to have a blast. They aren't at all interested in seeing the reptiles or the birds, or even the panda bears, but Chloe is fascinated by the big cats and Thomas could watch the howler monkeys all day long. One howls and he imitates the sound, which delights my daughter so much that he does it over and over again. And again.

"I . . . I'm g . . . gonna have a . . . a m . . . monkey . . . when we . . . we get our h . . . h . . . house," he keeps telling Chloe.

"No monkey!" she tells him. "Monkeys live in the cage. Monkeys don't live in the house."

We check out the monkeys for a while, then the big cats, then we go back to the monkey habitat again. Then we repeat the cycle after lunch. Mid-afternoon, it occurs to me that I should have brought a book. I could have just sat on a bench and read in the shade while they watched the lions or the monkeys.

It seems like it's going to be a calm, uneventful day. Then I make the mistake of leaving Chloe and Thomas in a long line to get Italian ices while I run to the restroom. My fifty-plus-year-old bladder just isn't what it used to be. When I return, I find passersby and people in line staring and pointing at my charges. They're kissing in full view of everyone, and we're not talking a peck on the cheek.

"Chloe!" I holler, wiping my wet hands on my shorts as I hurry toward them. "Chloe Mae Richards-Monroe!" When I reach them, they're still lip-locked. I'm pretty sure there's tongue involved. "That's inappropriate," I hiss as I grab her by the wrist. I know my face is bright red because I can feel the heat in my cheeks.

I pull her out of line and march her away. "Thomas!" I call.

"I w . . . want ice c . . . cream," Thomas hollers, following us.

"There's no kissing in public," I tell Chloe, leading her away from the Italian ice vendor, looking for a more private place where we can speak. And maybe can't be seen by everyone who caught a glimpse of a possibly R-rated show. "We talked about this, Chloe."

I find myself shaking.

I think part of the reason I'm upset is that people weren't just watching, they were laughing. They were snickering; they were making fun of the *retards* snogging. I'm almost positive I heard someone whisper the word *mongoloid*.

My baby. Someone was making fun of my sweet, darling *baby*.

You think we live in a modern society, that we're beyond making fun of people with mental disabilities. As an academic, I tell myself all the time that Americans are thinkers, that we're beyond such crap. I come to mankind's defense far more often than I should.

I'm surprised by the tears that sting my eyelids.

"K . . . Koey!" Thomas's backpack has come off one shoulder and is dangling off his elbow. "I w . . . w . . . want ice c . . . cream!"

I grab Thomas's arm, too, and march them farther down the

paved path. "Listen to me," I say as I pull them off a path to stand under the canopy of a shade tree.

But neither will. Thomas is still mumbling about wanting ice cream, and Chloe is trying to make him stand closer to her. When he doesn't move his feet quickly enough to satisfy her, she starts talking under her breath.

"Here, Thomas, here. I tell you stand here. Here."

"Thomas, Chloe, look at me," I say.

I can tell Chloe knows she's in trouble. She starts wiping her mouth with the back of her hand. As if she can wipe away what she did . . . what she was letting Thomas do.

I get control of my emotions. "Thomas, do your mother and father kiss like that in front of other people?"

He stares at me. Blinks. I think he's a little scared of me, which isn't my intention.

I look at Chloe, softening my tone. "Do Mr. and Mrs. Elden kiss in church in front of people?"

Chloe shakes her head no.

"They do not," I say. "It's *not appropriate*. Kissing is something *private* between a man and a woman."

Chloe is looking at me, but Thomas seems distracted. He's rubbing his lips together.

"Mrs. Elden says no kissing when we watch a movie," Chloe says. "In the living room."

I nod. "Okay, that's a rule in her house. A rule for when you're with her. My rule is no kissing while you're waiting to buy Italian ice. No kissing in front of other people. It makes people uncomfortable, Chloe."

"You . . . you t . . . taste good, K . . . Koey. L . . . like s . . . strawberries!" Thomas blurts out.

"Not strawberries. Cherries," she insists. She pulls her Chap-Stick out of the pocket of her shorts. "See?"

I catch her hand, taking the tube of lip balm. "Chloe, I need you to listen to me."

She slowly turns her head until she's looking at me. "No kissing," she says, with obvious resentment in her voice.

"Where did you learn that?" I ask, unable to help myself. I hand her back the ChapStick. "Who taught you to kiss that way?"

"No kissing in the living room," Chloe says. "No kissing at the zoo. No kissing at the bowling alley. No kissing at Miss Minnie's." She sets her chin the way she does when she's about to become obstinate. "When is the kissing?"

Her question . . . her ability to extrapolate to the point of being able to ask the question floors me.

Chloe's gaze meets mine. "When can I kiss Thomas?" she repeats stubbornly.

I think I knew then that I would cave. I think I knew then that I had lost my battle.

That night, Chloe sealed the deal. It was late. We were both sunburned and tired and she'd gone to bed while I was still downstairs responding to a few student e-mails. When I walked upstairs, shutting off lights as I went, I thought I heard her cat crying.

"Kitty, kitty?" I call. "Kitty?"

At the top of the stairs, I realize the sound I'm hearing is coming from behind Chloe's door. It isn't the cat crying. It's Chloe. I knock and go in. It's dark in her room, except for the band of light that shines from the bottom of the lamp on her nightstand—a nightlight for an adult.

"Chloe . . . honey?"

She sniffles. "Leave."

I hesitate. Do I respect her request for privacy? I take a step toward her and step on one of her sandals. She undressed just inside her door, leaving her shoes and clothes to lie where they hit the floor.

"Want to talk?"

She takes a great, shuddering breath.

"Didn't you have a good day at the zoo, sweetie? I had a good day." I walk to her bed and look at her.

Chloe's curled on her side, hugging one of her pillows. She's still wearing Thomas's dirty T-shirt. Her hair is a mess, some of it still in the elastic of her ponytail, but most of it sticking out all over the place. I smell her cherry lip balm as I cautiously ease myself onto her bed. And the suntan lotion I slathered all over her this morning. She has fair skin; she burns easily. Like her mother.

"Can you tell me?" I ask, unable to resist brushing a lock of red hair off her cheek.

She takes another ragged breath. "I miss him."

I pluck a tissue from the box on her nightstand. There's enough light coming from the lamp that I can see her cheeks are wet with tears.

"You miss . . . Thomas?" I ask.

That night, I remember that her pain felt so strong that I imagined a crack slowly making its way across my heart. That was before I understood what it truly meant to be heartsick. What the cold seizing of my heart would feel like.

"I . . . I miss him," she moans. And fresh tears run down her cheeks.

"Oh Chloe," I murmur, closing my arms around her. I rest my cheek on her shoulder and breathe deeply, remembering what it felt like to hold her in my arms when she was a child.

"My arms miss him," she cries, clutching the pillow. "They hurt."

I feel like my heart is lodged in my throat. "You really do love him, don't you?"

She nods.

"And you want to marry him?"

"Married means you . . . you can sleep together," she manages. "And kiss," she adds. She hiccups. "Right? If we get married, we can kiss. Like Ariel and Eric? In the end of the movie?"

I close my eyes and remember the final kiss in *The Little Mermaid*. It's a wedding scene. My girl knows her Disney. "Yes, you can kiss when you get married," I say softly. "But only in your room. No kissing at the zoo, okay?"

She snuggles against me. "No kissing at the zoo."

And for the briefest moment, we're both content.

∽ 16 ∾

The night I agreed that Chloe could marry Thomas was certainly a significant moment in my life. That one, I felt when it hit. For a second, I'm alone at Chloe's window, in the present, my fingers on her fingerprints on the cold pane of glass.

And then I tumble back in time again.

As I leave Chloe in her bed that night and go down the hall to my room, I recognize that, now that the decision has been made, I have two choices. I can be happy about Chloe's impending marriage and the joy it will bring her, or I can be unhappy about all the bad things I'm afraid might happen. I can try to help my daughter make this transition and support her and her husband in every way I can, or I can hang back and wait to be proven right.

What if I'm *not* right? What if Thomas *can* give Chloe the happiness I will never, *ever* be able to give her? No matter how desperately I want to? I owe it to Chloe. And somewhere, in the deep recesses of my guilt-ridden heart, I feel like I owe it to the child I *didn't* have.

I wanted that first baby so badly. In my heart. But my head told me it was the wrong time. Even though Randall and I had talked about marriage, he was still married. And I was still a student. It didn't make sense to have a baby at that point in my life.

We can have another, when the time is right, Randall had promised. He'd been so sweet, so attentive. I thought he was thinking of me. Only later did I realize it had been all about him. Because it was always all about him. He hadn't wanted his career or his image to be negatively affected. He didn't want physical proof of what a shit he was.

Even with all that logic behind me, the decision to have the abortion had been hard. But Randall had gone with me . . . and he'd promised me, as I walked into the procedure room, that our time would come. That we'd marry and I'd have a baby in my arms someday.

At least that part had been true. We did have a baby. We had our Chloe. But my arms never stopped aching for the first child.

As I climb into bed, not sure if the tears I'm fighting are of sadness or joy, I know that I'll continue to be Chloe's advocate, just as I've been since the day she was born. I'm her mother, and I love her more than anyone else in the world loves her. How can I not do everything I can for her until the day I die?

So I meet with Margaret and Danny the next day. The wedding date is set for December. I want to wait until spring. I think they should date longer, but Chloe wants to get married Wednesday. *This* Wednesday. Margaret is the one who suggests the compromise as we talk on the sidewalk when I pick Chloe up after church.

Margaret suggests that a December wedding would be beautiful in St. Mark's sanctuary. With all the LoGs present. In my head, I saw glimpses of a garden party wedding in our backyard, but Chloe's excitement is infectious and I get excited, too. As we stand there on the sidewalk in front of the church, she and Thomas hold hands and jump up and down and call each other *honey* and *baby*.

The second week of September, after my new classes are in full swing, I invite the Eldens to our house to make wedding plans. Margaret and Thomas will be here at seven. Danny is working the evening shift and can't make it.

I had asked Randall if he'd like to come; his response was typical. *He couldn't possibly.* He's all for Chloe getting married, as long as he doesn't have to be involved. I learn in our brief, awkward phone conversation that he and Kelly have officially separated and he's moving into a town house. I don't ask if there's another woman involved; I just don't care.

Jin wouldn't miss the wedding planning session for the world and arrives twenty minutes before Thomas and Margaret are expected. She's wearing a tie-dye sundress she made herself in a class this summer, and is carrying a homemade cheesecake. Chloe and I've made cookies, but we didn't have a lot of time this evening, so they're slice-and-bake. At least the kitchen smells good.

"I didn't have an afternoon class," Jin explains, carrying the cheesecake, with homemade blueberry topping, into my kitchen. "You don't mind?"

I laugh. "Your cheesecake? Believe me, I don't mind." I take glasses out of the cupboard. I've made decaf iced tea, and Chloe has made lemonade from a frozen mix. I keep checking the clock, oddly nervous.

"Thomas is coming," Chloe announces from her perch on a bar stool at the kitchen counter. She's busy arranging the cookies on a plate. "We're getting married, me and him."

"So I've heard," Jin says, her voice laced with amusement. "Congratulations, Chlo-bo."

"You can come." Chloe takes a bite of a cookie, and puts it back on the serving plate.

I reach across the counter, remove the cookie from the plate, and set it on the counter.

"Not everybody can come," Chloe continues. "Not the lady that works at Food Lion. But you can come."

"Huan and I are very excited." Jin grabs dessert plates. "I've already put it on the calendar." She looks at me. "Kitchen table or living room?"

"I was thinking kitchen table. To make it easy to write. To

take notes." I've already put two legal pads and two pens there. "Unless you think the living room is a better idea?"

"Kitchen is fine. It's warm. It's inviting."

"It's warm, all right." I fan myself with a kitchen towel. "The AC's on, but it still seems hot in here."

Jin carries the dessert plates to the table. "It's fine. You're just nervous. Why are you *nervous?*"

"People get nervous when they get married." Chloe giggles. "Because they get to kiss when the guy up front says *I do*. Me and Thomas are gonna kiss in front of *everybody!* I'm getting a new dress. But not with kittens on it." She slides off the stool, taking a cookie with her. She leaves the one with the bite out of it on the counter. "Thomas is coming. I'm gonna wait for Thomas." She walks out of the kitchen, munching on her cookie. "He always comes to the door."

"No kitten bridal gown?"

I cut my eyes at Jin. "Please tell me there's no such thing. I told her no one makes wedding gowns with kittens on the skirt."

Jin laughs. Then she glances in the direction Chloe's just gone. We can hear her singing in the living room. "Under the sea! Down where it's better and wetter . . ." She's got the lyrics wrong and the tempo is off, but it's from *The Little Mermaid*.

"So, you decide how you're going to handle the whole S-E-X thing?" Jin spells out the word.

I pour myself some iced tea. I wish I were pouring bourbon. "With Margaret? No. I'm not even sure I should."

"I meant with *Chloe*."

I groan and begin to fill the other glasses with ice at the dispenser in the refrigerator door. "Sort of. A little. I need to take Chloe to her gynecologist. She's due for a Pap smear anyway. And we need to talk about birth control."

"So you think they'll have sex?"

"If you saw the way the two of them were lip-locked at the zoo, you wouldn't be asking that question."

Jin leans on the counter and whispers, "You think they know *how?*"

"I guess that's what I need to talk to her about, but from what I've read on the Internet, even mentally challenged people . . ." I struggle to find the right words. "Figure it out."

Jin smiles.

"It's not funny." I hold one of the cold glasses to my forehead.

"I didn't say it was. I think it's sweet, actually."

"Mom! They're here!" Chloe screams from the front of the house. "They're here! Mom!"

They're early. Margaret is always early. I look at Jin. "I can't do this."

"You *can* do it. You'll be fine."

And I am fine. We go over the initial details that night at my kitchen table. Thomas and Chloe will be married at St. Mark's at three in the afternoon on December fourteenth. No bridesmaids or groomsmen; it will be hard enough to get just the two of them to stand at the altar long enough for the ceremony. Any friends they would ask are most likely more mentally challenged than they are. We're keeping it simple.

We divide up the jobs because, obviously, the bride and groom won't be making any arrangements. Jin volunteers to do all the things she knows I care about, but won't be good at: the invitations, the flowers, the decorations.

A reception will follow in the church hall. I thought a small, cozy reception here at our house might be better, but Margaret insists on finger foods, cake, and an apple juice toast at the church. She says she and Danny had a church reception, as did both her girls, and Thomas will have one, too. So I agree to the church reception, but offer to invite family and close friends back to my house for a light supper afterward.

Family. I don't have a lot of family: an aunt in Boston, an uncle on the West Coast, a couple of cousins. And my father . . . and his wife. I put off calling my dad for weeks after the date with the church is set. Finally, at Jin's insistence, Chloe and I call him the first Friday in October. The next day, Chloe, Jin, and I are planning on going wedding gown shopping in Philadelphia at one of those warehouse bridal stores. Jin says I can't buy my daughter a wedding gown without having told my father she's getting married.

Chloe says she wants to tell Grandpa, so I dial and hand her the phone. Gloria answers. She talks so loudly, I can hear her.

"Hello?"

"Hello," Chloe says, only the word is a little garbled. "Grandpa?"

"I'm sorry, you must have the wrong number."

I take the phone. "No, this is Alicia, Gloria. Chloe's calling. She wants to talk to Dad."

We're sitting side by side on the couch. Chloe leans over. "I want to talk to Grandpa! This is Chloe. About the wedding."

"Wedding?" Gloria says.

I'm now holding the phone between Chloe's ear and mine so we can both hear.

"Oh my goodness, Alicia! Congratulations. Arnie and I didn't even know you were seeing someone."

How would they know? Dad and I talk four or five times a year: Christmas, Father's Day, some birthdays, but not all of them. Gloria sends cards. Dad sends checks. There's not much talking. The talking that does take place isn't as personal as the conversations I have with Chloe's favorite food-sample lady at Costco.

"No, no, not me, Gloria." I look at Chloe. "You want to tell Grandma Gloria?"

Grandma Gloria. It was a concession. Mostly for my dad's sake. Randall was all for it, too, of course. He was entirely logical about the whole thing. Chloe was born after my mother was already dead. She never knew my mother. Gloria is Chloe's grandmother.

The only one she's got: Randall's mother had passed away before I met him. He never knew his father.

"Want to tell me? Tell me what?"

I can hear the uneasiness in Gloria's voice.

"Grandpa?" Chloe hollers into the phone. "Is Grandpa at the phone? This is Chloe Mae Richards-Monroe." It's a mouthful and her speech isn't all that clear.

It pains me that Chloe can't say her own name. She must be nervous. I know I am. "Gloria, can we talk to Dad?" I say. "Chloe has a surprise."

It takes my father a long time to get to the phone. Too long. I can't hear anything going on because Gloria's put us on hold or something.

"Is Grandpa there?" Chloe asks me after a minute or two. "Grandpa?"

I'm beginning to wonder if Gloria's disconnected us (accidentally or intentionally), and then the phone finally clicks.

"Hello?" my dad says. He sounds old. He'll be seventy-nine at Christmas. He is old. For some reason I feel a lump rise in my throat. I need to call him more often. I shouldn't wait for him to call me. To call us. I need to let my grudges go. It's not his fault Mom died. It's not his fault Chloe has Down syndrome and he's never known how to deal with that. It *is* his fault that he married my mother's hospice nurse four months after she died, but it's time for me to stop rehashing it. "Grandpa!" Chloe grabs the phone. "Me and Thomas, we're getting married." Of course she does the Elmer Fudd thing so it comes out more like *mah-wied*. "You can come!" she tells him excitedly.

There's a pause when my dad doesn't respond. Luckily, Chloe doesn't notice.

"I'm getting a dress. Me and Mom and Jin. At the store. No kittens. No Thomas the Train. It's called Thomas the Tank Engine but we don't say all of that."

I wonder how much of that conversation my dad got. He's hard of hearing, of course. Who isn't at his age?

Chloe waits. She might be mentally challenged, but she knows enough to know he should say something. A grandfather should say *something* when his only grandchild tells him she's getting married.

"Dad," I say finally. I shift the phone closer to my mouth. "Did you hear what Chloe said? She's getting married."

"Married?" he says into the phone. Then, "Gloria, did she say *Chloe's* getting married? I can't understand them. Connection must be bad."

I look at Chloe. She's so excited. And obviously disappointed that her grandfather isn't.

"Dad?"

There's another pause and then I hear Gloria again. "Sorry, I think his hearing aid needs a new battery. So, Chloe's getting married?"

"Yes." I find myself smiling. It's a sad smile, but it's a smile. "To a very nice young man she met at her daycare. His name is Thomas, and they're very much in love." I sound like the proud mama. "You'll be getting an invitation in the mail soon." Jin's hand-writing them, of course. She teaches calligraphy. "We just wanted . . . *Chloe* wanted to tell you the good news."

"Well, that *is* good news," Gloria says. Her words say one thing; her tone says something else entirely. "Arnie says that's great news. Your grandpa says that's great news, Chloe," she says loudly into the phone.

I can't tell if the volume is for my dad's sake or Chloe's. Gloria's always been uncomfortable around Chloe, even when she was small. Which I always found interesting because Gloria was a nurse. Not that Chloe has an illness, but . . . I let that thought drift away.

Chloe's still smiling, but it's not her real smile.

"Well," I say quickly. "We just wanted to call and tell you the good news. I'm sure you have things to do."

"Dishes," Gloria says. "We still have dishes to dry. And our show's coming on."

"Talk to you soon. Chloe, tell Grandma Gloria and Grandpa good-bye." I hold the phone out to her.

"Good-bye!" Chloe shouts.

I hang up. "So?" I ask her, sounding more enthusiastic than I feel. "What do you want to do now? You want to look at pictures of wedding gowns in the magazines we bought?"

She presses her lips together. "Can Thomas come over?"

I shake my head. "Nope. Too late tonight. We're going to get an early start tomorrow. It's going to be a busy day."

She thinks for a minute. Then her face lights up. "Can we watch *Pocahontas*?"

I attempt to hide my disappointment. I have several bride magazines on the coffee table. I recorded a couple of episodes of the TV show *Say Yes to the Dress*. I thought it might be fun to watch together.

Chloe sticks out her lower lip. "If Thomas can't come, I want to watch *Pocahontas*. He hates *Pocahontas* and he says when we get married, no more *Pocahontas*." She shakes her finger in my face, imitating him. "We're never watching it again."

Margaret and I have talked about Thomas moving in with us after the wedding. It's been decided. I guess I'd better buy them their own TV for their room.

The wedding dress shopping is fun. Chloe loses her patience pretty early in the day and I'm thankful for Jin's presence, but all in all the outing goes well. She/we choose a gorgeous, white A-line organza and chantilly lace gown with pearl accents. It has an empire waist, long sleeves, and a Queen Anne neckline, all as flattering on Chloe's short, round body as any dress could be. She says it's itchy, but I promise to buy her a slip so the lace won't touch the skin on her belly. The dress is five hundred dollars, a discontinued style, very reasonable, according to Jin, who has helped me through the day as much as she helped Chloe. We leave the dress for alterations and make an appointment to come back for it in November.

Our next big event/hurdle in the wedding plans is to get Chloe to the gynecologist. She had her first physical exam years ago and it was pretty traumatic. But she's so much more mature now than she was then. Surely it will go better.

Chloe knows she's going to the doctor because she has to before she gets married. She doesn't really know which doctor; it's easier on Chloe if she doesn't know so she doesn't have time to get too upset. I wait until we pull away from the curb at our house before I broach the subject.

"We're going to see Dr. Ellington. Do you remember him?"

She's buckled into the front seat. She's brought a book along; it's called *Puppies and Kittens Along the Way*. It's one of those board books with actual photographs and very little text. The book shows all the places a person can encounter a cat or a dog in a day. It's her new favorite book. Margaret bought it for her at the church yard sale.

"A cat in the bed. I have a cat in my bed. My cat," Chloe says.

"Dr. Ellington is the doctor that makes sure it's okay for you to get married . . . and kiss Thomas," I add.

She perks up when she hears the kissing Thomas part. She looks at me. "When we get married we can kiss whenever we want." There's defiance in her tone.

"In the privacy of your bedroom. That's right." I slow for a yellow traffic light. "Now, Chloe, Dr. Ellington has to examine your private parts. It's okay, because he's a doctor. And I'll be there with you. And there's a nurse." I just keep talking as if this is an everyday occurrence. "I don't know if you remember, but he examined you a couple of years ago."

"Do I have to get naked?"

So, apparently she does remember. "Yes, but there's a gown . . . like a dress that you can wear."

"I don't like dresses." She turns the page in her book. "I got a wedding dress. I like my wedding dress because I'm gonna marry Thomas in my wedding dress."

We're sitting at the red light. Chloe mentioned the word *naked*. This might be as close to the subject of S-E-X that Chloe's going to get on her own. I look at her and then the light. It turns green.

"Listen, hon, there's something I wanted to talk to you about. About being married." I press my lips together, wondering why this is so hard. I read up on how to talk to a mentally challenged person about sex. Same rules apply as talking to your kids. Keep it simple and honest. Use the proper anatomical words.

"You know, when a man and a woman get married, they sleep together in the same bed."

"Thomas is going to sleep in my bed." She points at her book. "A puppy in a box. Thomas is going to get a puppy when we get married."

"No puppy!" is on the end of my tongue, but I don't want to get off track. "Chloe . . . do you know about husbands and wives . . . kissing and touching each other in bed?"

She looks at me, then at the book. "Kissing." She purses her lips and makes a smacking sound.

"And touching," I say. "Once you're married, it's okay for Thomas to touch you. When you have your clothes off. And you can touch him."

She giggles and says something under her breath. It sounds like *peany*.

Against my will, my face gets hot. "Do you understand what I'm talking about?"

She stares at her book, but I can tell she's not really looking at it now. She nods over and over again.

"Married people make love, Chloe. It's a very special—"

"Don't say it!" She covers her ears and looks away. Her face is red, too, like mine, and she's giggling.

I take a deep breath and forge forward. It's only a ten-minute ride to the doctor's office. I don't have time to dawdle. "You know that men have different private parts. That women have vaginas and men have—"

"Peanies!" she blurts out. The puppies and kittens book falls to the floor. She's looking straight ahead. I can't tell if she's going to burst into laughter or tears.

I wonder if I should pull over to finish the conversation. But I don't want this to be a big deal. I don't want this talk to be traumatic. Sex is part of life. It can be a good part. Now that I've gotten used to the whole idea, I want Chloe to have the opportunity to experience the same pleasure any other wife would experience.

"Penises," I say. "Men have *penises.*" I can't help having a quick look at her. "How do you know about penises, Chloe?" Now I'm genuinely curious.

She giggles. "Thomas."

My eyes get big. "Thomas showed you his penis?"

More giggling. And, thankfully, a shake of her head. "He told me," she whispers. "But don't tell his mom. His mom says don't touch your peany, but he does." She pressed her finger to her lips. "A secret."

It takes me a moment to process that tidbit. I clear my throat. I wish I'd grabbed a water bottle on the way out the door. "What else did he tell you about his penis?"

She looks at me then back at the road. "Where it goes. When we're married." She points between her legs. And giggles again.

I'm caught between wanting to demand to know exactly what Thomas told my little girl, word for word . . . and being fascinated that they would have a conversation like that. I'm actually proud that my daughter *could* have a conversation like that . . . anytime.

"So . . . you understand?" I ask. "About sex. It's called *sex.*"

She covers her face with her hands. "Privacy." She giggles. "Me and Thomas, we're going to have *privacy* in my bedroom. Me and Thomas. Because he's my honey." She peeks at me, obviously tickled with the whole idea. "And you have to knock. On my door." She points accusingly.

I signal and pull into the parking lot of the medical center where Dr. Ellington's office is located. I slide into a parking space. Chloe gathers her library bag, containing more books, the kitten and puppy book, and a DVD box she's brought with her.

I get out of the car. I'm still not entirely sure Chloe understands the exact logistics of intercourse. But then I decide, as I walk around the back of the car, *What the hell?* She and Thomas will be married. They can do it however they want.

❧ 17 ❧

So, the sex talk, the talk I was so worried about, goes well. It's the discussion with her doctor that takes me by surprise.

Chloe and I go into the waiting room. I get the insurance forms to fill out, which annoys me because you would think all the info would be in the computer. Chloe is already a patient and Dr. Ellington is *my* GYN, too. Nothing has changed: not our insurance information, address, or phone number. I forego bucking the system and fill out the forms. Then the questionnaire. The questions are personal, of course. I just answer as best I can. These aren't the kind of questions I want to ask Chloe in public. Not after the *peany* discussion we just had in the car.

I find myself chuckling as I fill out the forms. I'm actually laughing inside. All this stress, all this worry, and Chloe's going to be fine. She knows what sex is; it sounds to me like she *wants* to have sex. Somehow, my daughter seems more normal than she ever has before. Everything's going to be fine. *Just fine.*

At the bottom of the questionnaire, where it asks the reason for the visit, I circle BIRTH CONTROL. I circle it twice for good measure. If I had a red pen, I'd use that, too. I know there are those in the world who would argue that Thomas and Chloe have the same right to reproduce as anyone, but I would wager those people have never come home to a house set on fire by their twenty-one-year-old Down syndrome child. I would bet those people don't have an adult child who still doesn't understand that moving cars are dangerous and you can't just walk in front of them to get something shiny on the street. A person who says the mentally challenged have the right to reproduce has never lain awake all night wondering what will happen to their child if they're killed in an automobile accident . . . or a freak mud slide.

Of course the chances Chloe could ever conceive, even if Thomas gets it in the right spot, are slim. For various reasons, Down syndrome women have a lower rate of conception. But my daughter can barely take care of herself; she can't take care of a baby. I can't leave this up to chance.

I turn in the stack of paperwork and sit there in a waiting room chair and pretend to leaf through a magazine. The room is about half full: an older woman in a business suit; a woman my age whom I vaguely recognize, from where I don't know; two women with big pregnant bellies, one with a toddler with her. There's also a young couple sitting very close to each other, hands clasped. They're happy and giggly. They keep looking at each other as if some miracle has just occurred; I'm guessing they're pregnant for the first time.

I glance at my daughter, beside me. She's still looking at her new book, but she's jiggling her leg. I know she's nervous.

I rest my hand on her knee. "This will be quick. Quick and easy-peasy," I assure her. "Then we'll stop at Taco Hell for dinner."

She twists her mouth. "That's a bad word. No bad words, Miss Margaret says. She'll wash your face. With soap."

I smile. Chloe really *is* funny.

Chloe's name is called. I get up, return the magazine, and look at her. She's still sitting, but I know she heard her name. I tilt my head. "Our turn," I say casually.

She shakes her head and looks down at the floor. I recognize the look on her face. Once she gets that *look*, she quickly becomes difficult to handle.

"You go," she says. "I sit here. Read my book." She doesn't look at me.

I take a step toward her. "Honey, you have to come. It's *your* doctor's appointment." I put on my *happy face*. "So you and Thomas can get married." Because there's no way in hell she's getting married without this appointment.

She thrusts out her lower lip. "I don't want to come." She whispers, "I don't want to get naked. I'm cold." She runs the zipper on her hoodie down a few inches, then up.

It's a warm October day. My students are still wearing shorts to class. She's not cold.

"Come on." I offer my hand. "I'll stay with you. I promise. First we talk to the doctor in his office. Then we go in the exam room." I glance up. People in the waiting room are starting to stare. "A quick exam and we're out of here. Double crunchy taco meal, here we come."

I'm supposed to be avoiding fast food. I'm hoping to lose a few pounds before the wedding, but I'll eat two double crunchy taco meals if that's what will get us through this.

"Chloe Monroe?" A nurse in peach scrubs sticks her head through the waiting room doorway. She's holding a chart.

I take Chloe's hand and pull. She resists. I hold my breath . . . and she slowly rises to her feet. I thank the Gods of Gynecology everywhere.

"This way," the nurse says with a genuine smile. She gets Chloe's weight and her blood pressure, and then leads us to Dr. Ellington's office.

"The doctor will be with you shortly." She closes the door behind us.

"We sit here." I take one of the two leather chairs in front of the huge executive desk. It's a typical physician's office: cherry furniture, medical textbooks on bookshelves, pictures of Dr.

Ellington's family on the wall. There's a large bridal portrait; I remember reading in the paper, a year or so ago, that his eldest, a medical student, had married. She's pretty. Not a great wedding gown, though. Chloe's is prettier.

I tap the chair next to me. "Right here, Chloe."

"I have to get naked now?" She clutches her canvas bag to her chest.

"Not yet, honey. Not here. First we talk to Dr. Ellington." I tap the seat of the chair beside me, again. "Then we go into the exam room and that's when you take off your clothes and put on the gown. I'll help you."

She sits, but she only perches on the edge of the chair. She slides her bag onto her lap. "Wedding girl," she points out.

"A bride. That's Dr. Ellington's daughter."

She stares at the portrait. "Are you going to get naked?"

I look at her. I'm used to Chloe's lack of segues, but this one's a doozy. "Not today. I had my appointment to get naked a few months ago."

There's a knock on the door, then it opens. It's Dr. Ellington. He's short and round, like Chloe . . . only without the Down's. Glasses and premature baldness.

"Alicia. Chloe." He tucks Chloe's medical record under his arm and shakes my hand. He offers his hand to Chloe, but she clutches her book bag for dear life. She knows how to shake someone's hand. We've practiced. But I don't push her. We've still got the exam to get through.

"So, how are you, Chloe?" He walks around the desk and takes his chair, which is oxblood leather like the ones we're sitting on, but taller and it swivels. "I hear you're getting married."

She keeps her gaze fixed on the front of his desk.

"Chloe," I say softly. "Dr. Ellington spoke to you."

"I'm getting married!" she says loudly.

"Congratulations." He's smiling. "A very exciting time. Exciting, indeed." He opens her chart. "So, I see you're here to discuss birth control methods." He looks across the desk at her, not me.

I don't wait long for Chloe to respond because I know from the *look* that she's teetering on a tantrum. It happens when she gets scared, or frustrated. "That's right," I say.

He glances at me, then Chloe. "You'd like a form of birth control, Chloe?"

She's jiggling her knee. "I have to go home," she mutters under her breath. "I forgot to feed my kitty. You have to feed a kitty. It's a lot of re-spon-ability."

"Chloe." I lay my hand on her arm. "Tell Dr. Ellington you'd like birth control." I look at him. "I'm not sure what's best. Maybe an IUD? Or Depo-Provera? Chloe's a brave girl, aren't you?" I rub her arm. "She's not afraid of immunizations."

He's looking at her, still. "I have to tell you the possible dangers of an intrauterine device, Chloe. IUDs prevent pregnancy by damaging or destroying sperm. There's the copper type and the type that releases hormones that affect the mucus in the cervix."

"I have to feed my kitty," Chloe says again, but her speech is garbled because she's not concentrating on her pronunciation now.

"Depo-Provera is given every three months, and has been found to be highly—"

Chloe shoots up out of her chair. "Bye!"

Dr. Ellington is obviously startled.

"Chloe, you can't go yet." I take her hand and hold her where she is. "Dr. Ellington, Chloe's very nervous. She's very uncomfortable. Could we move this along?"

He looks at me, and then my daughter. "Chloe, do you understand why you're here?"

I get up, but before I can get anything out of my mouth, he goes on.

"Your mother says you want birth control. Do you understand that birth control will prevent you and your husband from conceiving a child?"

"Dr. Ellington, you're using words Chloe doesn't—"

"Mrs. Richards," he says sharply. "I want to be certain my patient comprehends her treatment." He looks at her again. "Is that what you're saying, Chloe? You don't want a baby?"

She looks at me, then in his general direction. "We're getting a baby. And a puppy."

"No . . ." I squeeze her hand. "You're not getting a baby, Chloe. You're getting married."

"Mrs. Richards—"

"Thomas is getting a puppy when we get the wedding!" Chloe hollers at me. She's starting to cry. "And . . . and a baby!" She tries to maneuver around me because I'm standing between her and the door.

"Chloe." I grab her shoulders and attempt to get her to meet my gaze.

"Mrs. Richards, perhaps it would be better if—"

"Let go of me!" Chloe demands, flailing her arms.

She doesn't hit me on purpose, but as she struggles, she catches me on the chin with the back of her hand. It smarts.

"Mom! Mom! I want to go home! I don't want to get naked!" She's crying hard now; her nose is running. She's slowly bulldozing her way to the door.

"I'm sorry, Mrs. Richards." Dr. Ellington rises from behind his desk. "I won't be able to see Chloe—"

"Could you just give us a minute?" I'm physically holding my daughter back while trying to look like I'm not. "She's upset. If you could just give us a minute."

"I won't treat Chloe. She clearly doesn't understand what she's consenting to." He stands beside his desk looking completely awkward. It's obvious he just wants to get us out of there.

There's a knock on the door. "Dr. Ellington?" a female voice calls.

"It's fine! We're fine." He looks at me again. "I will not provide birth control to a young woman who doesn't understand what she's consenting to."

"Which is why I, as her mother and legal guardian, am giving *my* consent to have you provide her with birth control." I say it calmly, even though I want to scream at him.

Chloe isn't fighting me anymore. Now she's hanging on to me. Slobbering on me. My light blue cotton sweater is wet with her tears and snot. I pull her against me and smooth her messy hair. "It's okay, honey. Shhhh. It's going to be okay. Everything's going to be fine."

"I'm sorry, Mrs. Richards, I'll have to ask you to leave."

I look at him, my gaze meeting his. "You ought to be ashamed of yourself," I say. "Do you have any idea how catastrophic it would be for my daughter to get pregnant? Do you know the statistics on the outcome, should my daughter get pregnant? By her *mentally handicapped* husband?"

"Down syndrome men are rarely able to father—"

"Her fiancé doesn't have Down syndrome! He's GR. If my Chloe gets pregnant, she has about a seventy percent chance that her child will not be born of average intelligence!"

"The statistics aren't cl—"

"Dr. Ellington," I interrupt. "Do you have any idea—"

The door opens behind me. "Dr. Ellington."

"Megan, could you help Mrs. Richards out," Dr. Ellington says stiffly.

I put my arm around Chloe and guide her toward the open door. "It's *Doctor* Richards," I say.

"Pardon?" he calls after me.

"It's not *Mrs.* Richards, Dr. Ellington. It's *Dr.* Richards." I walk out the door with my melting mass of daughter in my arms. "Have a nice day."

Statistics say chances are slim Chloe and Thomas could conceive and have a child. Chloe and Thomas aren't the ones who are worried.

Jin meets me for a cup of coffee in the student center a couple of days after the scene Chloe and I cause in Dr. Ellington's office. Jin and I are both between classes. Jin already knows the story. I just need her to help me think through my next step. We both get lattes and take a small table against the wall. The student center is busy and loud, offering a certain amount of privacy.

"Maybe you need to talk to Margaret and Denny."

"Danny," I say.

Jin sips her latte. I dump a yellow packet into my cup.

"Maybe Danny needs to teach his son how to use condoms."

I sigh, take a sip of my coffee, and rip open another yellow packet. "Then that's depending on Thomas. I don't know if I can do that. Chloe's my daughter. If she gets pregnant, that baby is *my* responsibility."

"I did my Internet research, too." Jin unties a cute scarf from around her neck. It's autumn-brisk outside, but it's warm in the student center. "Chloe's not going to get pregnant." She lowers her voice and leans forward. "For all you know, he's going to put it in her ear."

She's trying to make me laugh. I don't. I rip open another packet of sweetener. "*My* responsibility. Another mentally handicapped child, Jin. I'm fifty-three. Can I raise another child at my age . . . when I'll already have two big kids in my house?"

She sips her latte and lets me go on. Jin's such a good listener. I need to remember to ask her later about how her date went last night with Abby. The romance is heating up, and I haven't gotten any of the juicy details. It seems like I'm always in crisis mode these days. I need to remember to take the time to listen to what's going on in Jin's life. Officially dating her ex and the mother of her son is a big deal.

"And what if I get sick and die?" I go on. I've been worrying about that a lot lately. It's something all parents of handicapped children worry about. Who will care for my child when I can't? Dr. Tamara's answer is that that's why Chloe should be in a group home. So she can easily transition when I kick the bucket.

"My mother died of ovarian cancer." I'm on a roll now. "Who would care for the three of them then? Margaret and Danny? They don't want the responsibility. They're tickled Thomas is moving in with me. That way, they can go right on pretending he's normal. They're not going to want to take care of another handicapped child. And Randall?" I snort. "How do you think Randall would do with Chloe *and* Thomas *and* a Downs baby in his town house? Where would his grad student sleep, for God's sake?"

Jin is quiet and calm. She reaches across the table and takes my hand. The student center is loud, but it seems suddenly to get quiet. My world becomes tiny. My heart is beating in my chest. I'm scared. I'm scared for my daughter, and I don't know what to do. I don't know what I *can* do.

"She probably won't get pregnant, but if she does, you could terminate the pregnancy," Jin says quietly.

My eyes cloud with tears and I look away. "I can't do that again," I whisper.

"A woman has a right to choose."

"This is not political. It's personal." I look at her again, taking comfort in her loving gaze. And Jin truly does love me. I don't have a man in my life, I don't have romantic love, but I have Jin. And that's a lot more than most people have. "*I can't do that again*." I enunciate each word.

I take a deep breath. Jin waits patiently. She knows I had an abortion, but she can't possibly know the pain it caused me. The sense of loss I feel, even after all these years. Because I'm still discovering how deeply it affected me.

I guess, for years, I was so busy with my career, with Chloe, with fighting with Randall that I was able to stifle these feelings. I covered them up, buried them deep, like foul pieces of rotting vegetables. I know now that I should never have had that abortion. It had been my choice to have it, and ultimately, though Randall had pressured me, I alone had made the decision to do it. I couldn't blame this one on Randall.

That's a large part of my pain, I think. The fact that *I* did it.

What's that old adage about "live and learn"? Well, I've lived and I've learned. I've lived with the abortion I had and I've learned I can't do it again. I can't do it, even if the child is in my daughter's womb.

"Chloe can't get pregnant," I say quietly.

She gives my hand a squeeze and lets go. "Okay." She raises her paper cup to her lips. "Then we do what most young girls do."

I raise an eyebrow, just the way Jin does it.

"We hit the Planned Parenthood office. The process is streamlined. She probably won't even need an exam." She rises. "I have to run, but you and me and Chloe, tomorrow. It's a date. I'll check the hours."

"You think they do Depo shots?"

She shrugs. "I don't know, but birth control pills for sure."

"I hadn't considered that," I think out loud. "She'd have to take them."

Jin shrugs. "She never misses a day with her vitamin."

"It's chewable and shaped like a cartoon character."

"Don't underestimate my Chlo-Bo."

I smile. "Thanks."

She walks away and I reach for my coffee, feeling a glimmer of hope, again. Everything really is going to be all right.

❦ 18 ❧

In the end, the whole birth control thing is anticlimactic. The women at the clinic are very pleasant, and a kind, patient female doctor deals well with Chloe. She talks to her, but also to me. I take along my guardianship papers for good measure. Chloe's on her best behavior and repeats clearly (we rehearsed this time) that she wants medicine so she doesn't make a baby. The clinic provides her with birth control pills. The bonus is that Chloe will go on a ninety-day cycle, which means fewer menstrual periods and less hassle for her and me.

Chloe and I talk extensively about the fact that she has to take the birth control pill *every day* so *Thomas doesn't make a baby in her*. Her words, not mine. I take the pills out of the little circular packet and put them, along with her chewable vitamin, in a days-of-the-week pillbox. We find a place, after trial and error, on her bathroom sink where the box is clearly visible. When she brushes her teeth in the morning, she takes her pills. I practice with her for a month, and then let her go on her own. Chloe doesn't know that I check every day to be sure the little pink pill for that day is gone. She feels independent, and I breathe easier.

The days leading up to the wedding go by faster than I can comprehend. At Miss Minnie's, they begin a countdown to the wedding on their classroom calendar, and Chloe wants to do the same on our calendar at home. She doesn't understand how a calendar year works, but eventually she gets the hang of marking an *X* in the next block every night after dinner.

I talk to Margaret regularly as the plans for the big day progress. She takes care of the church details; I make arrangements for the party at my house. We talk, but we don't *talk*. Shortly after the birth control fiasco, I try to broach the subject of sex between the newlyweds, but Margaret gets flustered and says something about God's wisdom and the marriage bed and then goes on to tell me about the party favors she's making that involve Jordan almonds and blue lace.

With the birth control issue under control, I just let the whole sex topic go. After all, I got what I wanted; Chloe will be safe from pregnancy. Margaret and I talk some about Thomas moving in with Chloe and me, but those conversations are superficial, too. She wants to send his Thomas the Tank Engine pillowcase and towels to make him feel more at home. She doesn't want to talk about helping Thomas and Chloe make the transition to married life, and honestly, I'm so busy and so tired with everything going on that I let Margaret slide there, too. If I can take care of Chloe, if I can make *her* happy, I can make Thomas happy, too, can't I? They can make each other happy.

The morning of the wedding, we forego tradition and let the *kids* see each other. We arrange for Margaret to bring Thomas over to move his last few things into Chloe's room. They'll spend their first night together as man and wife here. There's no honeymoon planned. Maybe a family trip to Disney World in the spring, but no definite plans. I'm a mess by the time they arrive at ten. I've had three hours' sleep, and I've already gotten into a silly argument with my father about breakfast, of all things. He and Gloria arrived yesterday and are staying in a local hotel. I didn't offer to let them stay here; they didn't ask.

So Dad wanted us to go out to breakfast. This morning. I explained that we couldn't possibly go this morning . . . the morning of the wedding. When the reception is at my house. Chloe and I have hair and makeup appointments at noon. I need to run out and buy pantyhose (I know they're not in style, but there's no way anyone is seeing these legs bare in December), and the caterers are arriving at one to set up.

I don't know who got snippy first. Maybe me. It was early when he called . . . when he had Gloria call for him. Chloe was still in bed watching *The Lion King*. I was already emotional—handicap aside, my daughter, my *only child*, was getting married. When Gloria called, I insisted she put Dad on. I thanked him for his invitation. I even invited him and Gloria over for coffee and Pop-Tarts. He said he didn't eat Pop-Tarts. He said he and Gloria were going to see friends in New Jersey tomorrow. That's probably when I got snippy. He was only staying two nights? Chloe and I haven't seen him in two years. We ended the conversation frostily, agreeing we would see each other at his only grand-daughter's wedding.

When the doorbell rings, I'm upstairs in my bedroom in a long-sleeved T-shirt without a bra. No pants. No underwear. My hair is wet and wrapped in a towel. Jin offered to be here when Margaret and Thomas came, but I insisted I didn't need her. I sent her off to the church to add the blue bows to the pews and perform whatever magic she intended to make in the sanctuary to make it more beautiful.

"Chloe!" I call down the hall from my doorway. "I think that's Thomas."

"Let him in," she hollers.

"I'm getting dressed." I rub my wet hair in the towel. "You let him in."

"No! You let him in," she calls back stubbornly.

I grab a pair of sweatpants from the top of the dirty clothes basket and pull them on before heading down the hallway. As I walk into her room, I pull the towel off my head. "Chloe, Margaret and Thomas have brought his things over. We talked about this. You're going to help him put his things in your room."

She's standing at the dresser Thomas and his father brought over the other night in their minivan. She's got the top drawer open. I can see that she's putting some of her own clothes in. There's a pile of humongous shirts on the floor.

"Chloe, what are you doing?" I hang my wet towel on her doorknob to grab on my way out. "That's Thomas's dresser. You have your own."

She ignores me, arranging one of her pink sweatshirts just so in the drawer.

I take a breath. At least she's dressed. She's wearing a white sweat suit Margaret gave her: white sweatshirt, white sweatpants. The sweatshirt says BRIDE in iron-on blue letters across the front. She's wearing rain boots, which seem odd for a bride, but might come in handy. There are snow flurries in the forecast.

The doorbell rings again.

I know it's important that I stay calm today. And patient. Chloe needs my patience. She deserves it. "Chloe, let's go let Thomas in."

"Me and him, we're getting married. Thomas."

"You are, indeed," I say. "He's waiting. You'd better go open the door before he leaves you at the altar." I chuckle.

She half-smiles the way she does when she understands I've made a joke, but she doesn't get the joke.

I lay my hand over hers on the dresser. "Go let him in," I say gently.

"So we can get married and kiss."

"So you can get married and kiss," I agree.

She leaves her bedroom, and I scoop up Thomas's shirts and stuff them in the top drawer and squeeze it shut.

"Hold your horses!" Chloe is shouting as she clomps down the stairs.

I follow her, deciding I won't go back to my room to dress more appropriately. What the hell, Thomas is going to be living with us. He's probably going to see me look worse than I do now. Margaret, too, at some point.

Chloe swings the door open and Thomas steps in, a big suitcase in his arms.

"N . . . knock, knock," he says.

"Who's there?" Chloe asks dutifully.

"C . . . cow."

"Cow who?" she says.

"Cows s . . . say m . . . mooooo!"

They both laugh hysterically.

Margaret walks in behind Thomas. She's carrying a suitcase and a small canvas duffel bag. "Good morning!" she says cheerfully.

I'm wishing I'd had a third cup of coffee. Maybe with a shot of bourbon. I smile, making a note that once Thomas moves in, I'm going to teach him some decent knock-knock jokes. "Come in, come in." I wave them in. "Cold out?"

"Brisk!" Margaret closes the front door behind her. She's wearing her winter uniform: flowered skirt, black tights, black shoes, and a long, thick sweater over some kind of top I can't see. She's also wearing big, fat, plastic curlers all over her head.

Thomas is wearing his red down jacket. When he puts down his suitcase and hugs Chloe, my daughter is engulfed in red. She looks so small compared to him. I don't know why, but a lump rises in my throat and I have to force it down.

I can see that he's wearing new, dark blue sweatpants. I'm guessing there's a sweatshirt under the coat that says GROOM.

"Coffee?" I ask.

"No, no." Margaret *pshaws* me. "We'll just unpack Tommy's things and get out of your hair. Busy day!"

"Thomas, get your suitcase." Chloe takes over, doing what she does best. "Take it upstairs. My room."

The four of us tromp up the stairs. I realize this is the first time Thomas has ever been upstairs in our house. I never really cared if Thomas was in Chloe's room, but out of respect for Margaret, I've made them stay downstairs when he was here. I think to myself that this is a lot for Thomas to take in in one day. But he seems to be doing fine. He seems excited.

"What a pretty room, Chloe!" Margaret exclaims as she lowers the suitcase to the floor.

"This is my room." Chloe walks over and pats her bed. She and I changed the sheets this morning and then made it. "My bed." She points. "My bathroom. I keep clean. Mom says I'm very clean."

"I know, dear. You're such a neatnik!" Margaret is smiling as she walks across the room. "I'll just put Tommy's toiletries in here where he can find them. No rush to put them away!"

Thomas drops the big suitcase in front of his dresser, then he flops it over, unzips it, and begins to pull out clothing.

"Here," Chloe tells him. She starts with the second drawer. "Put your clothes in here. My clothes are in there." She points to her dresser. "I have a closet."

"Y . . . you have a closet an . . . and we're gonna get . . . get married. N . . . now."

"In a few hours!" Margaret sings, coming out of the bathroom. "I left your toothbrush and toothpaste and deodorant and such in the bathroom, Tommy, honey."

"You're my honey," Chloe tells Thomas.

"You're my b . . . baby," he coos loudly.

He begins cramming his clothes in the drawers. Chloe stands there and watches, occasionally giving instructions. He's not doing it to suit her, but she's practicing patience, as well, this morning. I know that later she'll take it all out, fold it the best she can, and put it all back the way she wants it. But she seems to be tolerating his messiness well, for now.

"Your jammies are in here. And your robe and your slippers." Margaret carries the smaller of the suitcases to the bed, opens it, and pulls out a pair of men's red flannel pajamas, and a matching robe, and matching slippers. "And your pillow!"

I'm standing in the doorway, trying to give Chloe and Thomas a little space.

The decorative pillow is shaped like a generic train engine; it's blue and red and gray, but the blue is a different shade from the trademarked train engine I know so well.

Margaret lays it up against Chloe's four pillows that have been carefully arranged by Chloe this morning. Then carefully re-arranged. Twice.

"And just a few more things." Margaret carries socks and under-wear in her arms and dumps them into the drawer Thomas has open. "You and Chloe will have plenty of time to put things away the way you want them later."

His suitcase empty, Thomas slams the bottom drawer shut.

We're all quiet for a second. For me, the moment is surreal. A man is moving into my daughter's bedroom. He's putting his clothes in dresser drawers and his toothbrush beside hers in the bathroom.

"Well!" Margaret claps her hands together. "We should go. I know you ladies have plenty to do!" She gives Chloe a hug and kisses her cheek. "See you at the church, honey."

Then Thomas hugs Chloe, only he finishes off with a big, wet kiss on her lips. "S . . . see you at . . . at the ch . . . church, honey!"

My intention is to leave the beauty salon and go straight to the church. (Abby is handling the caterers.) There's a room there for Chloe and me to dress. The wedding gown and my mother-of-the-bride dress are already there; Jin dropped them off this morning when she went to decorate the sanctuary and the hall where the first reception will be held. I have it in my head that going from the salon to the church will make the day go smoother. It will give Chloe time to calm her nerves and watch a little *Princess and the Frog*. I've even got the wedding scene in the end cued up on my iPad. But I forget my shoes at home. Thank goodness I forget my shoes.

With my face painted, hair done, in clean sweatpants and sneakers, I trek back into the house. Chloe stays outside in the car, listening to the radio. I feel like I'm running on pure adrenaline. I'm excited. I'm scared. I'm so tired that I already feel dead on my feet. But I press on because it's what I do. It's who I am.

I check on the caterers in the kitchen. All's going well there. The house smells incredible, and Patricia and her staff have already transformed my dining room. Where stacks of books and paperwork usually sit, there are beautiful glass bowls and plates waiting to be heaped with delicious finger foods and desserts.

With a wave, I head up the stairs. I hear the water before I see it. It sounds like maybe Chloe didn't jiggle the toilet handle in her bathroom. I go into her room; no running toilet. I head for my bedroom and the adjacent bathroom. My toilet works fine; it doesn't need jiggling. But Chloe was in there, talking to me before we left. Maybe she left a faucet on. I don't make it to my bedroom. I see the water lying on the floor of the laundry room.

"Dammit!" I mutter. I was never much of a swearer. I always felt it beneath me. An English professor ought to have a better command of the English language. But the older I get, the more often I have to sometimes scan my brain for the right words and plain, old curse words come out. "Goddamn it!"

I stop at the doorway of the laundry room. The hardwood floor is shimmering with water. The only reason it hasn't run into the hallway yet is because of a little strip of wood on the floor in the doorway. "Goddamn it to hell!"

I can feel my face getting hot. I'm afraid I'm going to cry. I can hear water dripping, but I can't see where it's coming from and I don't want to wade in. I know how to turn off the water main, but there are caterers downstairs. How are they supposed to cater my daughter's wedding without water?

I go down the hall for the shoes I think I left in a cute little bag on the bed—where I would see it and not forget it. I fish my cell phone out of the kangaroo pocket of the Stone University hoodie I'm wearing. I speed-dial Mark. "Come on, come on," I murmur as I walk into my bedroom. Sure enough, my heels are there, right in the bag on my bed where I left them.

Third ring.

"Please, Mark," I whisper. "Answer this phone and I swear I'll make you a big plate of homemade chocolate chocolate chip cookies. I'll make a plate of cookies for you every day of the week for the next six months."

He must hear me because he picks up at the end of the fourth ring.

"Alicia."

"Mark," I exhale thankfully. "I'm so sorry to call you. I know you're probably getting dressed for the wedding."

He chuckles. "Nope. Paying bills. Guys don't take long to get ready. What's up?"

"A leak. In the laundry room. I can't tell—"

"I'll be right there with my wet vac and my toolbox."

"The caterers are already here and Chloe's supposed to be at the church and—"

"Alicia, go to the church," he says calmly. "You go to the church. I'll take care of the leak and I'll see you there."

"But you're a guest. I should call someone else, but I don't know—" Emotion catches in my throat.

"Go to the church," Mark repeats in the kindest voice. "Worst-case scenario, I'll see you at your house afterwards."

I want to argue. I'm not used to people doing things for me. Well, Jin, but she's different. She isn't *people*; she's Jin. But Mark is so nice and . . . and I need him to do this for me. I almost smile. "Thank you." I already feel better as I hurry out of my bedroom. "Thank you, thank you, thank you!" I walk right by the laundry room and don't even look at it.

"See you at the church," Mark says in my ear.

"See you at the church," I repeat. And then I take my daughter to the church to be married.

❧ 19 ❧

Chloe's only request when making plans for the wedding was that it be like Belle and the Beast's. Which was an interesting request, since, technically, Belle and the Beast don't marry in the movie. It ends with Belle and the prince dancing in a ballroom. What Chloe imagined was her wearing a big dress and her hero, Thomas, wearing a tux, I suppose. That request, I was able to grant.

Chloe's dress was white, not yellow like Belle's, but she was a beauty when I walked her down the aisle, her bouquet of calla lilies clutched in her sweaty palms. I fight tears through the entire ceremony as I listen to my dear daughter slowly, painstakingly repeat her wedding vows. Thomas, his voice booming, stuttered and stammered through the whole thing. That's when my tears spilled. At that moment I realized that he really did love my Chloe. And for that, I loved him that day.

Like the days leading up to the marriage, the wedding ceremony went by too quickly. One minute I was lowering Chloe's gown over her head in a little room off the narthex at St. Mark's. The next minute she and Thomas were walking up the aisle, arm in arm, the theme song from *Beauty and the Beast* playing on a violin. My Chloe was a married woman.

Instead of walking out of the sanctuary with Randall, who brought a date to his daughter's wedding (two guesses where he found her), I recessed on Jin's arm. Both of us wiped away tears and accepted congratulations. I ignored Randall and his twentysomething grad student. I refused to let him ruin my day.

The reception in the church hall was fine. It was just what Margaret wanted and it was perfect for Chloe's and Thomas's friends from Minnie's and from the LoGs. There were mini hot dogs wrapped in strips of piecrust, pieces of fruit on toothpicks, cheese and crackers and red punch out of a punchbowl. Chloe and Thomas held hands and laughed and accepted congratulations. They clapped when they saw the pile of wedding gifts on a table near the door.

"Those are for us?" Chloe asks me, her cheeks red with excitement.

"All for you and Thomas," I assure her.

Thomas stares at the piles of pretty boxes wrapped in silver and gold, with white ribbons. "I . . . I c . . . can open p . . . presents!"

"I open the presents!" Chloe insists, glaring at him. "I'm the bride, dummy head!"

"Now, now," I whisper under my breath. "You have to be nice to Thomas, Chloe. Thomas is your husband now."

"A . . . and you h . . . have to b . . . be nice t . . . to me," he says in her face.

"Let's cut the cake!" Margaret declares, standing at a table covered with a white paper tablecloth that held the three-tiered white cake trimmed in pale blue. It's in the same place the craft table had been the first time I brought Chloe to the LoGs almost two years ago.

Again, tears fill my eyes. I'm not a crier. I'd gotten over that after Chloe's birth. The business of living and caring for my daughter kept me from being a crier. But everything makes me cry today. I'm so happy for Chloe. So proud of her. So hopeful.

As I watch Chloe and Thomas cut the cake, with Margaret's

assistance, I think of my own mother and how happy it would have made her to see this moment. To share in this whole day with us. My mother was never anything like my father. She wouldn't be embarrassed by the idea of her Down syndrome granddaughter getting married, not the way my father seemed to be embarrassed today. She would never have been embarrassed by Chloe or by me or by the fact that I gave birth to a child who was less than perfect.

My mother wouldn't have seen Chloe that way. She would have seen Chloe for the perfect woman she is.

"Nice job," Jin whispers in my ear.

I press my lips together, watching Chloe and Thomas as they wield the cake knife together. Jin hands me a tissue to blot my eyes.

"You've handled this so well today," Jin goes on.

"I didn't have any choice."

"Sure you did." She stands beside me and slips her arm around my waist. "Even after you agreed to the marriage, you could have dragged your feet. You could have made life difficult for Chloe and Thomas. For Margaret." She chuckles. "For me."

I'm watching Chloe and Thomas still try to cut the cake. Cameras and iPhones are flashing. The photographer is maneuvering around the table. Everyone is laughing, including Chloe and Thomas. Everyone is so happy.

"You made the best of a less-than-ideal situation," Jin says.

"I don't know, maybe my fears will all prove to be unfounded. Look at them." I gesture, smiling. "How is this not an ideal situation?"

"Look at you, all mother-of-the-bride teary." Abby comes up from behind me and gives me a quick hug, then stands on the other side of me and I'm between her and Jin. They're both grinning at each other and I can't help but grin with them.

I dab at my eyes, hoping my mascara isn't running. "I didn't think I'd feel this way today."

"I think you need a drink."

"Not getting one here," Jin says under her breath. She had been appalled when I told her that there was no alcohol allowed in the church hall. *What's a wedding without friends and family getting hammered?* she'd asked me when she heard. "But I can guarantee you there'll be champagne back at the house."

Everyone crowded around the cake table erupts into applause as Chloe and Thomas manage to maneuver the beribboned cake knife through the cake. I clap, too. Randall is standing a few feet from me, and we make eye contact.

For a moment, he lets down his guard. He's smiling. At me. I see sadness in his eyes. Regret, maybe. The look on his face makes me wonder if maybe I've misjudged him all these years. Then his new girl appears at his side; she's not as pretty as they've been in the past. But for heaven's sake, he'll have to take Social Security soon! He looks at her and everything on his face changes. He's once again the arrogant man I know.

I return my attention to Chloe and Thomas. They look so sweet together, her in her wedding gown, him in his black tux and black tie. Margaret hands them a piece of cake on a plate. She's explaining to them what to do. They don't know the tradition of smashing cake in each other's faces, so it goes quickly and easily. Chloe is licking her lips; she has a little bit of blue icing on her upper lip. Thomas is stuffing more cake into his own mouth. There's more laughing. More clapping. Thomas's two sisters come up to give Chloe hugs and she's . . . glowing. There's no other word for it. My daughter, the bride, is glowing.

Within an hour of the cake cutting, the church reception is over. I thought Chloe and Thomas were going to ride with me, but a distant relative of Margaret's has surprised Thomas with a limo ride from the church to our house. We all go outside in the cold and the dark and throw birdseed and watch Chloe and Thomas climb into a stretch Hummer limo. Their departure is delayed. Thomas is so excited that we have to wait for him while his mother runs him back inside to use the restroom. Chloe waits for him inside the limo, keeping herself busy by running the automatic windows up and down.

The wedding guests wave farewell to the bride and groom, and the stretch limo pulls away. Mark appears at my side and walks me to my car. I saw him in the church. He made the wedding, but I haven't had a chance to speak to him. "My house flooded?" I ask him. I'm so happy that the wedding went well that I don't really care.

"Nope. Minor problem. A split hose on the back of the washing machine. Hose replaced. Water cleaned up. Don't you have a coat?" He removes his black wool dress coat and drops it over my shoulders.

"I . . ." I chuckle. "I guess I don't. I was in a sweat suit when I arrived at the church." I laugh again. That seems like a million years ago now.

"Smells like snow." He closes his eyes and lifts his face toward the sky.

I look up. "It does."

"Beautiful wedding." He presses his hand to the middle of my back as we cross an icy patch in the parking lot.

The parking lot is beginning to fill with people. Cars are backing out. Guests are calling to each other. Laughing. Everyone seems to have enjoyed the wedding.

"It really was beautiful, wasn't it?" I say. I realize Mark's coat smells good. Like him. He looks nice in his dark gray suit. His lavender and gray tie is a nice touch.

As we approach my Honda, I fumble for the keys in my black clutch. "Here I am." I click the fob to unlock the door. "Thanks for your coat." I start to slip it off, but he pulls it back over my shoulders.

"It'll be chilly in the car. You wear it home." He opens my door for me.

"You're coming back to the house, aren't you?" I slide into the car, feeling pretty in my sapphire blue dress and high heels.

"Wouldn't miss it. You owe me a glass of champagne. Maybe two."

Mark closes my door and walks away. As I start the engine, I watch him go. Was my plumber just flirting with me?

There were a hundred people at the church and the reception. There are probably only forty-five who come back to the house. Which is just fine with me. It's a perfect number. There are enough guests to entertain each other, but few enough that I can walk around and talk to everyone and thank them for coming.

After checking with the caterer and running upstairs to fix my makeup and take a bathroom break, I start mingling. I try to get Chloe and Thomas to walk around with me, but Chloe's getting a little cranky. I think she's just hungry, so I leave her sitting on one of the couches with Thomas and one of his sisters. The sister looks amazingly like Margaret, right down to the flowered dress. And she's every bit as kind and patient with Chloe and Thomas.

I leave Chloe and Thomas with big plates of food: sautéed shrimp, mini pita pizzas, tiny bison sliders. And glasses of chocolate milk. Their choice. I offered them champagne in champagne flutes, but both of them took one sip and wrinkled their noses. Which was okay with me. Mental disabilities and alcohol can be difficult to mix anyway.

Most of the LoGs haven't come back to the house, nor have Minnie's other students, but Minnie is there and we talk for a while. We've agreed that Chloe and Thomas should continue going to her, but there are details to be worked out. Thomas receives Social Security benefits, but Margaret has mentioned that his daycare costs are too high. She seems to think that Thomas and Chloe can learn to stay home alone with each other; I have my doubts. Minnie is hoping they can work something out with the state, but the system is complicated.

Abby joins us and we start talking about the state of care for the adult handicapped in the United States. I've always liked

Abby, but I find that I like her even better these days. She's changed. Mellowed a little. I guess life does that to us. I get so lost in the conversation that I almost miss my father and Gloria slipping out the front door. They're talking to Randall. His grad student is missing. Maybe past her bedtime?

"Will you excuse me?" I say. "I think my dad and his wife are leaving."

Abby and Minnie continue with their animated conversation.

"Dad. Gloria." I smile. "Going already?"

It's a silly question. They've both got their coats on. Gloria has a knit hat, scarf, and gloves on.

Gloria smiles. "The wedding was beautiful. The reception. Both of them. Beautiful." She opens her arms to hug me. "Everything was beautiful."

My dad and Randall are talking. They look a lot alike tonight. Both are wearing slacks and tweed sports jackets. Dad's wearing a porkpie hat. Both have gone gray, and both have more gut than they used to. My father is a retired high school teacher. Chemistry. I try not to think about the psychology of it all. Me marrying my father—or an image of him—after my mother's sudden death. It's all so . . . freshman psychology. And water under the bridge.

"I'm sorry you're going so soon, Dad." I give him a big hug, just because I need to. Despite all the things that have happened between us, he's still my dad. I'm still his girl.

"What a fine wedding. Chloe was beautiful." His hug is quick and not all that affectionate.

"She was, wasn't she?" I glance over my shoulder at her. She's sitting beside Thomas on the couch, still wearing her wedding gown. Her head is on Thomas's shoulder. I can see she's fading fast. It's been a long day. A long week. "You said good-bye?"

"We said good-bye," Gloria answers for him.

"You sure you can't stay another day?" I ask. "We're having brunch tomorrow. I'm sure Chloe would love for you to join us."

"We're meeting friends in Trenton." Gloria tightens the scarf around her neck. It's not that cold out. It's barely flurrying, but I guess it seems colder to those who live in warmer climates.

"Maybe stop on the way home?" They drove up. No flying for my father.

"You're busy. You'll be exhausted." Gloria rests her hand on the doorknob. "Such a beautiful wedding."

"Good to see you." Randall pumps my dad's hand. They always liked each other. Always got along.

"Good to see you, Randall. Congratulations."

Then my dad is gone and I'm standing at the door with my ex. I feel like I should say something to him. Our daughter got married today, something neither of us ever dreamed would happen. I forget sometimes that Randall was in that delivery room, too. When she was born.

But what do I say? I think he's thinking the same thing. We look at each other. Then I guess we both decide there really isn't anything we want to say.

"I think I'll get a plate." I point toward the dining room. "I'm starving and Chloe is going to be ready to go to bed soon."

"I'm getting more wine." He holds up his wineglass and then turns away.

I grab his tweed sleeve. "Thanks, Randall."

He turns. "For?"

"Sharing the expense of this. Making our daughter happy." My smile is genuine.

"I'm going to get that wine."

"You do that."

I intend to make my way to Chloe, but I keep stopping to talk to people. Someone gets me a glass of wine. I end up perched on a dining room chair against the wall, talking to one of my colleagues. Chloe finds me around eleven thirty.

"Mom," she whines. "I want to take it off." She shrugs her shoulders. "My dress. It's itchy."

I look up. Thomas is nowhere to be seen.

My colleague says something pleasant to Chloe and excuses herself as I get to my aching feet.

"Mom . . ."

I run my hand down her sleeve. "You want to change into something else and come back down? There's still quite a few people here. They'll all be gone when you get up in the morning. The wedding will be over."

My bride is drooping. Her veil is gone. Her *princess crown* is hanging off one side of her head, and she has several spots of food and drink on the bodice of her wedding gown.

"Or are you ready for bed?" I ask.

"I want to go to bed."

"Okay. Should we find Thomas?"

Chloe slumps against me. "I don't want to. It itches." She rubs against me.

"Okay, not a problem." I put my arm around her and gently guide her from the dining room into the living room. Thomas is sitting on one of the couches, staring straight ahead, his mouth hung open. He looks like I feel after crashing from a serious sugar high. Margaret is standing beside him, chatting with her daughters.

I guide Chloe through the living room, stopping in front of Thomas. "Chloe's beat," I say to Margaret, then to Thomas, "Chloe's ready to go to bed. How about if I help her get out of her wedding gown and into her pj's, and then you come up." I look back at Margaret. "Twenty minutes maybe?"

"I'm t . . . tired. I w . . . wanna go home." Thomas leans back on the couch. His bow tie is gone, as is his light blue pocket square. He's got food on the front of his white shirt, too.

"Not home, sweetie." Margaret puts her arm around him. "Remember, you and Chloe are married now. You're going to stay here with Mom Alicia and Chloe! Chloe's your wife!"

He looks at his mother, but doesn't answer. He's as tired as Chloe is.

"We'll see you upstairs in a few minutes," I say. Then Chloe and I weave our way through the guests, toward the staircase. "You want to say good night to anyone?"

Chloe shakes her head.

I give her a peck on the cheek. She's done so well today. I know it's been overwhelming for her: so many people, so much to do, just the idea of getting married. "You don't have to."

Inside her bedroom door, I kick off my heels. It feels heavenly to walk in my stockinged feet. I lead Chloe to her bed and pat it. "Sit down."

She drops to the edge of her bed.

I reach under the layers of tulle and pull off her white Keds sneakers that Margaret bedazzled for her.

"Don't throw them away!" Chloe hollers.

"I'm not going to throw them away. You can wear them tomorrow when we go to brunch." I peel off her white knee socks. "You can wear them every day if you want to."

"And my bride shirt. I want to wear my bride shirt. And my pants." She flops back on the bed and I'm enveloped in white tulle and lace.

I have no idea what we did with her sweatsuit. It was in a bag in the room we changed in at the church. I think Jin and Abby cleaned up the room. I'll have to check with one of them. Abby is spending the night tonight with Jin. I'm not sure who's happier about that, Jin or Huan, who came home for the weekend for Chloe's wedding.

"You can wear your bride shirt, too," I assure her. I grab her hands. "Now stand up. Let me take off your necklace." She's wearing the pearls my parents gave me for high school graduation. I wore them for my wedding, which took place at the courthouse between Randall's Greek and Roman Epics class and a staff meeting.

Chloe groans.

"Come on. You said the dress itches. You have to stand up for me to unbutton you."

She wiggles on the bed. "It's itchy."

I tug at her hands. "Stand up."

She slowly stands.

"Turn around."

Slowly she turns.

I slip the necklace off and lay it on the nightstand. She can keep the pearl stud earrings in her ears for tonight; they were too hard to get in. Then I start with the buttons at the top of Chloe's gown and work my way down. It takes me forever, especially with her wiggling.

"Almost done," I say, at least three times. Finally, she's unbuttoned. I realize there's no graceful way to get her out of the dress, so I spin her around so she's facing me again, grab it somewhere around the waist, and pull.

"Owww! You're hurting me."

"You're going to have to help me here."

"Owww! It's itchy. It hurts."

Finally, I get the thing off, and Chloe falls back onto the bed. She can be dramatic at times.

Not sure what to do with the dress now, I look around her room. She doesn't really have a chair or anything like that. She likes the room neat and empty. I end up tossing it over her wicker laundry basket. It will have to be dry-cleaned anyway.

"Take your slip off."

Chloe groans, but does it.

I get her new nightgown out of her dresser. It's white with tiny blue flowers. No kittens. "Go pee, brush your teeth, take your bra and underwear off, and put this on."

"I don't want to."

"Thomas will be up in a minute and he'll need to use the bathroom. Now go on. Then I'll tuck you in."

Chloe takes the nightgown and staggers toward her bathroom.

I'm pretty sure my daughter and her husband had plans of playing under the sheets tonight, but from the look on her face, I doubt there'll be much of that going on. I pick her slip up off the floor. But she wouldn't be the first bride not to consummate her marriage on her wedding night. There'll be plenty of time for that.

I hear the toilet flush. Chloe is running water in the sink when there's a knock at the door.

I'm smiling when I open it. "Thomas."

He's not smiling. He's pouting. Margaret and Danny are standing behind him.

"Tommy's worn out," Margaret explains. She sounds tired, too.

"Chloe, too. It's been a long day." I open the door farther for them. Kicking my shoes out of their way.

"I thought maybe Tom should come home with us," Danny suggests quietly from behind his son. "It's been a long day."

"Nonsense. Tommy's married now! He belongs with his wife!"

I'm trying to decide how to respond when the bathroom door swings open. "No! No! No!" Chloe shouts from the doorway. Then she hurls something at us.

We all duck or sway. The object hits the blue wall near the door, barely missing my head. It bounces to the floor. It's a Thomas the Tank Engine toothbrush.

Things pretty much go downhill from there.

❧ 20 ❧

"Not my toothbrush!" Chloe screams from the bathroom door. She's wearing the cute little nightgown I bought her.

I'm surprised by the realization that I've come to know Thomas's family well enough to not even be embarrassed. "Honey—"

"He can't come in here!" She disappears for a second. Before I reach the bathroom, a tube of toothpaste is ejected through the doorway, followed by a roll-on deodorant and a large pair of toenail clippers.

"S . . . stop!" Thomas yells from the hall doorway. He grabs his toothbrush, then goes after the deodorant, which has skittered across the floor in the direction of the closet. "K . . . Koey!"

"Chloe," I say sharply.

"No!" she screams. She throws the toiletries bag out next. "Not my bathroom! My bathroom."

I glance toward Margaret and Danny and indicate they should step inside and close the door. There are still guests downstairs.

"Chloe, listen to me," I say, turning back to her. I hear the door close behind me. "Thomas is allowed to put things in your bathroom. It's *his* bathroom, too, now. Remember? We talked about this. You and Thomas share a bedroom and a bathroom."

"Get out!" my sweet daughter in her nightgown shrieks. Spit flies from her mouth, she's so upset.

"Oh dear. Oh dear," Margaret is muttering.

"No, K . . . Koey! M . . . my t . . . toofpaste!"

"Maybe we should just take Thomas home. For tonight," Danny says quietly.

Chloe plants her hands on her hips. "Go home! Go home!"

I reach out to her, but she slaps my hands away. "No engine toothbrush! No toothpaste! My toothpaste! My sink!"

"Chloe!" I snap, looking her right in the eyes.

She bursts into a flood of tears. "No, no, no!"

She runs for her bed, to fling herself on it, I assume. Nope. She grabs Thomas's pillow and throws it at him. And hits him.

Thomas goes down with a cry. It couldn't possibly have hurt him. It's a pillow stuffed with little pieces of foam.

"Tommy!" Margaret runs for him.

"Chloe Mae Richards-Monroe," I say. "That's enough. Your behavior is inappropriate."

When I say *inappropriate*, that sets off another wave of tears, these born more of hurt than anger. We've been working on *inappropriate* for a long time. She knows "inappropriate" is bad. She doesn't want to disappoint me.

Margaret hovers over her son. "Tommy, are you all right?"

Danny walks over to his son. "He's all right."

Chloe is crying so hard that she's shaking. I pull her into my arms. "It's okay. It's okay," I soothe, stroking her hair, which has fallen from the beautiful curls my stylist created.

"My bathroom. My bathroom," she keeps saying.

"Get up," Danny tells his son. "Get off the floor."

Thomas gets on all fours and crawls toward the open closet door. He hunches behind it.

"Oh my goodness," Margaret mutters.

"Chloe." I press my hand to her face and make her look me in the eyes. "Thomas is supposed to sleep here tonight. Do you want him to sleep here, or do you want him to go home?"

"G . . . go h . . . home," Thomas blubbers from behind the closet door.

Danny's gaze meets mine. "We'll take him home. Bring him back tomorrow."

So my daughter's wedding ends in a bit of disaster, but I'm not disheartened. I'm committed. Chloe is wearing a thin white-gold wedding band to prove my commitment. And I'm not used to failure. So I let my son-in-law go home to his mom and dad's house and tell him to come back tomorrow.

I don't want him. I don't want him in my bathroom! I'm crying. I don't like crying. I'm not a baby head!

Mom says don't cry. She says Thomas can come back tomorrow. I told her good. But now I'm by myself in my room with my kitty.

I thought Thomas was going to sleep in my bed tonight. 'Cause we're married. He said if we were married his mom said he could touch my boobies.

I like when he touches my boobies. I don't like when he puts his toothbrush on my sink. His toothbrush is dirty. It will make my sink dirty.

Dummy Thomas Train toothbrush. Dummy head toothbrush!

I push my face in my pillow. I don't want to cry. But I'm sad. I'm sad and I don't know why I'm sad.

I liked my wedding when me and Thomas got married. He was cute. I was pretty. Like a princess. He whispered and told me when we were up there in the church that I was his baby. He said he was my honey.

I close my eyes because Mom told me to. She said not to worry. She said "go to sleep."

I decide I will go to sleep and Thomas can play with my boobies tomorrow. And we can watch *Beauty and the Beast*. But he can't put his toothbrush on my sink.

Tomorrow turns out to be a better day. Margaret and I agree to let the *kids* sleep in and we move brunch to eleven thirty, instead of ten. We all act as if nothing happened the night before and Chloe and Thomas are the happy couple at Friendly's. They hold hands and kiss often enough that Margaret and I both have to remind them about not kissing in public.

Thomas says good-bye to his parents after brunch, and he and Chloe ride home with me in the backseat of my car. By the time we get to the house, the caterers have been back, and like fairies, have cleaned up the mess and disappeared. My house looks as if the wedding never took place, except for the bridal bouquet in a vase in the middle of the coffee table in the living room, and the stack of bills in the kitchen drawer.

Once home, I do what every parent does when they're too tired to entertain their children. I turn on the TV and let them watch Disney movies all afternoon. We make dinner together: tacos, French fries, and mozzarella sticks, with leftover mini cheesecakes for dessert. Their menu choices. After dinner and cleanup, they go back into the living room to watch Animal Planet.

The phone rings while I'm pouring the last of a bottle of chardonnay into a wineglass. The caterers left a dozen opened wine bottles on the counter with their corks just stuck back in the neck. I feel obligated to drink some; it'll just go bad, won't it?

It's Margaret on the phone.

"Hi." I drop the empty wine bottle into the recycling bin.

"Hi! How are they?" she asks cheerily.

"Everything seems fine." I sit down on the bar stool. "No problems. Not even a hiccup. They've had dinner, and now they're watching something on TV on the secret life of cats. *Puppy Party* is coming on next."

"I knew they'd be fine. It was a long day yesterday."

"I appreciate your understanding." I sip my wine. "You know how Chloe can be. She really does love Thomas. I just think she was tired and . . ." I trail into silence. What else can I say? My daughter had a temper tantrum on her wedding night and sent her bridegroom packing.

"Well, I just wanted to check on Tommy!"

"Would you like to speak with him?" I hear the rumble of Danny's voice.

"Not tonight," Margaret says. "We'll talk in the morning!"

"Sounds good."

I'm checking out another open bottle of wine when I hear the front door open. I hear Jin's voice, then Chloe's, then footsteps.

"Aha," Jin says, coming into the kitchen. "Hitting the sauce."

I carry two corked bottles to the counter where I was sitting. "Get your own glass," I tell her.

"Or . . ." She grabs another bottle off the counter, pops the cork, and takes a swig out of it. "Mmm. California merlot. Nice."

I laugh and sit back down on my bar stool. I'm too tired to stand. "Abby gone?"

"Yup." Jin drops down on the bar stool beside me. "Some kind of legal brief due in the morning."

"And Huan made it safely back to school?"

"Yup."

I pour myself another third of a glass of wine, finishing off another bottle. It's another chardonnay. I look at her. "You good?"

Jin draws up one knee. She's smiling dreamily. "I'm good."

"Should I keep my mother-of-the-bride dress in the front of the closet?"

Another smile. "We're not there yet . . ."

"But?" I do the Jin brow thing.

"We'll see."

I nod. It's a good answer. I take another sip. "So, what's the fallout on my daughter's temper tantrum last night?"

Jin shrugs. "Not really any. The people who were still here

that late know Chloe. We love her. The wedding was beautiful, she was beautiful. It was a beautiful day. What's a little temper tantrum? We've all had them, or wish we had the guts to."

I nod.

"And Thomas's family?"

My turn to shrug. "They understand, of course. And things seem to be fine." I cock my head questioningly in the direction of the living room.

"Looked fine to me. They were all over each other when I came in." Jin flashes me a grin and I smile back at her, thankful she's here.

We finish off four partial bottles of wine and talk about stuff. I probably don't get more than a glass and a half, but eventually I start to feel sleepy. I check the clock. It's only nine-forty, but I don't want to let it get too late before I send Chloe and Thomas to bed. I don't want a repeat of the night before, and I know they both still have to be tired.

"You want to stick around?" I ask, taking my glass to the sink to rinse it out.

"You need me to?"

I think about it. "Nah. Little pink pill is missing from today's box. We're all good."

We walk out into the living room together. Jin tells Thomas and Chloe good night. It doesn't take much for me to get them to turn off the TV. To soften the transition, I have Thomas use the downstairs bathroom and put his pajamas on there. Chloe gets ready in her own bathroom. I escort Thomas to the bedroom door, in his red plaid wedding pajamas.

"Kitty in or kitty out?" I ask Chloe. It's a nightly question. Chloe likes her bedroom door closed. If she takes her cat to bed with her, it cries to get out in the middle of the night, waking my princess and annoying her. If the cat gets locked out, it wakes me up crying to get in.

Chloe's already in bed, in her nightgown, and she's all giggly. "Kitty out." She looks at Thomas. He's giggling, too. "Husband in!"

She really is funny, that girl of mine. "Good night," I call. I give Thomas a gentle nudge and close the door behind him.

I don't know what happened that night behind my daughter's bedroom door. I closed my door and put my earplugs in my ears.

But I can guess.

Christmas comes and Christmas goes. The first weeks of Chloe and Thomas's marriage are bumpy, but isn't any marriage that way? We're so busy with all the Yuletide hullabaloo, it's got to be hard to get into a routine, doesn't it?

Standing at Chloe's window now, my fingertips on the cold glass, I realize I was making excuses last winter. For Chloe and Thomas. For myself. I let myself live in Margaret's cheerful little world because it was comfortable there. Standing here now, I can see that the writing was on the wall. But just because I have a doctorate in comparative literature doesn't mean I always read the text correctly.

And, by then, I *so* wanted it to work out. We all did.

Thomas was happy to stay the first couple of nights. I knew very well it was because of the sex. I was diligent about checking on the birth control pills. I talked to Chloe and Thomas about the importance of them. I even showed him where they were in the little box on Chloe's sink, hoping that between the two of them, they could be sure she took one each day. Still, I breathed a sigh of relief when she had her period in January. It was awkward, explaining the whole thing to Thomas. I was annoyed that Margaret hadn't, but I felt as if I was now *his* parent, too, so I just sucked it up.

January was cold. Bitterly cold, with freezing winds and more snowfall than usual on the Chesapeake Bay. Mix freezing winds with a Victorian house and what do you get? Frozen water pipes. Broken water pipes.

Mark and I were already friends. We became better friends.

"I used some heat tape near the water pump. If it drops to a certain temperature under the house, the tape warms the pipes right up." He snaps his fingers. Which are red and look cold. We're standing at the back door.

"Come in." I wave him into the mudroom. I'm wearing jeans and a sweatshirt and my dirty hair is piled on top of my head because I had no water this morning to shower. Luckily, it's Sunday, so there's no school.

"I should let you get on with your day."

"Mark." I hold out my hand to take his coat.

He obediently hands it to me and leans down to unlace his boots. "Chloe and Thomas here?"

"Margaret is having them over for lunch after church." I hang his coat on a hook on the wall. "She'll bring them home sometime this afternoon. Whenever Chloe gets antsy. She used to like staying there, but now she's got it in her head that they have to be here all the time." I head into the kitchen and he follows. "I've got coffee. And quiche. Want some quiche?"

He makes a sound suggesting he won't eat.

"It's got mushrooms in it. And Swiss cheese," I explain, walking in my sheepskin slippers to the refrigerator. "No one here eats mushrooms and Swiss cheese but me."

"I love mushrooms."

"Exactly. And I can't eat it all." I pull the quiche out of the fridge.

Mark goes to the right cabinet and grabs himself a coffee mug. "Refill?"

I glance around for my cup as I pull the foil off the quiche dish. "Definitely. My cup." I point.

He pours coffee for both of us and even gets the milk out and adds some to my mug. "You're on your own on the sweetener," he tells me, taking one of the stools.

I smile. He's such a nice guy. I'm glad he's here. Not glad I had another broken pipe, but it's nice to see him. My life seems so hectic. As I anticipated, having Thomas here is stressful. I probably bring some of that on myself. But having Mark here, just having a cup of coffee together, makes me feel calmer. Better.

"So how's it going? Chloe and Thomas?"

It's on the tip of my tongue to give my usual reply, the one I use with colleagues, friends in the outer ring of my social circle, the friendly faces at LoGs. I meet his gaze. His damp hair is a little long around his ears, but it's not sloppy-looking. It's cute. And I like the way he looks at me when I'm talking. I like the way he listens.

I slide the cut slices of quiche onto two plates and pop one in the microwave. Then I turn to face him, reaching for a yellow packet in a container on the counter. "Okay."

He waits.

"About half the nights, Thomas asks to go home." I feel my cheeks get warm. "After they've been in bed awhile."

He nods, getting what I'm saying. It was just a theory at first, me thinking Thomas wanted to stay long enough for sex, but didn't want to sleep all night. But I've watched him set a pattern. It's not my imagination.

"This is a big adjustment. For everyone. Thomas's got to be homesick. Have you tried letting them stay at his parents'?"

I sigh, dumping the packet of white powder into my coffee. "Several times. Margaret even went out and bought a double bed for Thomas's old room. Chloe isn't going for it. She wants to sleep in her own bed. With her own sheets, her own pillows, her own bathroom. She wants to be here with me at night."

He sips his coffee. "But, being married? She happy with that decision?"

"Perfectly content. Nothing in her life has really changed for her other than the bed partner—she goes to Minnie's, we make tacos, she watches Disney movies. She just does it all with Thomas now."

"And how does she feel when he says he wants to go home?"

I hold my mug between my hands, savoring the warmth. The microwave beeps but I ignore it. I meet Mark's gaze. "She tells him to take his toothbrush."

"Things'll get better. They'll get easier."

I get his quiche out of the microwave. "Oh sure. Of course. We're in an adjustment period. It'll all work itself out." I grab a fork from the drawer. "It always does."

⚜ 21 ⚜

And sometimes it doesn't.

February brings a blizzard. Even though most students at Stone walk to class from dorms, the campus is closed and I have a weekend that stretches into five days. We lose water in the downstairs bathroom only, which has become Thomas's bathroom. We can deal. I call Mark to get on his calendar, but I insist he take care of his emergencies first. I know I have neighbors without any water at all until Mark comes to the rescue.

The city is slow to plow the roads because we're hit by two storms two days apart. They haven't cleared the snow from the first when the second hits. It's not that much: fourteen to sixteen inches, but our town isn't equipped for heavy snow. We have only two snowplows in the whole town and the county is too busy plowing the major roads to lend a hand.

The snow keeps Thomas from being able to go see his mom and dad. It's a bigger problem than him having to use Chloe's bathroom . . . or mine, depending on my daughter's mood. By day three, we're all cranky. When Jin saw the forecast, she hightailed it to Abby's and is snowed in there. So I'm stuck in the house, alone, with a grouchy newly married couple and a hundred boring papers to read and grade.

I'm trying to read a student's take on Jane Austen's hidden sexual content when I hear Chloe getting loud in the living room.

"*Aladdin!*"

"*C . . . Cars!*" Thomas shouts back.

"I said, *Aladdin!*"

I remove my reading glasses and walk out of the dining room, into the living room. "Hey, what's up?" I try to take on Margaret's cheery tone. I pull my sweater together tighter up at my throat. It's cold in the house even though the furnace is running as hard as it can.

Chloe is standing in front of the TV with both remote controls in her hands. She knows how to use only one of them. "I want to watch *Aladdin*." She thrusts out her lower lip. "He says no."

Thomas is wearing a hooded sweatshirt. He's got the hood up. He's also wearing wool slippers with pointy toes that his sister made and sent him for Christmas. Between the slippers and the conical hoodie, he looks like a giant elf.

"Whose turn is it to choose?"

"Mine," Chloe declares.

"M . . . mine, K . . . Koey. We . . . we watched s . . . stupid *S . . . Sleeping Beauty*. M . . . my turn."

I look at Chloe. She's putting on a little weight. I can see it in her face. It's my fault. Down syndrome people tend to get heavy if you're not vigilant; it's a combination of genetics and their general zeal for food. I've been letting Chloe and Thomas choose what to make for meals; they enjoy shopping and preparing them. It's something we can all do together. But Chloe's choices aren't all that healthful. I make a mental note to start buying more fruits and vegetables and working them into meals.

"Did you watch *Sleeping Beauty*?" I ask, knowing the answer. As soon as Thomas said it, I remember hearing it from the dining room. I know they're watching too much TV, but it's hard to come up with things for them to do independently. Especially in the winter. In a blizzard. And I can't be the cruise activities director all the time. I just can't.

Chloe doesn't respond. She just stares at the TV.

"Maybe you guys should do something else for a while. You could draw. Or make tissue roses. Your craft supplies are still on the kitchen table."

Chloe thrusts out her lower lip. "I wanna watch *Aladdin*."

Thomas stares at the floor. "I . . . I w . . . wanna g . . . go home."

Chloe marches to the couch and plops down. "He says that every time he gets mad!" She points at her husband. "He's a dummy head."

"Chloe, no name calling." I walk over to Thomas. "You can't go home today. The roads are too dangerous."

"He could walk," Chloe injects. "If he gets his boots."

I cut my eyes at her.

She looks down at the floor, knowing very well she shouldn't say things like that.

"Thomas, I'm sorry," I say quietly. I rub his shoulder. "We can't drive to your mom and dad's. The roads are closed and it's too far to walk. It's not really safe to walk on the roads, anyway. Not in bad weather like this."

"He could go on Wednesday," Chloe offers.

I exhale. Thomas is just staring at his big wool slippers. His eyes are teary.

"You miss your mom and dad?"

He nods.

"Would you like to call them?"

He thinks for a minute. "Dad . . . Dad s . . . says don't . . . call Mama. N . . . not all the days. He . . . he says I . . . I'm married. M . . . married m . . . men don't c . . . call their m . . . mama all the . . . the days."

His words break my heart. Thomas *is* a man. But as the mother of a mentally handicapped child, I also know he will always be Margaret's little boy.

"It's okay, Thomas." I give him a hug and he grabs me and

hugs me back. Hard. "You can talk to her if you want," I tell him. "We can call together."

"You can call Mom Margaret," Chloe throws in. "I can watch *Aladdin*."

"Chloe." I pull myself out of Thomas's arms. "You're not being very nice. You love Thomas. You have to be nice to him. We're nice to the people we love, right?"

"He's not nice to me." She tosses the remotes on the couch beside her.

Thomas stands in front of me, still looking dejected.

"Chloe, come tell Thomas you're sorry for being mean." I motion from her to him. "Give him a hug and make him feel better."

She hesitates, then slowly gets to her feet. Chloe has matured in so many ways in the last two years. But she can still be a little brat. I guess we all can.

"Sorry, Thomas," she mutters and throws her arms around him. She rests her cheek on his chest. "You want me to tell you a knock-knock joke?"

He shakes his head and lowers his cheek to her head.

"I'm sorry you're sad." She hesitates. "You wanna go in my room and close the door and—"

"I think maybe it would be fun to make tissue roses," I interrupt. I want to laugh. Maybe cry. It never occurred to me that my daughter would be such a sex fiend. That two mentally handicapped people would be so sexual. What kind of dummy head am I? When Randall and I were first together, when we first started having sex, we certainly would have taken the opportunity on a snowy Wednesday afternoon.

"You wanna make roses?" Chloe asks Thomas.

He nods.

I stand there, arms crossed over my chest, watching them. "Then maybe you can watch *Cars* later."

"You wanna make roses with us?" Chloe asks me.

I glance in the direction of my piles of term papers waiting to be read, then back at my daughter. "Sure. But I want to make the pink ones."

Chloe's twenty-eighth birthday comes and goes in March and by April, we begin to feel the warmth of the sun again, bringing with it the promise of summer. Thomas is still homesick and I'm at a loss as to what to do. Margaret and Danny have their own problems. Danny loses his job at the plant the first week of April and has to go on unemployment. The Eldens are struggling to make their mortgage. As planned, because I have taken on Thomas's day-to-day expenses: food, clothing, spending money, and of course the increase in my electric and water bill, Margaret gives me a check each month, money he receives from Social Security. But that's not enough to cover Thomas's days at Minnie's; daycare for mentally handicapped adults isn't cheap. Especially not a private facility like Minnie's. All this time, Margaret and Danny have been supplementing Thomas's income with their own, so he could attend Minnie's.

Margaret and I have lunch at the same Mexican restaurant where we lunched a year ago. She proposes that Thomas and Chloe start coming to her house every day instead of Minnie's. I don't like the idea of taking Chloe out of Minnie's. She's done so well there. She loves Minnie's. Of course, will she love it without Thomas?

In the end, I make the decision that Chloe will continue to go to Minnie's four days a week, two of which Thomas will accompany her. One day a week, she'll go to Margaret's with Thomas. Thomas will be with his mother three days a week, meaning Chloe and Thomas will be separated two days a week. I know Margaret isn't pleased with my decision. She brings up the fact that I would save money by letting Chloe go to her house more often. Her big problem with the new arrangement is that Thomas and Chloe will be separated two days a week. The way they've been fighting, I think it would be good for them. What young husband and wife spend seven days a week, twenty-four hours a day together?

Around the same time, Randall starts postponing, then cancelling his Chick-fil-A nights with Chloe. He never comes out and says so, but I think he's uncomfortable with Thomas. I'm too busy to get that annoyed with him. Chloe and Thomas just stay with Margaret through dinner on Tuesdays. Honestly, I don't think Chloe misses her dad; she certainly misses the chicken and fries.

When it gets warmer, I encourage Chloe and Thomas to go outside and get some exercise. I'm worried about her weight gain and wonder if I should take her to our doctor. But I can see why she's gaining weight. It's the French fries, mozzarella sticks, and all that pasta she eats with my healthy, homemade marinara.

So, we take walks around the block. Then I even let them walk around the block alone, as long as they check with me before they go and as soon as they get back. I get them a soccer ball and teach them the basics of the game . . . which I played a million years ago, and never well. They're not interested in trying to kick the ball into the goal I bought at Target, but they like kicking the ball back and forth.

One afternoon, in late April, Chloe begs me to come play soccer with them. Jin and Abby are in the backyard weeding an herb bed. It's a fun afternoon. Thomas gets sulky (he hates physical activity even more than Chloe) and ends up plunking down on Jin's back step, but Chloe and I kick the ball back and forth and laugh and fall in the grass. Jin goes into the house and comes back out with her good camera and takes pictures. Some are action shots; we mug for others. She prints them on her printer and brings them to me the next evening. I give most of them to Chloe, but there's one of the two of us, arms around each other. We're both laughing. Our hair is a mess and there are bits of grass clinging to our sweatpants. Chloe looks so happy. I put the picture on our refrigerator with a Stone University magnet and every day, when I get my milk for my coffee, I look at the picture and it makes me smile. I like it even better than the wedding pictures on the wall by the staircase. In the soccer pictures, Chloe's smile is genuine, not posed. She looks so happy. She *was* so happy that day.

My encouragement of Thomas and Chloe to get outside more leads to the *puppy incident*. Looking back, now, I think that was the beginning of the end. If I'd only known . . . no, I couldn't have done anything differently. Sadly, for all of us, I wouldn't have. A mother does what she thinks is best. I did what I thought was best for all of us.

Margaret had brought Thomas and Chloe home from Minnie's. It was a Wednesday. They stayed outside to look for toads, of all things. Margaret and I were talking in the front hall. She looked tired, and her voice didn't have the cheerfulness I've grown used to.

"So, still no luck on the job front?"

Margaret shakes her head. "He interviewed twice last week. But there are so many people looking for jobs. Just not enough jobs to go around."

I knew that Danny did something in the tool-and-die industry, but honestly, I didn't know what. "It's only been a few months," I say. "I'm sure something will come up."

"Lord willing," she agrees, raising her hand heavenward. "But Danny's having to go further afield." She shakes her head.

I want to ask her what that means, but Chloe bursts into the vestibule and presses her face to the window in our door. "Mom! Mom! Mom Margaret! Come quick!"

I can tell by her voice that she's excited, not scared. No one is hurt.

I wave for her to come in.

She shakes her head. "Come quick! Come see! We got a puppy!"

I meet Margaret's gaze and open the door. Chloe is already bounding across the vestibule and down the front steps. She leads us around to the backyard. There's an empty lot behind us and to the right. I see Thomas sitting in the grass in the lot, a puppy in his lap.

He spots us and waves. "M . . . Mama! I . . . I got m . . . me a p . . . puppy dog!"

"Oh my. Oh my goodness," Margaret exclaims.

The three of us trek across the yard, through the higher grass in the empty lot. The brown puppy in Thomas's lap is jumping up and down and licking his face and running around him and under his legs and over his lap.

Chloe jumps up and down and claps her hands. "I got Thomas a puppy!"

I look around in search of the answer to the most obvious question. One that would never occur to Chloe or Thomas to ask. I don't see any neighbors in their yards. No cars moving. It's only four thirty. Most people aren't home from work yet. As I get closer to Thomas and the puppy, I see that it's a little pit bull. Possibly a mix, but most definitely from the pit bull gene pool. I sigh. There was an article in the paper a few weeks ago about the number of people breeding pit bulls, people with no knowledge of breeding nor the financial means to care for the litters of dogs. The poor puppy is skinny and I see what looks like an abscess on its haunch. I get a sick feeling in the pit of my stomach.

"Do you know whose dog this is, Chloe?"

"Thomas's puppy." She grins.

"It's so cute," Margaret coos. "Such a cute puppy, Tommy." She leans over and scratches it behind its ear.

I glance around again. "It's not Thomas's puppy, hon. It belongs to someone. You can't take someone else's puppy."

"I w . . . want a p . . . puppy dog! This is *my* p . . . puppy d . . . dog," Thomas insists.

I look at Margaret, hoping for a little help here. She's busy petting the dog. Chloe joins them.

I stifle my impulse to tell Chloe not to touch the puppy. Not with an open sore like that. I have no doubt that those black dots on its back are fleas. "Where did you find him?"

"We found a dog here," Chloe says. "Thomas's puppy dog."

I spot Mark's white panel van coming down the street. I head for his driveway. He must see me, because he gets out and waits.

"Hey," he calls.

"Hey. You're home early."

"I just came back to get something. That new construction on Sycamore is running me ragged. Four baths."

"Big house." I glance in the direction of the empty lot. Thomas is now on his feet. He's running back and forth, getting the puppy to chase him. "Thomas found a puppy."

Mark groans.

"You know whose it is? Looks like a little pit bull."

"Jack, next door, called animal control yesterday. He said he thought someone dumped it. I saw the animal control van this morning. I guess they couldn't find it."

My turn to groan. "Thomas thinks it's *his* puppy."

Mark looks at me questioningly.

"I'm not having a dog." I raise both hands. "I just can't do it. And if I was, it wouldn't be a pit bull. Chloe's cat is ten years old. The dog would eat her."

"I hear pit bulls have gotten a bad rap. They can be very sweet dogs, apparently."

I look at him. "You want a pit bull?"

He laughs. "No thanks. Got one. Her name is Jennifer."

His ex-wife. I've met her. She's every bit as pleasant as he suggests. I sigh, hands on my hips. We both just stand there, watching Thomas run with the puppy. Now Chloe has joined in.

"This is the happiest I've seen him in weeks," I say.

"And now you're going to take his puppy away."

"Now I'm going to take his puppy away." I head back toward the lot. "Thanks."

"You bet," Mark calls after me. "If you need me to take the dog to the SPCA, just let me know."

I go back and stand next to Margaret and watch the kids play with the dog. "I can't have a pit bull in the house," I say quietly. "I don't want a dog. I . . . I really can't deal with a dog right now. A puppy is a lot of responsibility. House-training it, walking it."

"You don't think Tommy could take care of it?"

I can tell by Margaret's tone that she knows the answer, she just wishes she didn't.

I want to say, "Margaret, your son is wetting his pants, still, so I don't think he can handle the care of a puppy right now." But I feel like such an ogre already. "I just can't do it, Margaret," I say, instead. I look over at her. "You and Danny?"

She shakes her head. "Danny's allergic. We had Fritz back in Ohio and Danny was constantly sneezing. We're really not in a position."

I nod. "Mark says his neighbor called animal control. Someone who didn't want it must have dropped it off. The kids probably shouldn't be handling it."

"Fleas."

Or worse, I think. "Mark offered to take it to the SPCA. It's a no-kill." I look at her. "Someone will adopt it, I'm sure. He'll go to a good home."

Margaret just stands there, watching her son.

"You want me to talk to him?" I ask.

She shakes her head. "No, I'll do it."

"How about if Chloe and I go into the house and give you and Thomas a minute?"

She nods.

"Chloe!" I call. I wave to her. "Come on, let's go inside."

"I want to play with Thomas's puppy!"

I grab her hand and lead her back toward our house. "Thomas can't keep the puppy, Chloe. We've talked about this. No dog."

She keeps looking over her shoulder. "But Thomas wants a dog."

"I understand. But he can't take care of a dog."

"I can take care of a dog." She hurries to keep up with me. "I'm smart. I take care of Kitty. I feed her and brush her."

"You do take care of your cat. But a dog is a lot of work and that's going to be a very big dog, Chloe." We go in the back door.

"Thomas wants a puppy dog," Chloe repeats. "He's gonna be mad and be a crybaby." She gets milk and the chocolate syrup out of the refrigerator. "He's a big crybaby. He cries because he wants his mom. I don't cry because I want my mom."

I turn to her, watching her get a glass. "Go easy on the chocolate. What if you didn't live here, Chloe? Would you miss me? Would you cry then?"

"Thomas says I can go live with him and his mom and his dad when they go to Hi-O." She pours milk.

"When they go to Ohio? Are the Eldens going to Ohio for a visit?"

She shrugs and squirts a long stream of chocolate into her milk with one hand and stirs with a spoon with the other. "I told Thomas no. He's my honey. I'm his baby, but I don't like Hi-O." She continues to add chocolate to her milk. "I'm staying here with my mom. That's what I said." She takes a big slurp. "I told him he could go to Hi-O."

~ 22 ~

Thomas is inconsolable after I send the puppy off to the SPCA. I know Margaret understands, but I still feel guilty whenever we talk about it. I'm the one who suggests, after two days of constant tears, that Thomas might like to spend the night at home. Chloe agrees to go, then changes her mind at the last minute and refuses to. Thomas goes alone.

I don't ask Margaret or Thomas about Chloe's comment about Ohio. I can't imagine Margaret would think she could take my Chloe with her back to Ohio to live. Chloe obviously had the story wrong. What I suspect is that Danny is searching for a job closer and closer to their old hometown and if he finds one, decisions will have to be made. Someone was probably just feeling Thomas out and he and Chloe got the story wrong. I can't imagine how hard it will be for Thomas to have his parents living a day's drive away, if his father gets a job in Ohio, but I tell myself we can deal.

The thought that I have to just "deal" is going through my head two weeks later while I walk down the aisle at the grocery store. It's late April. April showers have hit hard. We're all in rain slickers: Thomas in yellow, me in green, Chloe in light blue. We're trudging down the aisles, going over what we might need at home. I know a list would be easier. Sometimes I make a list. But today, we don't need all that much. We're just killing time until we can go home and start dinner.

"Do we need coffee?"

"Nope," Chloe says.

"Tea?"

"Nope."

"Hot chocolate?"

"Yes!" Chloe cheers as if she's just hit bingo. "For my red cup."

"For your yellow cup?" We don't have any red cups. "Sure." I look at Thomas. "What do you think, Thomas?" I say, trying to draw him in. I feel so bad for him. I wish I knew how to help him. Margaret keeps talking about time to adjust. What if this is the adjustment? "Are we out of hot chocolate?"

He's pushing the cart, but without much enthusiasm.

"And marshmallows! Marshmallows!" Chloe cheers.

I glance at my already chubby daughter, who is still putting on weight. "Let's skip the marshmallows," I suggest. Sadly, Thomas looks like he could use a bag of marshmallows. His weight has been dropping since January. Last week, we had to buy him three new pairs of sweatpants. He's gone from XXL tall to just an XL tall. Margaret keeps patting his stomach and saying that married life agrees with him. I'm beginning to fear he's suffering from depression.

We make the turn into the next aisle. "Shaving cream, Thomas is still good. Toothpaste good. Mouthwash good," I say, thinking out loud.

Chloe drops back and is trying to help Thomas push the cart. He apparently doesn't want help.

"No pushing, ladies and gentlemen," I say, not paying much attention to them. The grocery store isn't busy; they're not bothering anyone.

"No pushing, ladies and gentlemen," Chloe repeats.

I stop in front of the feminine hygiene products. I think for a second. We haven't been here in months. I don't need the stuff anymore, and Chloe's on a three-month cycle. Two weeks ago, she took light blue pills for a week. Then she went back on the pink pills.

I look at Chloe. "You need tampons, hon? For next time?"

She's taken over the cart-pushing. Thomas is trailing behind. He looks scruffy. He needs a haircut. His mom cuts it for him. I make a mental note to remember to say something to her tomorrow.

"Chloe?"

"Nope. Marshmallows. I need marshmallows."

"No one *needs* marshmallows." I lower my voice, waiting for her to catch up. "You didn't use the whole box under your sink?"

"Nope." She pushes past me.

"But you *had* your period?" I ask.

She shrugs. "And Cheerios. Thomas wants Cheerios. And Cap'n Crunch." She reaches the end of the aisle and starts to make the turn. It's going to be wide. Thomas follows her.

I stare at the pink boxes and bags for a minute. I feel a flutter in my chest. A slight buzzing in my head. Then I realize I'm being paranoid. Chloe's never been good at remembering details. She couldn't always answer the question when her periods were monthly. I try to remember what's gone out in the trash, but Chloe and Thomas empty their own trash cans. It's one of the chores on a chart on the refrigerator. They always get stars in that category. And I never look into Chloe's drawers or under the sink. That's her personal territory. I just check the pillbox.

I make myself think about other things as we finish our shopping. Randall asked me this morning at a staff meeting, in front of everyone, if I was interested in taking a group of students to London for five weeks for a playwrights' seminar this summer. I wondered where he thought Chloe and Thomas were going to go. He knows Chloe won't spend even the night at the Eldens'. Maybe he was going to offer to stay with Chloe and Thomas at my house for five weeks? Take them to his town house? Not likely, since he can't seem to fit a trip to Chick-fil-A into his schedule. Or maybe he just thought I could tuck the two of them into my pockets and carry them to London with me? He took me completely off guard in the meeting. I said something to the effect that I didn't anticipate having that kind of time in my summer, but what I wanted to ask, in front of my colleagues, was if he had lost his *effing* mind.

Once we're home, I take my time overseeing the unloading of the groceries before I slip upstairs. I can hear Chloe's voice as I go into her bedroom, but I can't hear what she's saying. Thomas isn't talking; most of the time, she talks enough for both of them.

I check the pillbox first. Today's chewable vitamin and little pink pill are gone. I take a breath and open the door under the sink. I spot the big pink box. I feel a flood of relief as I see that the top has been ripped open. I specifically remember buying the box at Target in December; there was wrapping paper in the cart. Cars and trucks for Thomas, princesses for Chloe.

I grab the box and my heart sinks. It's open, but looks full. I count, then count again. Thirty-three little pink packages. The box holds thirty-five.

My hand is shaking when I quietly close the cabinet under Chloe's sink. I know this doesn't mean she's pregnant. There are several explanations. The doctor at the clinic made it clear that Chloe's cycle could change. Or . . . she probably had an open box already. Or maybe I bought two boxes that day. Maybe I overestimated how many she'd need in January and then again in April.

Besides, the doctor said there was little chance she could conceive. It said the same thing on the Internet.

So what do I do now? I think as I go down the hall.

I do what any rational woman would do. I call my best friend. Jin is in class. I have to call twice to get her to pick up. I give her a brief description of my terror and she promises to come right over, as soon as she dismisses her class.

I act like nothing is wrong. I help Chloe cut up chicken breasts for stir-fry for dinner. I cajole Thomas into washing broccoli and carrots and fresh snap peas. The stir-fry is on the table, Chloe is putting rice on our plates when I hear the front door open. I rush out into the living room.

"You're okay," Jin says calmly. She's wearing a bright patent-red raincoat and crazy red and yellow rubber boots.

"I'm not okay."

"You ask her any more questions?"

I shake my head. "She doesn't know. She wouldn't know. I won't trust her no matter what she says. You know how she is. She'll say what she thinks I want to hear."

Jin smiles at me and presses her palm to my cheek. "We're going to be okay. No matter what."

"You think she's pregnant," I groan. I feel weak-kneed.

"I do not."

"But you brought them?"

"I brought them." She clutches her shoulder bag to her chest. "A three-pack. Drugstore, not the dollar store, as requested."

"Dinner!" Chloe shouts from the kitchen.

I look over my shoulder, then back at Jin. "Think I can ask her to pee now?"

She exhales. "Sure. Otherwise, you won't be able to eat, will you?"

I shake my head.

Turns out, I don't eat anyway. I can't.

The plus sign comes up on the pink stick. Then a second time. I couldn't get Chloe to pee a third time. She said she was all out of pee. What was the point? I can read a pregnancy test. This one and the one in the trash can are both positive.

I sit on Chloe's bed, looking at the stick in my hand and thinking I'm going to throw up. Jin sits beside me, her arm brushing mine.

Chloe is standing in the middle of her bedroom. "Can I go eat? Thomas is going to eat all the chicken."

Thomas has been downstairs through all this.

I look up at her, my eyes brimming with tears. She doesn't understand the significance of peeing on a stick. She doesn't understand what the plus sign means. She won't understand when I tell her she's going to have a baby. Not really.

"Mom?"

Jin looks at her. "Go on downstairs, Chlo-Bo. Have your dinner. We'll be down in a minute."

Tears slip down my cheeks as my precious daughter waddles out of the room. She was gaining weight because she was eating too much. She was definitely eating too much. But she was also, apparently, gaining weight because she was pregnant.

"So, how pregnant do you think she is?" Jin asks me gently.

"She had her period in mid-January. I'm positive of that."

"So somewhere between a few weeks and three months?"

I shake my head. "How is this possible? How is this *even* possible? Chloe took the pills. I made sure she took the pills. I checked. Every day. Almost every day." Then I think, *What if I missed a day? What if this is my fault? What if I didn't do enough to protect my daughter?*

"Maybe the pregnancy isn't viable," Jin suggests quietly. "You said before, from what you read, that Down syndrome women can't always carry a pregnancy to full term."

I close my eyes. "How am I going to tell her? How am I going to make her understand?"

Jin takes my hand in hers. "First things first, she needs to go see an OB."

"I'm not taking her back to Dr. Ellington. He was a jerk. And I don't think she should go to the clinic. Not for this."

"So I'll call my GYN. She's a sweetheart. She'll run a blood test. Do an exam. We'll know more then."

I feel like my head is going to explode. "What am I going to do, Jin? What if she carries the baby to term?"

Jin squeezes my hand. "Then we're going to have a baby. And

we're going to love him or her, no matter what the disabilities are."

I so appreciate the fact that she doesn't bring up the possibility of termination. She knows how I feel, and whether she agrees with me or not, she doesn't bring it up. I open my eyes and meet Jin's dark-eyed gaze. "We're going to have a baby," I whisper.

Me and Thomas sit on my bed. We lean on the pillows and put our feet on my quilt. No shoes. I tell him all the time, no shoes on my bed.

He's being sulking. That's what Mom says when I'm mad because I don't get what I want. He *bees* sulking all the time.

Mom and Dad and Mom Margaret and Mr. Danny are downstairs in the living room. They're talking. For a long time. Mom keeps having wet eyes. I think she's sad about me. About that I peed on the stick. But she told me to.

I look at Thomas. "You wanna color?"

He shakes his head.

I look around in my room. It's pretty. Not as pretty like before because there's dummy head boy stuff, but the blue walls are pretty. I like blue walls. "We could watch a movie. On my DVD thing. We could watch *Hercules* if you want. You like *Hercules*."

He doesn't say anything, and that makes me mad. He used to say things to me. He doesn't like me anymore. I don't know why. I still like him. But not as much, maybe. "Wanna tell me a knock-knock joke? I'll laugh at you even if I don't understand."

He shakes his head.

"Are you mad?" I ask him. I take one of the pillows and hold it on my lap.

He just sits there on my bed and looks at the air.

"Are you mad because I got a baby in my belly?" I went to the doctor today. A lady doctor. A different lady doctor. She said there's a little baby in my belly.

"Y . . . you s . . . said when . . . when I m . . . moved here, w . . . we would get a p . . . puppy."

"I didn't say that! You said that!" He's making me madder. But I don't want him to look sad. "Babies are better," I tell him. "You can change the diaper."

"I . . . I don't . . . don't w . . . want a b . . . baby. I w . . . want a p . . . puppy."

I cross my arms over my chest. "I wasn't supposed to get a baby. Them pills are no baby pills. Boys put babies in girls."

"I . . . I ate the pills," he says.

I flop back on the bed and put the pillow on my face. "And we still got a baby."

"I think we take this for what it is, one of God's blessings," Margaret says.

I meet Randall's gaze across the coffee table. "What's done is done."

Danny says nothing. He looks thinner than when I first met him. Grayer. He says he has a couple of leads on jobs. I haven't asked where. It's been a week since Chloe took the first pregnancy test. She saw the OB/GYN this morning. Because of the special circumstances, meaning her handicap, they fit her in.

"Okay," I say, clasping my hands. "So . . . we've seen the doctor. She's just four weeks along." I assumed, from the weight gain, that she was further along, but that's neither here nor there.

Dr. Alvarez agrees that it was very unusual for a couple like Chloe and Thomas to conceive, but obviously possible. I tried to get her to explain how Chloe could have gotten pregnant taking the pill. She was very kind about it. Patient with me. She said I should try not to worry about it, at this point. A single pill dropped on the floor instead of taken, though rare, could result in a pregnancy. And the truth is, she explained gently, that the pill is still only 98 percent effective, when taken as prescribed. She *did* agree that we needed to talk about a safer form of birth control for Chloe, after the birth, but said there was plenty of time for that.

I liked Dr. Alvarez. I felt confident in her ability and relieved that Jin had found her for us. At least I wouldn't be worrying about Chloe's health during the pregnancy. At least not too much.

"A January baby!" Margaret exclaims.

I try not to be angry with her. She's very excited by the prospect of a baby. Of course, my guess is that she won't be the one up in the middle of the night with an infant . . . and neither will her son. Neither will my daughter, for that matter.

Randall clears his throat. The Eldens make him uncomfortable. I don't know if it's just because they're different from his circle of friends and acquaintances, or if it's something to do with the fact that their son has sex with his daughter. I had to threaten to tell the department he was going to be a grandfather to get him here tonight. "Chloe's health insurance is good, through the university, so at least we don't have to worry about that."

"Any more tea, anyone?" I indicate the teapot in the middle of the coffee table. There are cookies, too. Peanut butter, that Thomas and Chloe made all by themselves. Slice and bake. Thomas has learned to man the timer and is pretty darn good at it, although he has to stand there and watch it. "Thoughts? Questions? Concerns?"

No one takes more tea. Nor does anyone address the obvious: testing for mental disabilities. I know we all have to be thinking about it. How can we *not*? Obviously, the decision has been made that Chloe and Thomas will be having this baby, but that doesn't mean we don't want information.

I look at the three of them. Randall is sitting beside me on one of the couches; Danny and Margaret are sitting across from us. Everyone is obviously uncomfortable. I plow forward. If they're already uncomfortable, does it really matter what else I say?

"Dr. Alvarez says she'll run a series of blood tests around fourteen weeks. To look for possible genetic anomalies . . . like Down Syndrome."

"Is that necessary?" Danny asks. It's the first time he's initiated the conversation since they arrived. "I mean. We're keeping the baby. If the baby has Down's, we don't really care, do we?"

"She'll test for other things too: sickle cell, cystic fibrosis. There will also be routine ultrasounds to follow the formation of bones, the heart, that sort of thing. It's to give the OB and the pediatrician a heads-up, as much as anything."

"Thomas was a healthy baby." Margaret nibbles on a cookie. "And such a happy boy."

Randall looks at his wristwatch. "Well, I think we've covered everything here." He gets up. He hasn't touched his tea. "If you'll excuse me, I have an evening meeting to attend at the university."

He lets himself out without calling upstairs to say good-bye to Chloe. I look at my teacup and wonder if the Eldens partake, because I could use a hit of whiskey in my Earl Grey right now.

"So!" Margaret says, clasping her hands together. "We're going to have a baby!"

✆ 23 ✇

Chloe's pregnancy progresses uneventfully. Unlike the rest of our lives. Thomas becomes increasingly despondent. He misses his parents, his home, and his bed. Chloe just isn't enough for him. I'm not enough.

At my insistence, Margaret and I and Chloe and Thomas go to several sessions with Dr. Tamara for family counseling. He's not much help. He gives us *homework* and family-building *exercises*; he talks about the difficulties of any new marriage. But Thomas is uncooperative. The sad fact is (but no one wants to say it), Thomas thought he wanted to marry and live with Chloe and he doesn't. Thomas doesn't like change. He wants his mother. He wants things to be the way they always were, and not even the excitement of sex with my daughter is enough to make up for not being in his parents' home, in his own bed, with his own familiar possessions around him. The truth is that Thomas remains more child than man. I think he always will.

Margaret is beside herself. She wants so badly for this to work. We all do, at this point. She tries, but like me, she's at a loss as to what to do to help the unhappy couple. The thing that's hardest for me is that Chloe isn't all that unhappy. She's only unhappy when Thomas is. But out-of-sight, out-of-mind. Chloe doesn't protest anymore when Thomas wants to go home. She doesn't like the changes that have taken place in her life because of the marriage, either. She helps him pack his bag. Maybe, like me, she secretly sighs a breath of relief when he goes overnight to stay with his parents. I've come to love Thomas, I truly have, but the fact remains that it's hard to have him here with us all the time. Like Chloe, it can be mentally and physically challenging to take care of him day after day. And sometimes it's nice to have a break.

Chloe begins to show, even in her chubby state, by twenty weeks. I take off the whole summer, no classes, even though we could use the extra income with the coming baby. I try to do things with Thomas and Chloe that I think he'll like. I can occasionally get him to laugh or smile, but he's most happy when I pull up at his parents' house to let him out.

Thomas starts spending a few nights a week with his mom and dad, on a regular basis. Chloe flat-out refuses to stay overnight with them. She can't be reasoned with, coaxed, or bribed. If I try to make her stay with her husband at the Eldens', she throws a temper tantrum. Margaret doesn't know how to deal with her. Twice in the last month, Chloe and Thomas have gone to the Eldens', or somewhere with the Eldens, and Margaret has called me to come get her early.

On an August evening, Chloe goes up to bed after dinner to watch TV and rest her swollen feet and I'm left to do the dishes alone. Thomas has been with his mother for three days.

Mark taps on the back door about the time that Jin is walking in the front.

"I got those screens for the faucets." Mark stands in my doorway and jiggles a little paper bag in front of me. "I was in the neighborhood, so . . ."

I chuckle. I'm glad he's here. He's become a good friend, and I can use as many as I can get these days. The more pregnant Chloe becomes, the more scared I become. How am I going to do this? I'm fifty-three years old. How am I going to care for a newborn? A toddler? How am I going to take care of a baby, and Chloe and Thomas?

The prenatal screening blood tests have all come back negative. The baby doesn't have Down syndrome, which I think scares me more than if that blood test had just come back positive. I know how to deal with Trisomy 21. Thomas's type of retardation is harder for me; I guess just because I'm not as familiar with it. Jin keeps reminding me that the chances the baby will be handicapped are only 50 to 70 percent. Which means there's a 30 to 50 percent chance, maybe even higher since the baby doesn't have Down's, that the baby will be of average intelligence. I remind her regularly of the odds Chloe could have even gotten pregnant in the first place. Obviously the odds are against me.

"Iced tea or booze?" I ask Mark as we walk into the kitchen. Jin is already there, opening a bottle of wine.

"Gotta beer?" he asks, taking a stool at the counter.

"One beer, coming up." Jin grabs one out of the refrigerator and slides the unopened bottle across the granite countertop toward him. They're actually his beers, that he put there a few days ago. "Ally?"

"Let me finish loading the dishwasher and then I'll decide."

"Thomas back?" Jin pours herself a glass of shiraz.

"One more night, Margaret said. She called just before dinner. Chloe had made him hot dogs. We thought he was coming home."

Mark frowns as he opens his beer. "Chloe upset?"

"Not really." I think about it. "A little bit. I think she's hurt that he wanted to spend every waking moment with her in the beginning, and now . . . he doesn't. Of course she was also upset that I didn't let her eat his hot dogs."

Mark takes a sip of his beer. Nods with empathy.

Jin slides onto a stool. I'm on the other side of the counter, loading the last of the dirty dishes. I'm still debating whether I want the caffeine-free brewed iced tea or wine when the phone rings. I check the display before I pick up. It's Margaret. I wonder if Thomas has changed his mind and wants to sleep with his wife tonight. I haven't had anything to drink. If Jin can stay here with Chloe, I can run over and get him and save Margaret the gas. I know she worries about the money she spends driving him back and forth.

"Margaret?" I'm actually happy to hear from her. She's become part of my family, crazy skirts, T-shirts and all.

"Alicia! You're not going to believe the good news! Danny got a job!"

"Oh, Margaret, that's wonderful news. I know you're relieved. Please tell him congratulations for me."

"It is wonderful news, isn't it? The only downside is that it's in Canton," she bubbled on. "But our daughter Ruthie lives in Canton and it won't be a problem at all for him to stay there during the week."

Canton. *As in Ohio.* All I can think of is that Margaret and Danny are going to move away and leave Thomas with me to deal with on an everyday basis. "So . . ." I pace the kitchen. Jin and Mark watch me. "So, Danny will be in Ohio during the week—"

"And home on weekends!"

That doesn't sound realistic to me, but Margaret sounds so excited that I'm excited for her. And they'll work it out, won't they? I know that, in the present economy, there are plenty of families who live in less-than-ideal situations. They make it work. Danny and Margaret will make it work.

"Is Chloe available?" Margaret sings in my ear. "Thomas wants to tell her the good news."

"Hang on just a minute." I take the phone upstairs, knock on Chloe's door, and go in. She's lying on top of her bedspread on her side, a fan blowing directly on her. She's hot all the time now. No matter how low I set the thermostat on the central air. She's watching a movie: *101 Dalmatians*.

"Phone's for you, hon." I look at my daughter's pregnant belly, pushing against her kitty and balls of yarn T-shirt. She's going to have to go into maternity shirts soon. Luckily, her shorts have stretchy waistbands and she's just wearing them under her belly.

Chloe looks up. Cruella de Vil is singing. It's the Glenn Close version and not animated—a pretty wild step outside Chloe's box.

"It's Thomas." I bring the phone to my ear. "Here she is."

"K . . . Koey!" I hear as I pass her the phone.

"Thomas, honey," she says.

The tone of her voice makes me smile to myself. Neither Thomas nor Chloe have had much to say about the fact that they're going to have a baby. They just don't understand the impact it will have on their lives, on all our lives. But I can hear in their voices that they really do care about each other.

Maybe they're going to be okay. Maybe we're all going to be okay. Maybe I'm going to take to parenting this new baby, my grandchild, in ways I was never able to parent Chloe. A part of me is excited about the second chance. Now that I've had some time to get used to the idea. The first time I let too many people, too many things, influence me: Randall, my mother's death, Chloe's disability, the way people looked at me in the grocery store. I truly do feel that, with age, has come wisdom. It's not that I have any big regrets. But don't all parents, with adult children, sometimes wish they could rewind their lives?

I leave Chloe alone to talk to her husband. Downstairs, someone has finished the dishes for me. And poured me a glass of wine.

I lean against the counter and sip my wine. We're all quiet for a minute. It's nice to have friends that you can sit with in silence and not feel uncomfortable.

"So, Danny got a job," Jin says after a while.

I nod. "Canton."

Mark sips his beer. Takes his time. I like that he can do that. He isn't like me. He doesn't have to react to things immediately. "They moving, Danny and Margaret?"

"She says not." The wine is good. I pick pretty bottles, but Jin picks wine that tastes better.

Jin reaches across the counter and covers my hand with hers. "It's going to be fine."

Mark just sips his beer.

The days continue to fly by on my iCal. I measure their passing by the ever-increasing girth of my daughter's belly. She's a good sport about the whole thing. She tries to eat healthier and she's willing to gag down the enormous prenatal vitamins her OB has prescribed. I question her extensively about taking the little pink pills, because it still bugs me, but she never cracks.

"I ate them so I didn't get a baby" is all she ever says.

Just the same, I decide I'll dole out the prenatal vitamins myself. When Thomas is here, which turns into only three or four days a week, he gets a vitamin, too, because he insists he needs one to make the baby strong. It's easier than arguing with him, and multivitamins are cheap enough at the drugstore.

Danny starts his job in Ohio in late August. Jin and Abby make plans to move in together in September. Thomas continues to be unhappy at our house, but not any unhappier than he's been in months. I keep telling myself that things are going to change, that Thomas is going to get used to the new living arrangements.

Then he gets sick the first week of October. His cough is awful, his nose is running, and he runs a fever. It's a virus, according to his doctor. There's nothing to do but keep the fever down and let it run its course.

When Margaret suggests he come home to recuperate, I don't argue. At seven months pregnant, Chloe is robustly healthy. Pregnancy seems to agree with her: no morning sickness, no heartburn. Her doctor's only concern is an occasional elevation in her blood pressure. As healthy as she is, there's no need to risk having Chloe get sick. Sharing the same bed, not being extra careful with hygiene; it just makes sense for Thomas to go and Chloe to stay. I know Margaret is lonely, anyway. Danny can't come home every weekend, as they had anticipated; it's an eight-hour drive. But he likes his new job, and I know that Margaret is relieved not to be so worried about money.

We start buying things for the baby; we've chosen not to know its sex. I buy a crib that matches Chloe's bed. There are only two bedrooms upstairs because we made the third a laundry room, and the baby is certainly not sleeping with me. (At least I hope not.) Margaret gets a great deal on a changing table. I start picking up tiny T-shirts and sleepers. I look at diapers and wipes at the grocery store. I begin to take an interest in infants I see out in public. I even buy a book at a St. Mark's yard sale about what to expect in the first year of life. I know, I've had a baby before. But Chloe is twenty-eight years old. That was a long time ago.

I also do Internet reading about how to parent babies born with mental disabilities. Things have changed a lot in that area, I know, since Chloe was a baby. I find several online social networks dealing with parenting the mentally challenged. I realize I don't have to feel as alone as I did the first time around.

Thomas recovers from his illness, but he doesn't come back to our house. Chloe and I visit him at the Eldens'. She even stays for an afternoon. Finally I just come right out and tell Margaret that I think Thomas needs to come spend a few days with us. It's probably more me than Chloe; I feel he's neglecting my daughter. So Thomas comes home with us, but his reluctance is obvious.

I tell Jin and Abby about it that night. We're sitting around my kitchen table having a cup of herbal tea. Chloe and Thomas are in the living room. They're supposed to be choosing a movie, but so far, I don't hear anything coming from the TV.

I keep my voice low to prevent them from overhearing our conversation as I tell them how I manhandled Thomas and Margaret to get him here tonight.

Abby asks me an interesting question: "Why do you care?"

Jin looks at Abby, then at me, then stirs some more organic honey into her tea.

"Pardon?" I say, cupping my hands around my warm mug.

"Why do you care if he sleeps here?" Abby asks. She's sitting across the table from me, beside Jin. "Why do you care if he moves back in or not? You've said he's a lot of extra work. If they're happy living this way, why can't you be happy with it?"

"They're *married*," I argue. "He should be here with Chloe. Especially considering the *circumstances*."

Abby smiles at Jin. I see the emotional connection between them, and I'm just a little bit jealous.

"So this is about convention?" Abby asks.

I roll my eyes. "Is she like this all the time?" I ask Jin. "Is every conversation a courtroom argument?"

Jin chuckles and reaches for Abby's hand. "Pretty much."

Abby looks across the table at me. "I'm not trying to pick on you, Ally. I'm just saying that this doesn't have to be a conventional marriage. They don't have to sleep in the same house every night. Everyone has to make their own relationship work for them."

I think about Jin and Abby's relationship. It's unconventional for obvious reasons, but they're not living together twenty-four hours a day, either. When Abby moved in next door again, she kept her job in Baltimore, and her house. She still stays there three or four nights a week.

"Just something to think about," Abby says. "Especially with the baby coming. Your hands are going to be full with your classroom schedule and Chloe and the baby. Maybe you don't need Chloe's husband here every night."

I think about the Eldens' situation and my fear that Margaret will move to Ohio to be with Danny. Then I won't have an option, will I? Maybe Abby is right; maybe I need to loosen up a little. Thomas is obviously not going to be able to take responsibility for his child. Why am I pretending he is? Especially when I've secretly been critical of Margaret for that very same illusion—believing Thomas is more capable than he ever will be.

"Maybe you're right," I muse. "Maybe—"

"No!" Chloe screams from the living room. "Give it back!"

I look at Jin and Abby.

"No!" Chloe screeches.

"Excuse me," I say, pushing back my chair. I know Chloe is hormonal, but I'm frustrated with her temper tantrums. She doesn't seem to have an ounce of patience with Thomas lately, and she insists on having her own way entirely too often. "I'll be right back," I say to Abby and Jin, then, "Chloe!"

"I . . . I d . . . don't l . . . like it!" Thomas is shouting as I walk into the living room. The two of them are standing in front of the TV. Chloe snatches the *Aladdin* DVD box out of Thomas's hand.

"I . . . I wanna w . . . watch *T . . . Toy Story*!" He grabs wildly for the box, flailing both arms.

"No!" my awkwardly pregnant daughter screams in his face, stomping her foot as she moves the box just out of his reach. "It's my TV!"

He lunges for the box. She puts it behind her back.

"Chloe Mae—"

The words aren't out of my mouth before I see Thomas lunge forward and push Chloe back. There's only a few feet between us by then, but I can't get there fast enough and I watch my pregnant daughter fly backward into the TV cabinet.

❦ 24 ❧

The back of Chloe's head hits the open door of the TV cabinet hard. The door snaps back on its hinges. The DVD box flies from her hand, through the air.

"Chloe!" I cry, stepping in front of Thomas.

By the time I get to her, she's already scrambling up, arms pumping, screaming at Thomas. "I want *Aladdin*! Where's my *Aladdin*?"

I try to keep her from getting up so I can make sure she's okay, but she's strong and she's fighting me. I can't believe how strong she is. On her feet, she lunges toward Thomas.

He's sobbing. Cowering. "K . . . Koey. Koey."

He didn't do it on purpose. I *know* that. And he didn't hurt her; I can see that. But when I turn to him, I'm so angry. I'm so scared. "We do not push, Thomas! You do not push your pregnant wife!" I'm trying to grab Chloe, to pull her into my arms, but she throws herself at Thomas and shoves him hard. He goes down like a giant in a fairy tale, hitting his arm on the coffee table as he falls.

"Chloe!" I holler. "Enough!"

By now Jin and Abby are in the room. Abby drops to one knee to see to Thomas. Jin is trying to help me wrestle Chloe back.

I'm afraid if I don't get her attention, she's going to tackle him on the floor. I've never seen her so enraged.

"I want my *Aladdin*!" she screams. "I want Prince Ali!"

Jin has her arms around Chloe, around her big belly. "Chloe, Chloe, calm down. Listen to me."

I spot the DVD box on the floor. I take two steps and grab it. I take it to my daughter and place it in her hands. I'm shaking.

She's still screaming at Thomas.

"Come with me, Chloe," Jin insists, pulling her away from Thomas, who's still on the floor.

"*Aladdin*," Chloe sobs.

"Right here. Right here." Jin taps the box in Chloe's hands and ushers her toward the kitchen. "You okay?" she's saying. "Did you bump your head?"

When they disappear into the kitchen, Chloe is still going on about Prince Ali.

I look down at Thomas, on the floor. He's lying on his side, knees drawn up, holding his arm against his chest and rocking. I put my hand on the coffee table and squat down. Abby's behind him.

"Is he okay?" I ask.

She's rubbing his back. "He's okay. Thomas is okay," she says, soothing him. "You're going to be okay." She looks up at me. "Chloe?"

I swallow and nod. "She hit her head, but I think she's fine. She's too angry to be hurt."

Abby holds my gaze for a second. "You need to call Thomas's mom."

"I need to call his mom," I repeat, momentarily in a daze. "Right. I should call Margaret." I look down at Thomas. He's still sobbing, his eyes squeezed shut. As I get up, I smell urine. I see the stain on his pants.

I grab the cordless phone off the end table near one of the couches and head upstairs to get Thomas a clean pair of sweatpants. I realize I'm still shaking when Margaret picks up.

"Margaret," I say.

"Is everything all right? The baby?" She can hear the distress in my voice.

"Everything is okay," I say. I take a deep breath. "But I need you to come get Thomas." As I pull a pair of pants out of Thomas's dresser, I relay what happened.

By the time Margaret arrives, red-eyed, Thomas is sitting on one couch, in clean underwear and sweatpants. Chloe is sitting on the opposite couch, glaring at him. I'm making her hold a bag of frozen peas to the knot on the back of her head, so she's not happy with me right now, either.

Thomas has tried to apologize to Chloe and to me several times. He knows he did something wrong. My darling, on the other hand, doesn't seem to get that this is bad. It's very bad. She has no idea what domestic violence is, nor does she understand that she could have been seriously injured. What if she'd been at the top of the staircase when he pushed her?

I know that Thomas only reacted to her taunting. He didn't mean to hurt her; he would never hurt her intentionally. But he's so big.

"I just . . . I don't know what's gotten into you, Tommy." Margaret sits down beside her son; she's still wearing her coat. She looks at me, sitting beside Chloe.

Jin and Abby have gone home.

"I don't understand what got into him," Margaret says to me.

I know exactly what got into him. I glance at Chloe. "Put the peas back on your head," I tell her.

She makes a face but does as she's told. I return my attention to Margaret. "As I said on the phone, I know he didn't do it intentionally. He was upset. They were both upset."

"But we can't have pushing or hitting." Now *her* voice is shaky.

"No. We can't have pushing or hitting," I agree.

She looks at Thomas. "We should go, son. And let Chloe get some rest."

Thomas gets to his feet awkwardly. We all go to the door, and I take his coat off the coatrack and help him into it.

"Bye, honey," Chloe says and lifts up on her toes.

"B . . . bye . . . baby," he says softly. He kisses her on the lips.

Tears spring in my eyes. Standing there watching them, I think I knew in my heart where this was going. It was just so sad. So unfair.

"I'll call you," Margaret says and they hurry out into the cold.

Chloe closes the door behind them and waddles away, the bag of frozen peas in her hand. "I'm watching *Aladdin*."

Margaret calls the next day. There are no long, drawn-out discussions. No argument from either side. She's talked to Danny. He thinks she and Thomas should go to Ohio for a while. I speak briefly to Randall. He hints around that I may have caused the unrest between Chloe and Thomas because I didn't let them function more independently from me. But in the end, he's just not all that interested. He offers to pick up Chloe on Tuesday and take her to Chick-fil-A.

Margaret and Thomas come by to get his things. I hadn't noticed, but apparently he'd slowly taken most of his belongings home. They carry a suitcase and a laundry basket out.

Chloe waves from the vestibule door. I don't think she understands the seriousness of Thomas's departure. I do think she knows I'm sad, though, because she slips her small hand into mine. Together, we watch Thomas and Margaret load his things and pull away from the curb. He waves.

She lifts her hand and lets it fall.

Thomas went away. Because there's no hitting and no pushing. We hit and we pushed. That was bad. But he made me mad. He wanted to watch dummy head movies. He cried because he wanted his mom. All the days. Now I can watch movies I want.

Sometimes I'm sad because Thomas isn't sleeping in my bed.

He was warm and he put his hand in my nightgown when we went sleeping. But now I'm fat because I have a baby in my belly. It wiggles in my belly. I can't sleep good. Thomas would have to sleep on the floor so it's good he went to Hi-O.

When I have a baby maybe he'll come and kiss it. You kiss your baby. And change the diaper. If it pees or poops.

Thomas has to change the diaper if it poops. Maybe he'll come on Wednesday.

Life goes back to the way it was before Thomas came into our lives two and a half years ago. Except, of course, for the obvious: Chloe's big belly and the looming, momentous change the birth will bring into our lives. Margaret calls every day for a few days, then every other day. Then only twice a week. I understand why she thinks a separation between Thomas and Chloe, for a while, is a good idea, but I don't understand her flagging interest in the baby.

"It's her grandchild!" I tell Jin, trying to keep my voice down, so Chloe doesn't hear me. She's in the kitchen, making a snack for us. We're in the living room. Abby has flown to the West Coast to visit her parents. Huan is with his new girlfriend in Philadelphia (a Chinese American girl!). Mark is spending a week with his kids in Vermont, skiing. It's quiet here. A little lonely, because we've made quite a family in the last few months, the five of us: Abby and Jin, Mark, Chloe, and me.

The house is decorated for Christmas. We put a tree up yesterday and have started decorating it. Chloe and I have a tradition of hanging mostly homemade ornaments on our tree. I have boxes of paper cup and noodle ornaments she's made over the years.

Chloe is excited about the presents under the tree. There are several for Thomas. We picked them out and wrapped them together, but she hasn't asked if he's coming for Christmas. There had been discussion that the Eldens might, but that was when they first went to Ohio. Margaret hasn't called in over a week, and I feel guilty because I haven't called her . . . but not guilty enough to call her.

"I'm sure she still feels bad about what happened." Jin is threading popcorn on fishing line.

I pick through a bowl of cranberries, looking for ones that aren't too squishy. I must have bought a bad bag because most of them seem soft. "But this is her grandchild," I repeat.

Jin looks at me. "Maybe she can't handle it, Ally."

"What do you mean?"

"I mean, maybe having a handicapped grandchild is more than she can handle. Maybe she's distancing herself because she just can't take it emotionally. Especially with the marriage now being over."

I look at the cranberries in the bowl. I want to argue that the marriage isn't over. But it is. I know it. When I first realized it, I was upset, not because it was over but because I ever let it take place to begin with. Mark was the one who talked me down off that ledge. He was so sweet. He said, as a parent, I did the right thing at the time. He said that there was no way I could have anticipated that Thomas wouldn't be able to adjust to the marriage and all it entailed. It was nice of him to say it that way because we both know Chloe didn't adjust all that well, either. Her way of adjusting was simply to resist any change, and I probably didn't do enough to facilitate change in our house, for Thomas's benefit.

Mark also said that I couldn't blame myself for the pregnancy. He reminded me that it could have easily happened without nuptials. The way he'd said it had me smiling for days. Mark made an additional comment that day when he ended up helping me box stained-glass sugar cookies for my colleagues. He said that I shouldn't assume that the baby was a bad thing. He said maybe the marriage didn't fail. Maybe the arrival of the baby was supposed to be the end result, all along. Not the union between Chloe and Thomas.

I think maybe he'd had one beer too many.

I look at Jin, sitting across from me on the couch. I listen to my daughter singing "Dalmatian Plantation," at the top of her lungs. I smell the heady scent of the fresh pine tree and feel the warmth of the fire on the hearth. I imagine holding an infant in my arms, an infant that looks at me with the same love in her eyes that I saw in Chloe's eyes as a baby. Her disability never impeded her love for me.

I'm not the kind of person who believes in fate, but maybe this really *is* what is meant to be.

Christmas comes and goes, and Thomas's gifts remain unopened under the tree. I finally buckle and call Margaret on the pretext of giving her a report on Chloe's pregnancy. She doesn't pick up her cell phone. I leave a message: "Just wanted to let you know that Chloe's appointment went well today. Baby's heartbeat is great. Chloe's blood pressure was okay. So . . . no news is good news. I hope you all had a nice Christmas. Chloe was hoping we would see you, but . . ." I hesitate. "But maybe we should send Thomas's gifts?" I sound cheery. "We'll . . . talk to you soon."

Margaret doesn't call for several days. I'm already back in school: a new semester, new classes, new students. I've made arrangements for Sue Chou to cover my classes when the baby is born. I've started the process of finding someone to care for the baby. Chloe is still going to Minnie's, still participating in all the activities. The pregnancy really doesn't seem to have slowed her down all that much.

I smile when I see the name on the caller ID. "It's Mom Margaret." It's after dinner and Chloe and I are sitting on my bed, folding tiny flannel receiving blankets and towels with hoods.

"Thomas," she says, holding up a white T-shirt with pink and blue kittens all over it. "He's my honey."

"Margaret, good to hear from you," I say into the phone. "I hope you—"

"Alicia—" She sounds upset.

"Is everything okay? We were worried when we didn't hear from you—"

"Alicia, we need to talk about the kids."

I glance at Chloe, wondering if I should get up and go down the hall. "Okay . . ."

"Tommy's in a new daycare, he's doing great, and while Danny and I don't usually agree with divorce—"

She continues to talk, but I don't really listen after that. I didn't see this coming. I mean . . . I suppose I did. The fact that the Eldens went for a *visit* to Ohio and didn't come back was a clue, but . . . divorce?

I look at my daughter, with her enormous belly. She's trying to fold a little yellow thermal blanket. She folds it, unfolds it, then folds it again. I notice her wedding band on her finger; there's no way I'm going to get her to take it off.

Margaret is still talking.

A *divorce?* That would certainly cut the ties between us, but how Margaret and Danny . . . I can't wrap my head around it.

They're abandoning Chloe. Their grandchild. I can't decide if I'm hurt or angry. Both, I suppose. I could never forsake my grandchild, no matter what the circumstances. I understand that having my daughter pregnant brings the whole situation closer to me, but even if Thomas was my son and Chloe was Margaret's daughter, I wouldn't walk away. I could never walk away.

I think about what Jin said. About the possibility that Margaret and Danny just don't have the emotional capacity to handle another handicapped child. About how they might not be strong enough.

I realize, then, that I'm strong. I never thought I was, but as I listen to Margaret, now little more than a buzz in my ear, I come to the full realization of my strength. I'm fifty-three. Young. I can take care of this baby *and* my daughter. We don't need Thomas. We don't need the Eldens. We don't even need Randall.

"I understand," I say softly. I think I've cut Margaret off.

"I'm so sorry," she says.

And I know that she is. She's sorry. I'm sorry. We're all sorry. We wanted our children to be happy, so we let them get married. It was a mistake. We made a mistake.

I don't let myself think about the fact that I *knew* it was a mistake. That I knew, in my heart of hearts, that Chloe and Thomas weren't capable of having a married relationship. I caved because of the pressure from others . . . and because I wanted Chloe to be happy. She was so happy in the beginning.

I can't talk to Margaret anymore. "Just send the paperwork," I hear myself say.

"Just send it?" She sounds like she's going to cry.

"Just send it." I hesitate, then ask the question that has to be asked. I'm not even sure what I want the answer to be. "Will Thomas be giving up his paternal rights?"

She's quiet for a moment. "I think it's best, Alicia, don't you?"

I hang up. I know it's petty, but I hang up on her.

"Look, Mom! I folded it pretty." Chloe holds up the yellow receiving blanket and she has, indeed, folded it nicely.

I can't take my eyes off her. My beautiful, clever, funny Chloe. "You know something," I say.

"Know something?" she echoes, reaching for another clean blanket from the pile.

"I love you, Chloe Mae Richards-Monroe."

She looks up and smiles, the biggest, sweetest smile.

ᘇ 25 ᘒ

I can't sleep because my belly hurts. It hurts in my baby. I roll over on my back and I look at the roof in my room. I can see it because the bathroom light is on. I leave the bathroom light on because I have to pee a lot of times at night.

Mom says we have to paint the roof in my room because it's getting peely. I wonder if I can paint it blue and make clouds. The baby will sleep in my room. I don't know if it's a girl baby or a boy baby. If it's a girl baby I think it will like clouds on the roof. I don't know what boy babies like.

My belly really hurts. If Thomas was here I would tell him. He doesn't live here anymore. He had to go to Hi-O. He didn't like it here. I like it here with my mom. Maybe someday me and Mom will go to Hi-O and see Thomas. Maybe Wednesday.

My belly hurts worse and worse. I rub it, but it still hurts. I get out of bed slow. "Mom?" It hurts so bad then when I get to my door I have to lean on it. Then it stops hurting. Mom says it hurts a little to get a baby, but then the baby will come out and it won't hurt.

I turn on the light in the hall and walk down the hall. "Mom! My belly hurts!"

"Chloe?"

I hear her. I feel bad because she was asleep. But she said if my belly hurts, to wake her up.

"Chloe? What's the matter, hon?"

Mom comes out in the hall. She's wearing the pj's me and Jin gave her for Christmas. They have Christmas kittens on them. I clapped when she opened her present. I love kitten pajamas.

"Mom, my belly hurts," I tell her. When I walk, water runs down my legs and scares me. I look down. "I didn't pee! I didn't."

Mom laughs, but she looks like she's going to cry. "Oh Chloe, honey, it's okay." She hugs me. She doesn't even care if she gets in the wet on the floor. "It's the baby!" she says. "The baby is coming."

Do more women go into labor at night, or does it just seem that way because it causes more disruption? Chloe wakes me at four thirty in the morning. It's January eleventh. A good day to have a baby. I'm excited as I help her get dressed and bundle her into the car. I'm scared, too. I call Jin on our way to the hospital because I promised her I would, but I tell her to go back to sleep. This is a first baby. Who knows how long it will take for Chloe to deliver?

After Chloe is admitted and settled into her cozy pink and blue labor and delivery room, with a couch for me to rest on, I call Randall. It's seven by now. A decent hour. He doesn't answer. I leave a message. Then I call Margaret. I leave a message there, too. On impulse, I call Mark. He picks up on the second ring.

"I wake you?" I say.

"Nope. Already on the road." I hear him swallow a mouthful of coffee. "Got a toilet overflow situation at an insurance agency in town."

"Well, I'll let you get to that," I say, leaning against the wall in the hall outside Chloe's room. "I just wanted to let you know that Chloe's officially in labor and has been admitted."

"So this is it," he says.

"This is it." I sound up. I feel up. I can do this. I can do it with the help of my friends. I'm learning to accept their help. Maybe it will even be nice to not feel like I have to do everything alone.

"You want me to come over? Just for moral support?"

"Oh no. There's no need. She's only two centimeters. This is going to be a long day. Chloe's doctor hasn't been in yet, but the nurse has already said we can expect a long day."

"You're sure? I can bring you a cup of coffee."

I laugh. "I'm fine. Thanks."

"Talk to you later?"

I smile. "Talk to you later."

Jin shows up after her 1 p.m. class. I'm glad to see her because Chloe isn't dealing well with the labor contractions. She's crying. We had a kicking episode. Dr. Alvarez comes in between seeing patients in her office, examines Chloe, and explains to me that it's still too soon to give her an epidural. The epidural would relieve the pain of the contractions, but it's hard to judge how much longer Chloe will be in labor and the spinal anesthesia could only be administered for a certain length of time. Giving it to her too soon can mean having to push with no pain medication.

I try to remain patient with Dr. Alvarez. I understand what she's saying, but Chloe is not the average mother in childbirth. She doesn't understand what's going on. Not really.

Dr. Alvarez promises to stop back in after her end-of-the-day appointments, and I go back into the room where Jin is sitting with Chloe.

My daughter's face is swollen from crying. She's already pulled her IV out once so she has a bandage on one arm, an IV in the other. The nurse mumbles something about restraints. I don't want Chloe restrained, so Jin and I take turns sitting next to her, trying to keep her calm. We try to show her how to breathe through the contractions, but as soon as they get rough, she can't concentrate and starts to cry and fight the contraction.

Jin slips out of the chair when she sees me. "I'm going to give Abby a call."

"Any word?" I ask as we pass. A couple of hours ago, Abby got a call that her father had had a stroke. Abby was already at the airport, trying to catch a flight to the West Coast.

Jin shakes her head.

I move into the chair next to Chloe's bed. Chloe's lying there under the sheets, a wide elastic belt around her belly. The monitors and the IV pump beep. Her red eyes are squeezed shut.

"Mom," she says, half-opening her eyes. "It hurts."

"I'm here." I take her hand, which is missing her wedding ring. One of the nurses made her remove it; it's in my bag for safekeeping. "Soon the doctor will give you some medicine and it won't hurt as much."

"I don't want a baby." She thrusts her lower lip out. "I don't want it."

I smile to myself. Don't all mothers in labor think that, at some point? "It's going to be okay," I say. "This will all be over in a few hours and then we'll have a cute little baby to hold."

"I can hold a baby." She closes her eyes. "But you have to change the diaper. I don't like a stinky diaper."

"Sure. I'll change the diaper," I say.

And the hours pass. Slowly. Chloe's labor progresses . . . slowly. The pain begins to wear on me, after a while. My daughter's in pain and I can't alleviate it.

Randall comes by, but he only stays five minutes. He's obviously uncomfortable in the labor room with his daughter in the bed and me pacing. I'm not upset that he doesn't stay. It's not like I want him here for the delivery. He tells me to call him and let me know what happens. He mentions he has an early class tomorrow. I'm not sure what I'm supposed to do with that information. Jin says that means don't call him after 10 p.m.; he needs his beauty sleep. Jin has never liked Randall and never pretended to.

When the nurse comes in to check on Chloe at 9 p.m., I get snarky with her. I'm tired and I'm worried. The nurses say eighteen hours isn't unusual for labor, but it seems like it's been so long. And I don't see the end in sight right now.

"Seven centimeters!" she says cheerfully. The way she says it, she reminds me of Margaret. Who left me a very brief message this morning promising to pray for the baby's safe delivery and who hasn't called back since.

"That's far enough along for the epidural, right?" I say to the nurse.

The blonde in the pink scrubs snaps off her disposable gloves. "I'll have to check with her doctor."

"I understand that. I understand you can't administer the epidural, personally. But could you call Dr. Alvarez?" There's an edge to my voice. "Could you do that?"

"If Dr. Alvarez gives the okay. But then I'll have to call over to anesthesia."

The monitor that shows Chloe's contractions begins to hum and Chloe moans. "Mom . . ."

I lean over Chloe, getting my face right in hers. "Okay, here comes another. Take my hand and get a deep breath." I breathe in deeply, hoping she'll imitate me.

"No . . ." Chloe groans. "I don't want a baby." Her voice becomes high-pitched as the contraction gets stronger. "Mom! Make it stop! It hurts . . . Make the baby stop!"

Holding Chloe's hand, I turn to the nurse. "Call the doctor, call the anesthesiologist, call the hospital director, if you have to!" I'm getting loud. "I want my daughter to have that epidural. Now! Do you understand me? Right now!"

The young woman hustles out. Thirty minutes later, the anesthesiologist appears. He administers the epidural and Chloe's pain subsides considerably. I apologize to the nurse. Twice. She tells me not to worry about it.

Jin stays with me. Mark comes. He brings me coffee and a chicken salad sandwich he made himself. With a pickle. He's not uncomfortable hanging out in the labor room with me. He's sweet to Chloe. He goes home because I tell him to, but he makes it clear that I can call him if I need him. Or if I need another chicken salad sandwich. It doesn't matter how late or how early it is.

Chloe starts pushing at 2:35 a.m. It's hard, but she's a trooper. Jin stands on one side of her, I stand on the other. With every push, I feel like I'm pushing, too. I don't think about what kind of mental disabilities the baby will have, or how I'll deal. I just want to get this over with. I just want to help Chloe get through it.

The baby boy is born at 3:47 a.m. He's almost eight pounds. Chubby. With big blue eyes and no eye folds, no shortened limbs, no disproportionate head. I know the test came back negative for Down syndrome, but I didn't trust it. I trust what I see. I can't catch my breath. He looks like a normal newborn.

"There you go, Chloe! Congratulations," Dr. Alvarez declares. She wraps the slippery infant in a receiving blanket. "Would you like to cut the cord, Alicia?"

I'm crying so hard that I can barely see to take the scissors.

"You want to hold him, Chloe?" Dr. Alvarez asks as the baby is separated from her body.

Chloe shakes her head. She doesn't really even look at her little boy. "I'm thirsty. Can I have a drink?" She looks at Jin. "Can I have Gatorade now, Aunt Jin?"

Dr. Alvarez looks at me. "Would you like to hold him for a minute, Alicia? Before the peds nurses have a look at him?"

I'm too choked up to speak. Then he's in my arms, looking up at me with big, dark blue eyes. Eyes that seem to see me. Eyes that speak to me.

I feel like I can't breathe. He looks so normal. He *feels* normal. His muscle tone seems right. I meet Dr. Alvarez's gaze. "He looks—"

"Perfectly healthy baby boy," she says softly. "We can run tests, of course, but—"

Suddenly a loud beeping comes from one of the monitors behind Chloe's bed. Everything happens so quickly then. It's a blur.

It was all a blur then. It's all still a blur.

I close my eyes and rest my forehead on the cold windowpane in Chloe's room. I don't know what's happening. Everyone in the delivery room was so happy and smiling one second, and then the next, they aren't.

Someone sweeps the baby out of my arms. Jin and I are pushed back from the bed where Chloe lays. I don't see her close her eyes. If she's had some sort of convulsion or something, I don't see it.

Dr. Alvarez hollers for a crash cart. Everyone crowds around the bed. I can't see my Chloe anymore. A code blue is called over the intercom to Chloe's room number.

"What's happening? What's happening?" I keep saying.

Somehow Jin gets to me in the room full of doctors and nurses. She pulls me into her arms. We're both crying. Someone pushes us out into the hall. The door keeps opening and closing. People coming and going. Rushing.

I don't know how much time passes. A long time, I think. Maybe an hour?

Even though it's only been three days since it happened, I can't remember exactly what Dr. Alvarez said when she came out into the hall. Her mask was gone. She was still wearing a yellow disposable gown over her scrubs. There were tears in her eyes.

"No, no," I remember whispering. You see this scene in movies. You read them in novels. You think you know how it will feel. You think you can imagine the pain. But you can't imagine the depth of the pain.

Jin had her arms around me. She was holding me. Keeping me upright, I think.

"Would you like to step into a room?" Dr. Alvarez asks me, pulling a surgery cap off her dark head. "A place more private?"

I remember shaking my head. Feeling numb. "Right here is

fine." I don't think I could have moved. I knew what she was going to say. In my mother's heart, I knew.

"I'm so sorry, Alicia. Chloe's dead. Of cardiomyopathy," she told me, mincing no words. "We did everything we could."

"A heart attack? A heart attack?" I know I said it several times. Jin was crying. Still holding me.

"But . . . she had no history," I remember saying. "Down syndrome people . . . they have cardiac issues. But not Chloe. Chloe didn't have anything wrong with her heart."

Dr. Alvarez took one of my hands. She looked into my eyes. "There was no indication there was a problem. This is very rare with mothers, Alicia. But it happens."

I remember trying to breathe. I couldn't think. I remember asking about the baby. Dr. Alvarez assured me he was fine. Healthy and fine. She told me that he scored a perfect ten on his APGAR. She said that I could certainly have him tested when he got older, but she saw no evidence of mental retardation. She said that the pediatrician on call had confirmed her observation.

So my twenty-eight-year-old daughter was dead, and I was the grandmother of a healthy baby boy.

And now here I am, standing at Chloe's window, with a newborn asleep in the crib against the wall. Jin and I brought him home this morning. The hospital offered to keep him a few more days. Just until after the funeral, but I need him here. I know he can't fix this feeling that my heart has seized up . . . but I couldn't sleep last night with him in the hospital. My Chloe's little boy. I need him here.

I hear the front door open. It can't be Jin because she just left to get more diapers and formula. Whoever it is, I don't want to see them. I don't want to see anyone. I don't want to talk to anyone. Not Randall, who seems more pitiful than useless to me now. Not Margaret and her platitudes. Not any of my well-meaning colleagues, who don't know what to say, leaving me not knowing what to say to them.

"Alicia?"

I'm still resting my forehead on the windowpane. I open my eyes. It's flurrying now. The grass in the backyard is brown and brittle, with a dusting of white. I remember playing soccer in the yard with Chloe. The picture Jin took of us is still downstairs on the refrigerator.

I've cried so much in the last three days that I'm out of tears.

"Alicia?" Mark's voice drifts up the stairs.

The baby is stirring, but I can't seem to move away from the window. "Up here." My voice cracks.

I hear him on the stairs. He comes up the hall and walks into Chloe's room. He walks up behind me, stands there for a minute, then puts his hand on my shoulder.

The baby starts to whimper.

We just stand there for a minute, then he moves away from me. I hear him walk to the crib. He's making soothing little cooing sounds, the kind you make to babies. Words that don't really mean anything.

The baby quiets and Mark walks back to me, rocking a bundle of flannel blankets in his arms. Now the baby is making little mewing sounds.

"There's a pacifier," I say.

"Got it."

I don't want to look at him. I don't want to feel this tenderness in my heart because, somehow, I feel like it's a betrayal of my love for Chloe. But I can't help myself.

I turn away from the cold window and look at the baby Mark's cradling. He looks good with a baby in his arms. With my baby.

I touch the infant's cheek. I inhale his newborn scent. "I'm going to call him Adam," I say.

Mark rocks Adam gently and the baby sucks on the pacifier, looking up at me with those big blue eyes. Chloe's eyes.

"I can do this," I whisper, smiling through my tears as I lean to brush my lips against Adam's soft cheek.

Mark switches Adam to one arm and puts the other around my shoulders, hugging me against him. He kisses the top of my head. "We can do this."

Please turn the page for a very special
Q&A with Colleen Faulkner!

1. What made you decide to write about the subject of a parent caring for an adult child with an intellectual disability?

I like women's fiction that deals with real, present-day problems. I look at friends and family members who are dealing with issues that seem overwhelming to me and admire the strength I see in them. As a mother of four adults, I can only imagine how difficult it must be to make decisions for an adult child who can't necessarily make her own decisions. I wanted to write about a woman I could laugh with and cry with . . . and admire.

2. Are you and Alicia similar people?

As a writer, I create fictitious characters, so no, Alicia isn't me and I would not necessarily have made the choices she made. But I think there's always a part of me in my female protagonists. Alicia has my practicality. There are times when I think Alicia could have fallen apart, but the practical side of her pushed through the pain or uncertainty because she felt she had no choice. Chloe had no one but Alicia. Alicia's responsibility as a parent was to do the best she could for her child.

3. Did you do research for the book, or do you have personal experience with people with intellectual disabilities?

I did a lot of research on the subject of adults with mental challenges and the choices their caregivers have to make. I also read a lot about sexuality and adults with intellectual disability and talked at length with a friend who works in a group home for these special people. She's had so many amazing experiences; she gave me a better understanding of the practical side of Alicia and Chloe's life. I also grew up with family members my own age who are intellectually challenged, so I've seen the joy and the sadness in being a parent of such special sons and daughters.

4. What next for Colleen Faulkner?

One Last Summer tells the story of four women: Aurora, McKenzie, Janine, and Lilly, bound by friendship and tragedy as preteens, who have remained friends as adults. Now, in their forties, they've gathered at the beach for one last summer vacation together. McKenzie is dying. This will be their last chance to share their laughter and tears, revisit the past, and look to the future, which will not be what anyone expects.

JUST LIKE OTHER DAUGHTERS

COLLEEN FAULKNER

ABOUT THIS GUIDE

The suggested questions are included to enhance your group's
reading of Colleen Faulkner's *Just Like Other Daughters*!

1. When the book opens, do you feel that Alicia is giving Chloe the independence she needs/deserves? If not, give an example.

2. Would you have responded differently than Alicia when Chloe first came home saying she and Thomas were going to get married?

3. Do you think Randall loved his daughter? Why do you think he wasn't more involved in her life? Was Alicia responsible for his lack of involvement? Do you think Randall's relationship with Chloe would have been different had Chloe not had an intellectual disability?

4. Do you think Alicia should have allowed Chloe to get married? Should Margaret have allowed Thomas to get married? Would there have been a better option?

5. Do you think having Chloe and Thomas move into Alicia's house after they were married was a good idea? Would the marriage have survived had they moved into Margaret's house? A group home?

6. How could Alicia have prevented Chloe and Thomas's marriage from failing? Margaret?

7. What would you have done if Chloe had been your daughter and become pregnant? How do you think others would have reacted to your choice?

8. How do you think Alicia's story will end?